I0742407

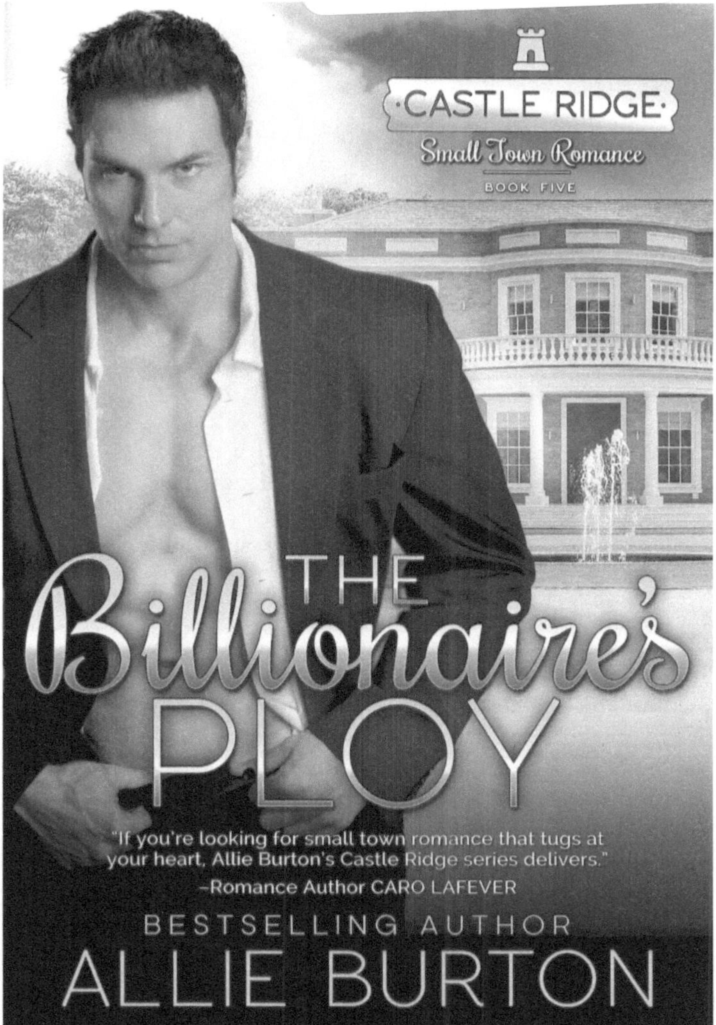

CASTLE RIDGE
Small Town Romance
BOOK FIVE

THE
Billionaire's
PLOY

"If you're looking for small town romance that tugs at
your heart, Allie Burton's Castle Ridge series delivers."
—Romance Author CARO LAFEVER

BESTSELLING AUTHOR
ALLIE BURTON

THE BILLIONAIRE'S PLOY
A Castle Ridge Small Town Romance Book 5

Copyright © 2017 by Alice Fairbanks-Burton

Published by Alice Fairbanks-Burton
ISBN-13: 978-1-7326764-7-3
Cover by The Killion Group, Inc.
Interior Design by Author E.M.S.

For my dad,
who always said you should love what you do,
motivating me to continue writing
even through the struggles.
Hope he's enjoying himself in heaven.

THE
Billionaire's
PLOY

ALLIE BURTON

Chapter One

"How're we going to get those kids back together?" George Webber took a puff on his cigar. The man's desperation scratched down Jackson Croft's spine, causing a shiver of misgiving.

Ensconced in plush leather chairs in the men's grill at the Castle Ridge Country Club, the stink of the cigar circled around his head, suffocating him. It was either the smoke or their current discussion.

Those kids were fully-grown adults. His brother, Ryder, was only a year younger than himself. George's daughter, Shey, had a Master's degree from Harvard.

"My brother is twenty-eight. I can't force him to do anything." Jackson clutched the drink in his hand. A glass of bourbon—an old man's drink George had ordered for him. What Jackson wanted was a beer.

He loved his brother, but he wasn't Ryder's father, and didn't hold the key to his wealth. Jackson had hoped once Ryder married he'd settle down, find his place in the company and in the world. Like their mom had asked for on her deathbed.

She'd asked things of Jackson, too. Things he couldn't give. A chill ran through him, as if his mom's cold hand glided across his skin.

The recent break-up of his brother and Shey had thrown a wrench in the plans. Business plans for Jackson and personal plans for his brother. He'd told his brother to grovel and get the woman back.

"Even if the kids," Jackson spat the word and re-tightened his tie, "don't get married, we can go ahead with the deal."

The merger between Webber Resorts and Croft Industries was an important deal. The crown on his father's legacy. A local connection showcasing the company. The final proof to the other business executives Jackson wasn't some kid who could be pushed around, who'd been handed Daddy's company.

Which he had.

Those same executives never realized the terrible shape the company had been in, and how he'd made them successful again. And they never would. As a tribute to his father.

Pinching the leather of the chair, he calmed himself.

He'd worked his ass off for the past seven years. While learning the ropes, he'd discovered the horrible financial state of Croft Industries. He'd rebuilt block by block, and stock by stock, taking the company public. His dad's second wife had never known, his brother had never known, and his stepsister had never known.

His muscles hardened, chasing away the chill. He'd used risky and manipulative practices to protect the company and his family.

He tilted forward to emphasize his point. "Together, we can build an even greater company. With Croft Industries' financial backing, Webber Resorts can become a premiere destination-resort chain."

George's ruddy cheeks swelled, making him resemble an evil Santa Claus. "Who else are you lining up deals with? Are you buying too many companies? Stretching your assets?"

"Excuse me?"

"I've heard rumors." The white of his eyebrows flattened into a threatening line.

Alarm pierced, and Jackson glanced around the dark, wood-paneled room at the other occupants, searching for corporate spies. "Rumors? What rumors?"

"Croft Industries' stock prices are going up fast."

"A good thing."

"Too fast."

He'd noticed the fluctuating stock prices. Between the paperwork for the merger and his brother's never-happening engagement, he hadn't had time to investigate.

"Croft Industries is a good buy. A strong company. Investors are noticing." He spoke loudly, wanting the group of early-spring golfers to hear.

"Webber Resorts doesn't want to be another purchase on your ledgers."

He knew Webber Resorts had other companies interested in buying them. None of the discussions had gone as far. The relationship between his brother and George's daughter had practically sealed the deal.

Until the relationship ended.

"I don't need to be bought by you." George's superior expression ground into Jackson's psyche.

The same expression he'd received across a dozen boardroom tables, at charity events, at this country club and the club he belonged to in Denver.

"Webber Resorts has other suitors." The man made it sound like a marriage contract.

His muscles tensed, knowing he'd have to play the bad guy again. It was his role. Something he did well, even if he hated the act. "*Right now*, you have other companies interested. Things could change."

George's gaze grew wary. Suspicious. "Change how?"

"Anything can happen to a resort company. Norovirus, death on a chairlift." Jackson could hire someone to make one of these events happen. "Even a bad ski season because of poor snow conditions."

"You might think you're a god, but you can't control the weather." George got to his feet unsteadily. Pivoting to face Jackson, he loomed above in a threatening pose. "While I control my company, my business contacts, and my daughter."

The old man called his bluff. An equal nemesis, if not a bit too sentimental.

Jackson forced his body to relax. He turned his lips up in a cool, calculating smile. "Croft Industries buying a controlling interest in Webber Resorts will be a great partnership."

"So will the merger of Shey and your brother." George downed the bourbon in his glass, and slammed the glass on a nearby table. "I'm doing this deal for Shey. One of my kids needs to get married and give me grandchildren."

Jackson shook his head at the contradiction in terms. The old man was doing it for himself because he wanted grandchildren, while Jackson was so far from even thinking about grandchildren. He'd have to have children first, and a wife, even a girlfriend. Except he was too damn busy and didn't have time for such frivolities. That was his brother's job.

He needed to get this conversation back on track. "Even if Shey and Ryder get back together and eventually get married, they might not have kids."

George's cheeks became redder. His gaze narrowed. "They will."

How was the old man going to guarantee it? Talk about someone believing they were a god. It was good Jackson had never had a long-term girlfriend. In-laws would be an added complication.

"Calm down." He advised, while his own nerves attempted to run riot. "We'll figure this out. Is Shey coming to the reception tonight?"

"She was supposed to be Ryder's date. They broke up." As if that explained everything.

"She can still come. You're coming."

"She and her girlfriends decided to take a weekend trip to the Caribbean."

"She's perfect for Ryder." Jackson's sarcasm and disrespect slipped out. He'd coddled his brother too much, trying to protect him from things Jackson had witnessed. And when Ryder had graduated a year later, he'd been able to make his own decisions about a career because Jackson hadn't been allowed a choice.

Big mistake. One of many he'd made. Years later after graduate school, Ryder was still deciding what he wanted to be when he grew up. If he ever grew up.

"My daughter is a very hard worker." George's offense glanced off Jackson. "She helps run Webber Resorts."

Ryder was a vice president at Croft Industries. Didn't mean he showed up to work every day. In fact, he never showed. Jackson knew, because he was there seven days a week. The unfairness roiled inside.

"Call me a romantic old fool." George's expression became indulgent. "She loves your brother. Always has."

Jackson ground his teeth together, putting on his negotiating face. "We've put a lot of work into this deal. Do you really want to see it go south because of the whim of *the kids*?"

His opponent's lips firmed and his expression hardened. "No engagement. No deal."

"But George. Our companies can do great things together. I've got this new avalanche safety device we're developing, and it can be available at your resorts first."

The old man leaned back in the chair. "No."

So that was that. Get Ryder and Shey engaged, or there'd be no merger. Jackson was a businessman, not a matchmaker.

A businessman who wanted this deal.

Determination surged through his veins and every muscle in his body hardened. Shey was good for his brother. It was time Ryder stepped up to the plate and helped with the business. Maybe marrying her would finally force him to join the adult world.

Jackson held out his hand for a firm handshake. "Okay. I'll get those kids back together, whatever it takes."

Emory Reese Barrington strutted through the quaint streets of downtown Castle Ridge a different woman. A worldly, mature, twenty-four-year-old, wearing high-heeled designer boots, a pencil-slim skirt and silk blouse, and a tailored wool coat. Her style was so different from the hand-me-down clothes she'd worn the last time she'd strolled Main Street.

An unstoppable smile bloomed on her face, lighting up her insides. She was home for good.

The air smelled of spring, melting snow, and mountains. Pulling her roller board suitcase across the sidewalk, she was careful to miss the puddles. The town hadn't changed much over the years. Main Street's wide sidewalks welcomed locals and tourists. Most of the quaint shops had been here for years. The street was dominated at the end by the Castle Ridge Lodge. She was used to crowded European cities with attitude and less altitude.

She'd arrived a day early to surprise her mother, unable to wait to be held in her mother's arms. To have her favorite meal cooked, and sleep in the small twin bed she'd used as a child. To feel welcomed and loved.

A red Maserati careened around the corner. Not a sensible car in the mountains. Her ex-boyfriend owned a fancy sports car and drove maniacally. This driver was probably a jerk, too.

The car flew past and hit a pothole in the road. Murky snowmelt splashed out of the rut and sprayed. Into the air, onto the sidewalk.

Onto her.

Her chest clutched. The dirty water hit her beautiful coat, staining the fine white wool. She jerked backwards too late. Her jaw dropped and she seethed. "Oh!"

The blackish-gray spots soaked into the wool and spread, resembling a sponge mopping up dirt. The stain became as large as a throw pillow. The coat was ruined. Anger spread like the muddy spot on her coat. If she ever saw the driver of the Maserati again she was going to give him a piece of her mind. He should be driving slower and avoiding the potholes.

And this was the only heavy coat she owned. Today might be warm, but the spring storms were some of the snowiest. Colorado weather always surprised.

She grabbed a tissue out of her oversized briefcase and dabbed at the stain. Pointless. She'd wanted to arrive home looking stylish and elegant, not dirty and disheveled. The inconsiderate Maserati driver had ruined the first impression she'd make on her mom.

The Maserati backed up, and parked by the red curb. The male driver jumped out of the car, wearing sweats and a long-sleeved black T-shirt. Casual clothes that screamed expensive.

He had light-brown hair, and a scruffy beard. The kind of scruff male models sported. "Sorry. I'll pay for the dry cleaning."

"Dry cleaning?" Instead of steam rising from the wet coat, it rose from inside her. Dry cleaning wasn't going to fix this. She crushed the tissue in her fist and lifted her head to glare at the careless driver. "Do you know how much this coat..."

He removed his sunglasses and sunlight glinted off his gray eyes. Familiar eyes. Eyes she'd dreamt of as a teenager. Except he wasn't a boy any longer. He was all man.

His shoulders were broader. His chest more defined, wearing the tight T-shirt. His brown hair wasn't combed. The strands were long and wild and reckless. And his gaze pierced through, her making her knees quiver.

Like they always had.

He ran a hand through his thick hair, messing it even more. "I didn't see the pothole, or realize how much water was—"

"Ryder?" Her voice was huskier than usual, with a slight tremble. The trembling was normal talking to her teenage crush. The huskiness was new. Surprisingly, new.

Maybe because she'd changed so much in the past few years. She was no longer just the housekeeper's daughter. The young girl who lived in the shadows of the same great house. The girl who'd crushed on Ryder Croft for years.

Okay, she still did have a crush.

Her cheeks flushed at her silliness. How could she not crush? He was gorgeous, and had only gotten better with age. And he'd always treated his high school girlfriends well.

The reason she'd been so bowled over by Alejandro.

"Yeah. I'm Ryder." His sharp gaze sized her up, and goosebumps raced across her skin. He'd never looked at her in that way before. As if he was interested.

Probably because she'd been a pimply-faced teen with long, frazzled hair. She'd recently cut her hair short, and she'd grown out of the acne.

"I can't believe you're here." Her teenage dreams were playing out in her mind.

She, hanging out on Main Street. Him, seeing her and stopping to help her out.

He glanced up and down the sidewalk and back at her. "How are you?" He sounded unsure, afraid to ask because of the ruined coat.

"I'm good." What was a coat when Ryder Croft was paying attention? Reverting back to her teenage self, she didn't know if she should hug him or kiss him senseless like she'd always wanted.

"You're wet and dirty." Real concern rattled in his voice. "What can I do to help? I have a beach towel in the car."

She'd imagined this moment a little differently when she'd first gone away to college. She'd come home first semester for break, and he'd get down on his knee and tell her how much he missed her and couldn't live without her. *Ha.* Internally, she giggled at the romantic winsomeness of the dream.

Instead, he'd been skiing in France, and she'd never seen him. In fact, she'd rarely seen him during her college years, and the two years in Spain completing an interior design internship.

His gaze raked her from top to bottom, causing nerves to flutter. Her confidence from minutes earlier was gone. His first impression of her was one of a drowned rat. Yes, she was thinking melodramatically. That's how she'd related to him as a lovesick teen. She needed to pull herself together. She wasn't a besotted girl any longer.

"Um." She unbuttoned and removed the coat so she'd at least appear presentable.

He moved toward the car, and opened the small trunk. "Here's the towel." Handing her the beach towel with a large beer logo emblazoned on it, he studied her again, taking his time, and lingering on certain parts of her anatomy.

The nerves increased, creating tingles that wouldn't settle.

Quirking his head, he grinned. His eyebrows wiggled up and down. "Do you need a ride someplace? You know, since we know each other."

The tingles crisscrossed her body, warmed her even without the coat. Much better than the offer of a towel.

"Or we could go for drinks." His suggestion caused the tingles to overlap and overheat.

"This early in the day?" The idea was tempting, except she hadn't slept well on the plane, and her mother would kill her if she found out she went for drinks before seeing her. "Are you going home?"

"Yeah, after I—" Pointing at the local jewelry store, his cheeks flushed.

"Buying jewelry for one of your many girlfriends?" She kept her tone light, teasing, even while jealousy chilled the earlier warmth.

So typically Ryder. He'd frequently buy his girlfriends gifts. He was so nice and thoughtful. She'd always fantasized about receiving one of those presents for what it represented—a relationship of any kind with him.

He tilted his chin. "How do you know…? Never mind."

She'd never tell him she'd studied him, followed him around, spied on him, dreamed about him.

"I'm returning something." His curtness was a warning not to ask questions. "Here, let me take your bag." He took her suitcase, put it in the trunk, and held the passenger door open. "I'll give you a ride."

"That would be great." Holding in her squeal, she stepped off the sidewalk, trying to be graceful. She slid into the passenger seat acting cool, attempting to return to her sophisticated self from moments before.

Moments before running into Ryder.

"I'll be right back." He jerked his head in the direction of the store. "Two minutes."

Once the door was closed, she screamed. "Ah! I can't believe it! I'm riding in a car with Ryder Croft!" She reverted to her thirteen-year-old self.

She relaxed into the leather seat. So much nicer than the coach seats on the plane, and the bus from Denver to Castle Ridge. She understood and appreciated fine materials after her interior design internship. She'd helped decorate some of the largest homes in Barcelona. Had been in the middle of decorating a Vizconde's mansion when she'd left the country. Bitterness twinged inside threatening gloom.

Don't think about that. Not now.

Taking a deep breath, she appreciated the smell of leather and Ryder's lingering, evergreen scent in the car. The same cologne he'd used throughout high school and college. Probably a little too much cologne, because she used to follow his scent around the large house.

Seconds later, he trotted in front of his car and got in the driver's seat. "Everything okay?"

"Yes. Why?"

"You had a funny expression."

She smashed her lips together, trying to control her facial muscles. She didn't want him to know about her silly crush. "It's been awhile since I've been in a car."

"Really?" He tossed his should-be-patented lethal smile, and her head spun. "Why?"

"I've been living in Europe." Why didn't he know? Her mom must've said something about where she'd been for the past two years.

He gunned the engine. "Where to?"

Her shoulders dropped and irritation burned through her lungs. He had no idea who she was. Her cheeks heated. Why would she expect otherwise? Ryder had never noticed her around the house. And yet, he'd noticed her today. His slow perusal had traveled across her body and appreciated. He'd asked her out for drinks. Would he have offered her a ride if he knew?

Maybe he didn't recognize her, but he was attracted to the more polished Emory.

She straightened and slipped a teasing smile on her face. For a little while it would be fun to pretend. He'd find out soon enough who she really was. "You said you were going home."

"I am."

Her irritation twisted into teasing payback. Tell him who she was and see disappointment on his face, or play the mysterious visitor for a short time? Her smile deepened. "Perfect."

"You live near me?" Curiosity showed in his angled mouth.

"Yes." Satisfaction settled inside her. Playing the mystery woman would be fun.

"You're not going to tell me who you are?"

"Nope."

"You're not a serial killer, are you?"

"Do I look like a serial killer?" She waved her hand indicating her body.

"Not at all." The appreciation in his voice went a long way to pumping her ego.

They left Main Street and headed out of town, deeper into the mountains. Evergreen trees lined the curvy road, so different from the highways around Barcelona. More comforting, more homey. Mounds of snow edged the road, with bare spots where the snow had melted.

The scenery wasn't as interesting as Ryder. He'd always held her attention, and she wanted to know what he'd been up to recently. "What were you returning in the jewelry shop?"

"An engagement ring."

The size of the large diamond he probably bought and returned dropped into Emory's gut. Ryder was engaged. The burning she'd felt earlier erupted again.

Her mother had never mentioned the engagement in their calls, texts, or letters. Shifting in her seat, she decided to face the truth. Just because she'd loved Ryder since she was twelve didn't mean she loved him anymore. She'd even had a serious relationship with a man from Spain. She might've fallen into her old patterns when they'd first met, but she needed to keep this light.

"Your fiancée obviously has better taste than you." She forced the friendly tease, the I-don't-care-you're-in-love-with-someone-else intonation. "She didn't like the ring."

Because why else would a woman not say yes to Ryder?

He shot her a dark glance. "She never saw the ring."

Hope flared inside Emory. Ryder wasn't engaged. He'd ogled her in town. He was gorgeous and fun. They could date. A great start to her return home for good.

She squashed her silly, childish fantasy. Even if he wasn't engaged, he'd considered it. "You chickened out asking?"

"She broke up with me before I had the chance to ask." His quiet timbre echoed in the small car. His expression thundered into a frown. He flashed his trademark grin again, except it appeared less bright. "Guess I got off a life sentence."

Emory empathized with his sadness. Who was crazy enough to break up with Ryder Croft? It was usually the other way around.

They turned onto the winding road leading up toward the enclave where his family's large mansion had been built. Twining her fingers together, she watched the scenery fly by way too fast. She needed to change the subject and not talk about his love life.

"I was sorry to hear about Lexi's mom." Not the most uplifting comment, but she meant it. She'd always liked the second Mrs. Croft and her daughter.

"We miss her. She was ready to go." He kept his gaze on the road, filled with his own sadness about the loss of his stepmother. He gave her a triumphant leer. "A-ha! So you're friends with my sister, Lexi."

Emory couldn't stop the mysterious smile from flitting on her face. Being unknown, she wasn't automatically the housekeeper's daughter, or the poor girl. She wasn't the ugly duckling in a house full of swans. "We grew up together."

In an upstairs-downstairs way.

"How's Lexi holding up?" Emory couldn't imagine losing her mom so early. Even though they hadn't been living close to each other while she'd been in Spain, they kept in contact.

Excited tremors ran through her. She was enjoying the ride, but she couldn't wait to see her mom. Couldn't wait to be held and comforted. To get her opinion on her hair and her business plans. To share everything with her.

"She's doing okay. Thanks to Dax O'Donnell."

Emory had heard about the whirlwind romance. "I'm glad they're happy."

"What road should I turn on?" Ryder glanced her way again, trying to figure out who she was.

She enjoyed the sensation of being the beautiful, mysterious woman and wanted to draw this out. Once he realized she was pesky Emory Barrington, her fantasy would end. "You don't remember me yet?"

"Of course, I do." He ran a hand through his hair and peered her way again. Confused and unsure made him even cuter. "You're the girl who lives near my house."

She laughed, enjoying the relaxation of flirting with a handsome man without worrying about anything else. Or anyone else. "You don't know who I am."

His glanced at her again. "Give me a clue."

"This is too much fun." She ran a finger down his arm, playing her flirtatious role. Not being herself.

She was touching Ryder Croft, she screamed inside. Flirting with him, laughing with him. She'd dreamt of this moment. This was like being at a costume party and playing a role.

His brows knitted together. "Did we ever date?"

"No."

His expression loosened. "That's good."

She arched her eyebrows at him slightly insulted. "Why?"

"What I mean is, I'd feel terrible if we dated and I couldn't remember your name." Even when he broke up with a girl he'd been nice and considerate about it. He was a sweet guy. "Did you go to Highlands?"

The ultra-private high school the Crofts had attended. "No."

He surveyed her again. "How long were you in Europe for?"

"There's your turn." She pointed at the long driveway leading to the house.

Excitement about seeing her mother eclipsed the

attraction brewing between them. She was almost home. She'd be seeing her mom in seconds.

"You definitely know where I live." His relaxed smile curled in her stomach. "How about stopping for drinks at my house?"

"Great idea."

He drove up the long driveway, and around the circle in front of the house.

Mansion, really.

The exterior was rough-hewn stone and wood, with large glass windows. A perfect combination blending with the surrounding trees and mountains. Stone steps led to the dark wood of the large, double front door. The doors stood open displaying a glimpse of marble floors and a large chandelier. It hadn't changed much.

Catering and tent rental trucks were parked in the driveway. Workers unloaded white chairs and canopies. The noise covered up the tinkling of the cascading fountain in the middle of the circular drive. A stage had been constructed on the side lawn, and outdoor heaters were spread around the grassy area. Her mom would be busy working tonight.

"You're having a party." She'd always loved the Croft parties.

From a distance.

"Tonight." Cutting the engine, he placed his arm along the back of her seat. "It's my sister's wedding reception."

"I thought Lexi already got married?" Emory couldn't hold back her surprise. Her mom never mentioned an upcoming reception.

"Lexi secretly eloped, and this is the extravagant party after the fact." His lips twisted together in an ironic smirk. "For someone so cautious, she rushed into this marriage."

He got out of the car and hurried around to her side and opened the door, a true gentleman. This is how he treated his dates, not the lowly housekeeper's daughter. She enjoyed the attention.

"You're not upset about the quick marriage." She got out of the car, holding her ruined coat.

"They're good together." Satisfaction oozed in his tone. He regarded her. "It's tonight. You should come."

Her spirits flew. All her teenage fantasies about attending one of the Croft events burst into an explosion of light. Excitement shot through her entire body. *Ryder Croft invited me, Emory Reese Barrington, to a Croft party.*

Jeez, quit acting like a child. She shouldn't be impressed. She'd been to lots of fancy parties in Spain. She was a special guest at a Vizconde's party. Her thoughts soured. One of many of his *special* guests.

"You're inviting me to your sister's wedding reception? Isn't it too late to RSVP?" Except he wasn't inviting Emory, he didn't know who he spoke to.

"There will be hundreds. One more person won't be noticed." He took her hand and rubbed his thumb against her skin. "We could dance."

This should be where she swooned. Clutching the coat tighter between her hands, she imagined holding Ryder in her arms while they danced, of him walking her through their elaborate gardens as he'd done with other girls, of him kissing her.

Ryder would be disappointed when he found out her name. For now, for this one moment in time, she could feel special. "I'd love to."

"Great." An uneasiness slid into his gaze, and she wondered if he was picturing the woman he'd planned to propose to. He opened the trunk, taking out her suitcase.

"Hello, Emory." An even deeper, masculine voice rumbled.

Her heart leapt to her throat, blocking the passage of air. She pivoted around at the greeting. Her fantasy to pretend for a little while longer died by two words from the frightening, older brother. She'd hoped Ryder wouldn't learn who she was until tonight at the party. When she was dressed up and looking her best.

It was too late now. "Hello, Jackson."

Wearing a suit and tie on a Saturday afternoon, he strolled from his boring sedan parked ahead of them. His brown hair had been slicked back from his forehead in perfect grooming. A couple of new lines had formed on his forehead. Only a year older than Ryder, he acted at least five years older. Because he never had fun, his only interest being the family business.

"Emory?" Ryder raised his brown eyebrows into high arches. He hadn't guessed who she was after spending thirty minutes in her company.

Her flying spirits took a dive and crashed to the ground. Had she been so unnoticeable as a kid? Jackson had recognized her immediately.

He signed off on a clipboard a worker gave him, barely glancing at her. "How was Barcelona?"

She angled her chin, surprised he remembered where she'd gone, and that she'd been gone at all. Their paths didn't cross frequently in the past, on purpose. She'd avoided him and his overbearing attitude. "Good."

The work experience had been great. The personal life, not so much. She wasn't going to go into detail. Not with Jackson.

"Emory?" Ryder's jaw dropped.

"Your mother is going to be glad you're home." Jackson considered her and his brother. His expression went quizzical. "Good to see you," he said, before heading up the stairs and through the front door.

"Emory?" Ryder shook his head trying to get her name straight.

Her shoulders dropped farther every time he said her name. Her fantasy had ended sooner than expected. "I suppose your invitation to the party has been withdrawn, now you know who I am."

"No." He shook his head again. "No. Of course not."

She raised her brows. "Are you sure? Do you want to dance with the housekeeper's daughter?"

He waved a hand in front of his face, and his expression cleared. He assessed her shape. "This is the twenty-first century."

She squirmed with misgiving. Not really an answer to her question.

Chapter Two

"Emory! You're home early!" Her mom's joyous shout echoed through the front courtyard.

Margaret Barrington sprinted forward, her arms open wide. Her short, gray hair bobbed with the quick trot, and her uniform fluttered in the breeze. She had a slim, petite frame, probably because she never sat still.

"Mom." Emory's chest wanted to explode with the happiness bursting inside. It had been two years since she'd last seen her mother. She hurried forward, forgetting about Ryder and the invitation.

Her mom wrapped her arms around her. The scent of cleaning polish and sugar cookies welcomed, bringing back fond memories. Since her father died when she was five, they'd been a team. She'd helped her clean and cook. Her mother taught her to sew, and to appreciate nice things. It was the creativity plus the practicality that had her deciding on interior design for a career.

"I missed you so much." Her mom leaned back and

squeezed her upper arms, studying her with tears in her violet eyes. "I'm so excited you're here to stay."

"Me, too."

"I thought you weren't supposed to come in until tomorrow?" Her mom wrapped a tight arm around her, not wanting to let go.

"I caught an earlier flight." She refused to think about the reasons why during her reunion with her mom.

Her mom fingered the short hair. "You cut your hair. It's beautiful."

"Thanks, Mom."

"Let's get you unpacked." Mom let go of her, and grabbed the handle of the roller board. She turned toward a frozen Ryder. "Thanks for giving my baby a ride."

Emory's skin warmed. She didn't need her mother reminding him how she used to look. "Yes, thanks. I'll see you later."

"Yes. Later." He gave them a slight wave before disappearing into the front door of the mansion. Even knowing who she was, he'd said he wanted her to go to the party, right?

She firmed her muscles, not giving in to uncertainty. "Yes, let's unpack. I need to find a nice dress for tonight."

"Tonight?"

Together, they sauntered into the house, through the busy kitchen filled with temporary help for the party. Granite counters gleamed, and stainless-steel appliances shone. Trays were laid out on the counter as the workers prepared. It was the same scene before every Croft party. The workers were in motion, and her mom's job was to supervise.

"I've been invited to the party." She rambled behind her mother, taking in the familiar sights and sounds. They headed toward the back wing of the large Croft mansion, to the suite she'd lived in since her mom had taken the job for the first Mrs. Croft.

That woman had been a nightmare.

Amazing how well Ryder had turned out, with such a terrible mother. Light, fun, and charming. While Jackson had ended up intimidating, overbearing, and too serious. And he obviously noticed details, because he'd recognized Emory the moment he saw her.

How had he known it was her?

Her mother opened the door and led her inside.

The suite of rooms looked the same as when she'd graduated college two years ago. A small living room decorated in soothing pastels, attached to an efficient kitchenette with a counter and small kitchen table. Large windows letting in light gave the place an airiness. The short hallway led to two bedroom doors. The one to the left was her mother's, with an en suite bathroom, and the one to the right had been hers since she was five years old.

Entering her bedroom, a comfortable familiarity settled around her. The room had changed over the years, but it was her space. From a place filled with stuffed animals and dolls, to walls decorated with pop stars, to the more simple tastes of a woman in college. The four-poster bed sported an Indian-print bedspread she'd found at a local flea market, and bought with money she'd earned in high school. She'd thought it exotic and interesting and stylish. The top of the tall dresser had an expensive Rococo Revival Gilt Gesso mirror the first Mrs. Croft had thrown away. Emory couldn't stand the thought of something so precious being at the junkyard, so she'd saved the mirror. She loved mixing different styles together, and creating something new.

Her mother opened the curtains to a lovely view of a small side garden, where a few early-spring flowers bloomed. "What's this about you going to Lexi's wedding reception tonight?"

Emory flopped onto her bed like the teenager she'd once been. Excited jitters danced with unease in an unusual partnering. Maybe Ryder had only been being nice by standing by the invitation.

"Ryder invited me." Her voice rose. She jumped off the bed and grabbed her suitcase. "Can you believe it? He said we were going to dance. Together."

Mom frowned, and tiny wrinkles appeared around her mouth. Wrinkles that hadn't been there two years ago. "What about Shey?"

"Shey?" Emory opened her suitcase and yanked clothes out, throwing them around the room. Normally, she was a pretty neat person—her mom was a housekeeper, after all—but she couldn't contain the frazzled energy.

"His girlfriend." Her mom snatched up one of the flying items and started to fold.

"They broke up." She spotted the gold dress she'd worn to one of Alejandro's many parties. Events where she'd wanted to look rich, sophisticated, and sexy. Pulling it out, she held it to her shoulders. "What do you think? Is it nice enough for a Croft event?"

"You talk as if you were invited to a king's castle." Her mom chided. "It's the same house you've lived in since you were a child."

Her nerves escalated, remembering how she'd felt as a kid. "Lived in, but never belonged."

Ryder had teased her as kids. Between his many girlfriends and sports, he hadn't hung around the house much. Jackson had been too busy with school and then work, barely noticing she existed. Which was probably because she hid whenever he was around.

When Lexi had moved in with her mother, Emory had thought they could be friends. Except Lexi had been quiet and studious, her head always buried in a book or doing experiments and tinkering with things in the garage. Emory had been too awkward and shy to make the first approach.

Mom picked a shirt off the floor and hung it on a hangar. "I thought you were done with this childish obsession of Ryder."

"It wasn't childish." Emory swung the dress around. "It was *looove.*"

Or so she'd thought, when she was thirteen. Now, it was hero worship, and a need to have fun. And attraction. She'd sensed the chemistry the second he'd stared into her eyes. Well, even if he hadn't realized they were *her* eyes. She swung the dress back and forth thinking about already dancing with her Prince Charming.

Mom snatched the dress out of her hands, and

shook the fabric out. "I heard Ryder and Shey were about to get engaged."

"They broke up before he asked her to marry him."

"How do you know so much when you've only been home minutes?"

"Ryder told me on the drive from town." An amazing drive.

He'd become her knight in shining armor not only because of the ride home, but because he'd made her realize she could be interested in men again. After the terrible breakup with Alejandro, she'd been afraid to flirt, afraid of being hurt.

Mom stopped moving, and studied Emory with a knowing expression. "He was thinking about marriage, which means he was serious about Shey."

Emory had thought the same thing. Since breaking up with Alejandro, she hadn't wanted to dive into any kind of dating or relationship. Ryder was getting over someone, too. They could console each other and have fun. "It's one party. Can't you let me enjoy myself?"

"I don't want to see your heart broken, or you pining for a man you can never have." Her mom's gaze softened, and she had a pleading expression.

She remembered her pangs of longing from the teenage years, remembered how desolate she'd felt alone at college, knowing he was out partying and having a good time, remembered her crazy fantasies about him missing her and coming to find her at school.

None of it had happened.

But now? She had one magical evening to spend with Ryder. Something she'd dreamed of since she was a kid. Her mother had no right to take it away. This wasn't Europe with its strict class system. Here, anyone could become anything, marry anyone.

"Why? Because I'm the housekeeper's daughter?" How dare her mom be so *classist*?

Hadn't she accused Ryder of the exact same thing?

"No. Dignity is required to serve." Her mom used her lecture tone, the one she'd heard so many times before, when kids made fun of her for being the maid's daughter.

Past insecurities punctured holes in her self-esteem. What if she didn't fit in? What if Ryder didn't really want her to come to the party now he knew who she was? Had he just been being polite?

Her mom hung up the dress, giving up her objections. "What about Alejandro?"

"I told you, he and I are done." She hadn't shared the details of his cheating ways. She'd been too miserable and angry. Still wasn't ready to discuss the situation with her mother.

Nodding, her mom ran a hand down the gold dress. "I can steam this, and it should look fine for tonight."

She pushed her doubts aside and hugged her mom, grateful this wouldn't become an issue. "Thanks, Mom."

"Does Jackson know you're attending?"

Her nerves doubled, tying a knot in Emory's belly. "No. I don't know. Maybe Ryder told him."

She could imagine Jackson's snobbiness at a mere housekeeper's daughter attending his sister's wedding reception. He always insisted on the formalities. His scowl would be legendary. She imagined his face. Handsome, stern, mature. Maybe he'd changed. Loosened up. "Does Jackson have a girlfriend?"

"No. Why?"

"I thought a girlfriend might have relaxed him over the years."

She had to wonder what type of woman would date a man like Jackson.

Emory waltzed into the elegant backyard party. Anxiety fluttered similar to the decorative butterflies hanging from the lower tree branches. She smoothed the skirt of her dress and surveyed the guests, trying to spot Ryder. Or anyone she knew.

The backyard garden had been transformed into a fairytale glen. Tiny, twinkling lights wove in the trees. Lanterns lined the walkway. Music drifted on the light breeze. For early May, the weather was warm, with a hint of crispness in the air.

Faltering, she stopped. What was she doing here? She didn't belong in this fantasy world. She was used to watching their parties from a distance, perched in a tree, or behind a serving cart. Fantasizing, not living.

This was real. Anxiety flared into excitement, charring her self-doubt. She pinched her arm. She was going to enjoy herself.

She moved forward with determined steps. Spotting the bride, she worked her way in that direction. She needed to say congratulations, because she hadn't brought a gift. Etiquette dictated she had a year, so she'd find something chic and elegant for their new home, and mail it to the happy couple. A calling card for her new business.

Lexi's bright-red hair shone. Her face beamed as she greeted guests. The tall man beside her had blond hair and tanned skin. He contemplated his bride with an expression of love. They both appeared deliriously happy.

Emory dreamed of a man looking at her in that way. She'd thought maybe Alejandro would be the guy. He'd been her only serious relationship. It turned out he looked at a lot of women that way.

Drawing closer, her stomach twisted. She hoped the bride wasn't upset at her presence. "Congratulations. I don't know if you recognize me." Ryder hadn't. "I'm—"

"Emory." The bride hugged her, as if wanting to spread her joy. "I'm so glad you're home. How was Barcelona?"

Her nerves relaxed a little. She was remembered and welcomed. "Good."

"This is Dax O'Donnell, my husband." Lexi spoke the last word with pride.

"Hi. Nice to meet you." He gave her a short, nervous smile. "I'm a little out of my element, with all of Lexi's people."

"Me, too." Emory couldn't help empathizing with the man. At least she wasn't the main attraction with the wealthy friends and family of the Crofts.

"They're your people, too, now." Lexi took hold of his hand.

He studied the ground in an aw-shucks demeanor. "I'm just a ski patrol paramedic."

A humble man. A rare quality in the Croft household. Emory liked him on the spot.

"Dax is starting a new enterprise. A fabulous mountain avalanche safety class." The bride's pride extended to the groom's accomplishments.

"What a great idea." She remembered the story of how Lexi's father had died, and understood her appreciation for the class.

"What do you do, Emory?" Dax steered the conversation away from him.

"I'm an interior designer." She'd worked hard at school, and at her internship in Spain. She planned to start her own firm in Castle Ridge.

"You need to meet Dani Marstrand. She's opening a bed-and-breakfast, and will need help with decorating the rooms." Lexi waved at a shorter, brown-haired woman standing farther back in the reception line. "Dani, meet Emory Barrington. She's an interior designer."

"You're just the person I need to talk to." The woman's grin calmed the last of her nerves.

She was going to be accepted into the Croft realm, and maybe she could make some contacts to get her business kickstarted. "Lexi tells me you're opening a bed-and-breakfast."

"This fall. Do you have a business card?"

Why hadn't Emory come prepared? "Not yet. I moved back from Europe today."

"Here's mine." Dani took a card out of her purse, and handed it to her. "I'd love to show you my lodge and get ideas. Luke and I have so much work to do."

The woman filled her in on the location and their

plans, while Emory scanned the crowd. Her adrenaline scrambled when she saw Ryder. He was talking to an older man with a balding head and large paunch. Ryder wore a scowl, and his lips pinched in an angry shape. Must not be a pleasant conversation.

Grabbing a glass of champagne off the tray of a passing waiter, he swiveled away from the man and headed toward where the bride and groom stood under a white canopy. He downed the entire glass in one gulp. Guess he was used to good champagne and didn't feel the need to sip and appreciate. Staring in her direction, he stopped. His eyes widened when he spotted her.

Anticipation thrummed through her. Anticipation of a fun evening with a handsome man. She just needed *to not* revert to her star-struck, teenage self.

He peered behind him with a furtive glance, and moved forward with large steps in a straight line toward her. "You look amazing, Emory."

The way he said her name with an air of distinction and a hint of swagger had her knees trembling. "Thank you. So do you."

Amazing was only the beginning of how he appeared. He resembled a model from a magazine. His longer hair had been groomed, and loose curls fell from the end. His gray orbs sparked with a troublemaking light, hinting he was up to no good. His strong chin and prominent nose imitated statues carved by Michelangelo himself.

He was perfect.

The custom black tuxedo fit his frame, highlighting broad shoulders and a trim waist. He eschewed the normal bow tie for a bolo tie with a horseshoe clasp. He didn't take himself too seriously. Unlike his brother.

"I'm going to go find Luke." Dani's parting comment was lost on Emory because Ryder held out his hand.

"Do you want to dance?"

To her! Her entire body wilted, and she wanted to cling to a nearby pole for support.

She was having an out-of-body experience. It was the only way to explain what was happening. *Be cool. You are sophisticated and worldly.*

Putting her hand in his, she noticed how dark and strong and manly his hand was, compared to her small, white one. To heck with sophisticated. She wanted to live out her teenage fantasy. She deserved it, after her breakup with Alejandro. Fun and flirty. Nothing serious.

He led her toward the temporary dance floor, and the crowd parted, as if this was a movie. Ryder Croft was about to put his arms around her. She struggled to breathe. He would hold her close to his Greek-god body. She would press up against him and freely inhale his piney scent.

He swung her around, and placed one hand at her waist. "How was Spain?"

He'd asked her a question. She couldn't think or comprehend. He swayed to the music, and she tried to follow the rhythm.

"What?" What if he thought she was deaf? Or stupid?

Flames of mortification erupted inside her. What if she said something dumb? She might revert to her teenage feelings for this man, but she didn't want to seem like a teenager.

"How was Spain? My brother said you'd just returned." He repeated himself because she was an idiot.

"Spain? It was good. Good." If she babbled any more, she'd sound like a baby proving she was too immature for this man. What had happened to the sophisticated and mysterious woman from the car? Ryder was probably asking the same question. She needed to pull herself together.

So what if this was the boy she'd had a crush on forever? They were both mature adults. She'd had a real relationship with a man. Ryder had had dozens.

"I love Madrid. And the coast. Wonderful beaches." His voice was a beachy breeze, warm and soothing.

She stepped on his foot. "Sorry."

"No worries." He was so nice.

"I haven't danced much recently."

"We'll have to remedy that while you're here." He swung her into a low dip.

Her head buzzed. Did he mean he wanted to see her again? Her teenage fantasy was about to come true.

Jackson stood near the bar, a sentry watching the crowd. He'd already pulled several business associates into his home office to talk about Asian markets and trade deals. He'd cornered a wily investor, and got him to verbally agree to a deal. All in all, Lexi's wedding reception had been an excellent business investment.

Of course, he'd give his stepsister whatever she wanted. Technically, she was his partner in her new avalanche safety device. And she was extremely happy with Dax O'Donnell. The man had even stood up to Jackson's scrutiny.

"Who the hell is Ryder with?" George nudged with his shoulder, and pointed his fourth glass of bourbon at the dance floor.

Scanning the crowd, Jackson made out his brother's head bending to talk to a slip of a girl. A girl with dark, short hair that waved around her face like a frame unable to contain the beauty.

He sucked in a sharp breath. Not because he was taken with her, but because he was shocked.

He'd recognized Emory the minute he saw her standing by his brother's car this afternoon. His brother had seemed surprised he'd driven the girl home, as if he hadn't realized who he'd picked up. Par for the course, Ryder was always picking up strange women.

Then again, Emory used to have long, kinky hair, glasses, and no shape whatsoever. Her eyes had been the same. Violet with a twinkle. Jackson's mind had been on other things this afternoon, and he hadn't taken the opportunity to really study her. She'd gone from no curves, to maximum curves. The acne and glasses were gone. And the hair had been styled into an elegant 'do, shaping her pixie face with the slight, upturned nose.

"Well?" George's demand brought Jackson back to the moment.

"That's Emory. She's our housekeeper's daughter." Nothing for anyone to worry about. She was just a girl.

A girl who'd lived in their home since she was a small child. Who hid around corners, watching everything and everyone. Who stood on tiptoes at this second and kissed Ryder on the mouth in front of everyone on the dance floor.

Adrenaline rushed through Jackson's veins. He couldn't let her interfere with the Webber deal. He'd caught her kissing his brother once before. She'd been around twelve and had been dusting the formal living room. She'd picked up Ryder's photo and kissed the glass.

"She's cleaning his lips." The old man's anger cut through his shock.

"Ryder's known her since she was a child. They're like siblings." Even though Jackson never felt like her sibling. He'd always sensed her presence in the house, yet rarely saw her. She must've run away when he was around. He furrowed his brow, thinking she'd been shy or he'd scared her. "It was only a peck."

That's all the kiss was. That's all it could be. A friendly, sisterly peck.

"My daughter's heart is broken, and your brother is picking up women." George shifted to nasty. "I'm not so sure I want them getting back together."

Jackson ground his fist into his other hand. His brother loved Shey Webber, and he couldn't lose this deal. Not because of a slip of girl who meant nothing to his brother. "Of course, you do. *The kids* are good together. They had a minor misunderstanding. I'm going to clear this situation up right now."

"You better."

The threat rubbed against his raw nerves. The discussion they'd had earlier today fresh in his mind. He understood the ramifications of losing the deal. He'd put hours into the negotiations, and thousands into the lawyer fees.

Marching to the dance floor, Jackson tapped his brother on the shoulder. "Excuse me."

The girl—no, woman—lifted her head. Her expression went from dreamy to startled, staring at him with those big, violet eyes. He could imagine the way a Renaissance painter would capture her full lips shaped in an attractive bow. The smooth stroke of a brush representing her ivory skin.

"What do you want?" His brother's sharp question chased him out of his contemplation of the ingénue.

He forced the fanciful image away and glared. "We need to talk. In private."

"Whatever you have to say to me, you can say in front of Emory." Did his brother already think of them as a pair?

Ridiculous. Not going to happen. Keeping his brother away from alluring young women should not be part of his job description. And yet, it was. He gripped his brother's upper arm and tugged, keeping a tight rein on his annoyance. "Excuse us."

"Grab a bottle of champagne, and I'll meet you in the rose garden in ten minutes." Ryder's voice rose, and he peered in the direction of the bar.

The last spot his future father-in-law had been standing.

Was flirting with Emory a plan to make Shey jealous?

A chest-thumping smile bloomed on Emory's face in acceptance of the invitation. She'd be in the garden waiting, and Ryder would break her heart. If Jackson allowed it. Which he wouldn't.

Although she was not his concern. His concern was Croft Industries, and the pending deal with Webber. And his brother.

He hustled his brother into his office, and closed the sliding glass door. "What do you think you're doing?"

"Dancing. Enjoying our sister's wedding reception. Unlike you." The challenge in Ryder's pitch surprised. He leaned against the back end of the couch and crossed his arms. "How many business discussions have you had tonight?"

Jackson refused to let his brother make him feel guilty. He'd use the party the way he wanted. If he reached out to business contacts, so be it. "How many hearts are you going to break tonight?"

"What's that supposed to mean?" The snarl in his brother's tone, told him he understood the direction of the conversation. His brother picked at the metal stud on the leather couch.

"You're playing with Emory's affections." An unusual sensation seared his lungs. It wasn't worry about the girl, it was worry about the deal.

"Do you think she's not good enough for me, because she's the housekeeper's daughter? You always were stuffy."

The insult bounced off him. He had the utmost respect for the household staff and their children. Unfortunately, he was the head of the family, and had to enforce rules and make decisions that were best for the entire family. And the staff.

"This has nothing to do with her being Mrs. Barrington's daughter. Or maybe it does." Because he had a soft spot for the woman and her daughter. A soft enough spot where he'd anonymously awarded Emory a college scholarship. "You know the girl has had a crush on you since middle school."

He'd seen it in the way she'd followed his brother around the house. How she'd watched his brother more than anyone else. His muscles tensed. It appeared she still had a crush on Ryder.

Ryder's brows arched, and his mouth rounded into a surprised *O*. "She has?"

Jackson paced to the small side table in his office. How could his brother be so obtuse? "And your future father-in-law is here, wondering why Emory is kissing you."

His brother stood straight with a jerky motion, and stomped toward the desk. "George is not my future father-in-law. Shey and I broke up."

"Why did you break up with her?"

The couple had been happy and in love.

"She broke up with me." Ryder's voice cracked. He picked up a financial newspaper off the desk, rolled it up, and smacked the desk.

"What did you do?" Jackson couldn't stop the accusation, even though he sensed the distress in his brother's voice.

"*I* didn't do anything." His brother spun around and paced back toward the sliding glass doors, surveying the party out the window. "She said she believed we were a merger, not a marriage."

The words struck like lightning. Guilt sizzled in his gut. His and George's fault. All their talk about pre-nups, contracts, stocks, and portfolios.

"Can I go back to Emory now?"

He hated the obedience in Ryder's tone.

Facing away from his brother, Jackson noted the small bar. He needed a drink. But he needed to deal with the Emory situation before things got out of hand. Before she was hurt, and before the damage was too great for his brother to get back together with Shey.

Ryder needed to wallow in his feelings for Shey, not get distracted by another woman. He needed time, and Jackson needed his brother out of the way. Considering the decanters and glasses on the bar again, he spotted the open bottle of clam juice from the Bloody Marys one of his Japanese business associates had mixed.

He immediately dismissed the idea. He couldn't.

"In a minute."

Ryder wouldn't die because of a few drops of clam juice. His shellfish allergy wasn't too severe. He'd be sick for a few days, giving Jackson time to fix the situation, getting the deal and the engagement back on track.

This was his brother, though. Deliberately exposing him to an allergen would be terrible. Yet, he'd done other terrible things in his business dealings before.

Had needed to, in order to survive. In a way, he was helping his brother. Giving Ryder time to think about his love for Shey. Giving Shey a reason to contact Ryder because of his illness.

Jackson's hand trembled, picking up a clean glass. "Have a drink with me."

Chapter Three

With his back blocking his brother's view, Jackson splashed a little of the clam juice into a glass. He opened the decanter of bourbon and filled the glass, making sure the juice wasn't noticeable. Then, he filled his own glass to the top. He was going to need more than a glass of bourbon before tonight ended.

"Let's drink to Lexi." He handed his brother the spiked glass, and picked up his own. Guilt churned, creating a maelstrom in his midsection. He brushed it aside. The family doctor was a guest tonight. Medical help was nearby.

"To Lexi." Ryder raised the glass and took a long swallow.

Jackson sipped, and he couldn't help himself, he one-arm hugged his brother. He loved his siblings. He was the one who'd cared for them financially and made sure there was money for college and fun. He was helping Ryder tonight. Not torturing him. "To your new freedom."

"To my new freedom." Ryder took an even longer swallow, and another.

Panic flared. That couldn't be good. Jackson only wanted his brother to get a small taste. To make him sick a few days, not forever. Not to need an emergency room, or hospitalization.

"Hold up there. You don't need to drink it all at once." A muscle spasmed in Jackson's cheek. Snatching the glass away, he downed the rest of his brother's drink. "How about a beer?"

Searching for signs of discomfort, he studied his brother. Maybe there hadn't been enough clam juice to make an impact. Maybe he hadn't done a terrible thing.

He got two beers from the small fridge behind his desk. Opening them, he handed one to his brother. "Do you know where Shey is tonight?" He wanted his brother's mind back on one woman.

"Island getaway." Ryder snarled and slammed the beer on the counter. "I need to get back to the party."

"Spend a few minutes with your older brother." Jackson needed to watch Ryder.

"My lips feel funny." He thumbed his mouth. "Tingly and *nuuumb*." The last word slurred. "What's going on?" His eyes flew open and panic flashed. "What was in the drink?"

"Only bourbon." Jackson's stomach turned. He tried to play innocent, even though he was guilty as the devil. His experience with a poker face in the boardroom helped, although he'd never been nauseous in the boardroom. At least not any more. "You okay?"

"I'm dizzy." His brother smashed his hand onto a small table and collapsed into a chair.

His turning stomach vaulted, as if he'd drank poison. "Some of the glasses are dirty. Maybe I poured into a dirty glass with something in it. We should call the doctor." He whipped out his cell phone, and dialed their personal physician. After explaining what happened, including the shellfish allergy, he hung up. "The doctor will be here any second. He was dancing. Let me get you water."

The doctor would give Ryder something to stop the allergic reaction from being deathly. Jackson wouldn't be the monster of a brother.

Ryder's pale face shone with sweat. "What about Emory?"

"What about her?" Jackson's voice hardened. This wasn't about the girl. It was about his brother and Shey. It was about a merger. And a marriage. And a love existing between the *two kids*. He clenched his teeth.

"I was supposed to meet Emory in the rose garden." His brother slumped on the chair, breathing heavily. "I don't want her to think I stood her up."

"I'll meet her. Tell her you got sick." Put an end to this silly crush.

The doctor hurried in with his small medical bag. "A shot of epinephrine, and then I'll take him to his room before he gets sicker."

"How sick?" Ryder slurred the question.

Worry crashed into guilt, making Jackson's head pound. He'd done this to his own brother. What kind of a man was he? But if it was for Ryder's own good, if he and Shey reconciled, did it matter how it happened?

"Good thing you thought about his allergy." The doctor's efficient moves put Jackson's mind at ease, not his conscience.

"People were making Bloody Marys earlier. I think maybe one of the glasses was dirty and had clam juice at the bottom. Of the glass." He over-explained, sounding more and more guilty. "Will Ryder be okay?"

The doctor already had the syringe in his hand. "He'll be fine."

The pounding stopped. He'd already committed the sinister act. "My brother's kind of a wimp. Give him a large dose so he can sleep through the discomfort and the itching all night and most of tomorrow."

The doctor's brows crinkled with concern. "Your brother's an adult. He doesn't need—"

"Do it." No one questioned his commands.

The doctor jerked back, before nodding.

"Do you need help with him?" It was the least Jackson could do, after poisoning his brother and threatening the doctor.

"No. I've got him." The doctor got his brother to his feet. "I'll leave instructions behind."

"Okay." After he cleared up the Emory situation, he'd take the best care of Ryder ever. Hire the best nurses, make sure he took whatever he was supposed to, and ate well. Jackson would ask Mrs. Barrington to make his brother's favorites.

And he'd call Shey and let her know Ryder was sick and needed her.

Jackson sunk into his desk chair, and downed the rest of his bourbon. The sour taste burned his throat and sank in his gut. Opening a desk drawer, he took out his personal checkbook and slipped it into his suit pocket. He was a snake getting ready to bite. Dread anchored him to the chair. When had he become this horrible person?

Part of the job description. He'd done it to business opponents in the past. Even innocents.

Early on, a young accountant had noted the inconsistencies in the financial statements. He'd met with her privately and asked who else she'd discussed the information with. When she'd said no one, he'd known what had to be done. He'd told her boss she'd acted inappropriately toward him, and she was taken off the account. And the boss had never believed the jilted woman's word over his.

He slammed the drawer shut, and headed out of his office toward the rose garden. An appropriate place for a slithering snake about to take down an innocent.

Emory stood in the garden, surrounded by roses of varying colors. None of them were as bright as her. Which was ridiculous. She wore a shimmery dress that hugged her curves and flared out in a short skirt. She resembled a fairy, light and innocent. He was about to bring a shadow to her fairytale world.

If she'd been waiting for him, he wouldn't have taken this long. He would've rushed to her side. He pushed the fanciful thought away. Women like her didn't wait for men like him. She was too young, too inexperienced, too in love with love.

He cleared his throat, cleared his emotions. "Emory."

"Jackson?" She peered at him with wary eyes. Eyes darting around, searching for an escape, as she'd done when she'd found herself alone in a room with him when she was younger. He'd felt like an ogre then, and did now. "Where's Ryder?"

Jackson wanted to capture the innocence. Splash it on a canvas to remind him of how innocent life had been before his father died. Before he'd been exposed to the cutthroat business world. Before he'd learned of the desperate financial status of Croft Industries.

Maybe he'd never been that naïve.

"My brother couldn't make it." Guilt slithered across his skin, making him feel slimy. He was the reason his brother couldn't make the rendezvous.

"Why? Is something wrong?" She worried about his brother, when they'd only been together for a few minutes.

A ray of green envy sliced him inside. Ryder had the life. A beautiful woman caring about him. Shey in love with him. The opportunity to choose what he wanted to do with his career.

Stepping forward, Emory made to go around.

Jackson stopped her with his hand, grazing the bare skin on her arm. Soft skin. Silky skin. He should remove his hand from her. He didn't.

"Ryder's sick. The doctor took him to his bedroom."

"A doctor?" Her gaze widened, and he saw specks of black, hinting at a depth he could only imagine. "That's serious."

"An allergic reaction." He tried to shake off the

sliminess, wanting to grow a second skin. "He'll be fine. He sent me instead."

"Sent you?" She licked her lips showing her nervousness.

Frowning, a blackness dimmed the twinkling lights around them. She was afraid of him, even now. A sharp pang ripped through his chest. For good reason. He always knew she was smart. And especially attractive tonight. "To give you a message."

Her black eyebrows rose in skepticism. A variety of colorful, flowery scents circled around, with a touch of apples. Hers? Must be the rose garden. He wasn't close enough to smell her. Leaning in a little closer, he couldn't stop himself from taking a tantalizing sniff.

Apples, yes. And something more exotic.

"What's the message?" Her stilted voice reminded him of the reason he was here.

It wasn't to smell her or paint her or be tempted by her.

"Ryder's not available tonight. Or ever." Jackson used the guilt and the pain and the jealousy to deliver the harsh blow. He'd hurt people before, made grown men cry. Heck, he'd made his brother ill, yet he'd never experienced this gut-wrenching emotion the moment before he slashed an opponent down.

Her eyes shimmered and her chin quivered. She flattened her lips together as if trying to hold in a cry.

He didn't want to hurt her, and yet, by her expression, she already hated him. Why not go for broke? She tempted him as he'd never been tempted before. He understood why his brother was interested. "But I am."

"You are what?"

"Available." With quick reflexes, he bent his head and locked his lips onto her soft and surprised ones.

Magnetic energy sparked through him. He molded her body to his, lining up the interesting parts in all the right places. His mouth pressed against her shocked seam. Her lips were moist and yielding. He couldn't stop himself from using his tongue to get a little taste. A taste of heaven.

For a second.

She broke away and slapped his cheek. "You jerk. What the heck were you doing?"

The sting on his skin was what he deserved. He was a dirty, jaded man. A guilty man. He deserved to be slugged or shot. He'd afflicted the man she was supposed to meet and expected to take his place? The thought scarred. He hadn't been thinking when he kissed her. Only feeling and sensing and seeing.

High flags of righteous red shone on her cheeks. Her gaze turned stormy and dark. With a simple kiss, he'd changed her from light and innocent to shady and somber. That's what he did to people. It's what he'd done to himself.

He couldn't show what he felt. He put a sneer on his face. "I wasn't sure if it mattered which Croft brother you kissed."

Except he knew it mattered.

But his brother loved Shey. They'd get back together soon, and it would be Emory's heart hurting. In a way, he was doing her a favor. Stopping this attraction between her and Ryder before it got started.

"You surprised me." She swiped her mouth with the back of her hand and glared. "And it matters."

Music from the party intruded into their silence. Wind blew through the budding trees. Her scent must have stuck to his skin when he'd pressed her body against his, because he still smelled apples. She continued to glare, completely unaffected by his kiss.

The checkbook burned against his chest, reminding him of his goal. "You're correct. It does matter. My brother isn't right for you."

"And you are?" She scoffed.

"I'm not right for anyone." Darkness surrounded his soul at the truth of his statement. He didn't have the time, or the inclination, for a relationship. He certainly wasn't worthy of her, especially after his next action. He took out the checkbook and pen. "How much will it take for this little flirtation to disappear?"

She reeled back and her eyes grew darker, except for the bright flash of anger. "You're paying me off?"

"Twenty thousand? Fifty thousand?" The dollar amount meant nothing. He needed to save the merger. Save the marriage between Ryder and Shey.

Emory tilted her chin up in the habitual way, exhibiting curiosity and intelligence. "You're joking, right? All we did was dance."

"A dance. A kiss." Jackson controlled the spear of jealousy remembering their kiss. "I'm trying to save an important merger."

She shook her head in slow motion. "I have nothing to do with a merger."

"Ryder does. If he and Shey don't get married I've easily lost a million dollars, and even more if the merger doesn't go through." Jackson had to remember. This was for the merger and his brother's future.

"The deal's worth a million dollars?" The awe in Emory's tone told him he'd won.

Everyone had a price, even innocent fairies.

Disappointment left him sluggish. He clicked his pen and started to write out the check. "I'll write this for one hundred thousand."

She slapped the checkbook out of his hand, and it hit a puddle with a splash. "You couldn't buy me with all of your wealth."

Chapter Four

Emory clenched and unclenched her hands, taking in slow, deep breaths.

She was a bug. A small, smashed, not-even-worthy-of-being-stepped-on bug. Low and unworthy. Identical to the bug sloshing in the mud puddle where Jackson's fat checkbook lay. How dare Jackson believe she'd accept a bribe.

Her eyes burned. She refused to cry in front of this man. She wouldn't make his victory complete. Making her feel inconsequential. Making her believe she didn't belong with these lofty people. Making him believe she'd skulk away and leave Ryder alone.

Ryder hadn't kissed her back. Even so, he'd asked her to meet him in the garden. That must mean something.

Jackson hadn't won anything. She had more self-respect than that to be bought off like a common hooker. She'd worked hard in school, earning a full scholarship to college. She'd excelled in her college courses, winning a prestigious international internship. She had plans for a future.

So what if her past wasn't as exalted as his, her family wasn't as rich as his? She'd never stoop to his low-level tactics. "I've done nothing wrong."

Just as she'd done nothing wrong in Barcelona.

She held her head high, studying his gray eyes. Ryder had the same color, yet the inflections were different. His eyes were fun and light and mischievous. Jackson's eyes were slate cold.

"Everyone has a price. Even if it's not money." Sad he believed his statement.

"You're wrong about me and others." She wanted to prove his view of the world was skewed. Everyone didn't behave in ways he expected. "You need new friends."

His eyebrows flew high at her comments, shocked she should be so bold. His friends must not be honest, either.

"I'm sorry." His deep timbre rolled across her, trying to persuade her to believe that he actually was sorry.

Hah! It was another misdirection.

Glancing away so she wasn't persuaded, she fidgeted with the gold skirt of her dress. She'd been so excited to attend this party, to meet the people Ryder called friends, to be in his glamorous world. Now, not so much. "Ryder asked me to go dancing in the future. A date."

Well, he hadn't been quite that specific, but she refused to bend to pressure. She wasn't scared of Jackson anymore. She wasn't.

"My brother won't be going dancing for a while."

A muscle ticked in his cheek, showing the hint of dimples.

The mighty Jackson Croft had a tell.

"I want to see Ryder. And you're not going to stop me." Her childish demand had her wanting to cover her face.

"He's sleeping now. The doctor gave him something." Jackson's cheek ticked again. "Can you wait until morning?"

Did the tell signal discomfort or lying? Why was he suddenly being so accommodating? He'd gone from trying to buy her off, to acquiescence. His calm expression, except for the tic, gave nothing away. The steel of his gaze tried to force his will onto hers. She could wait until morning because she didn't want to barge into a bedroom, not because of Jackson's request.

"You can buy *me* off, dear Jackson." The scratchy, feminine voice interrupted Emory's contemplation of the man's eyes.

Dear Jackson? Could this be one of his paramours? Had the woman heard their confrontation? Witnessed the kiss?

The woman who'd spoken wore a pink sheath dress enveloping her slight frame. Her blonde hair hung low on her back in a long, sleek ponytail. Her flawless skin hinted at age on closer inspection. The forehead was too tight, and tiny wrinkles presented around her painted lips.

"What're you doing here?" His tone hardened, and yet his face paled as if he were seeing a ghost.

This woman wasn't welcome. Just like Emory.

"Don't stare at me, son." The woman tapped a long, painted nail on her cheek. "Kiss your mother hello."

Emory's breath snagged. This was the first Mrs. Croft. Her appearance had been altered with what had to be extensions, and lots of makeup.

Victoria Croft. The woman who'd treated the help like slaves, bossing them around and never saying thank you. Emory remembered running from the kitchen whenever this woman was around. She'd been only nine when the divorce had happened, and hadn't seen the woman since.

"I'm not going to kiss you." Jackson sounded cold and calm, except the tic in his cheek switched on. "I haven't seen you in fifteen years."

The first Mrs. Croft must be in her late fifties, yet she resembled a thirty-year-old. Emory might not remember how the woman looked, but even so, she remembered the tension in the house—and especially in her mother—when the woman was home.

"I'm still your mother." Victoria's gaze narrowed, and she surveyed the two of them, assessing and coming up with the wrong conclusion.

Emory's stomach swirled. She was not with Jackson, and never would be. Even though he'd recognized her when Ryder hadn't.

"I asked, what're you doing here?" Jackson bent down and picked up the checkbook, shaking off the water.

She smashed her lips together, feeling bad for putting him at a disadvantage in front of this evil woman. Because she'd heard stories and witnessed the woman's cruelty and neglect. She remembered seeing her mom in tears after an altercation.

"I was in town and heard about your little party." Mrs. Croft's flat smile didn't reach her eyes. "Of course, once I got here, I learned it was a party for that harlot's daughter—"

"Heather was not a harlot. She and Father met after the divorce." His defense of his second mother warmed Emory. "And Lexi is my sister."

"That woman ran Croft Industries into the ground by spending boatloads of money."

Emory didn't understand the accusation. Croft Industries was a respected company with a large and diverse portfolio. The second Mrs. Croft had never participated in the business.

"You don't know what you're talking about." His gaze darted to Emory and back to his mother.

She scrunched her shoulders, trying to make herself smaller. She didn't want to intrude on a family fight. "I should go."

"Yes. You should." His agreement should've had her hurrying away.

For some strange reason, she didn't want to abandon him. Although he didn't need help dealing with his own mother. He didn't need help dealing with anyone.

"You were going to pay this little hussy off. I want my fair share." The woman's calculating tone sent a shiver through her.

She remembered the tone berating her mother. The ear-splitting resonance brought back childish insecurities she'd fought hard to erase from her mind.

She was not lower class. She was this woman's equal.

"She's not a hussy." Jackson's defense of her was as quick as his defense of his sister. "You overheard a misunderstanding."

Emory stood a little taller, hoping that's what he believed. She was worthy of defense, and worthy of his brother. They'd had a misunderstanding. And he wouldn't interfere with her going on a date with Ryder.

Right?

Jackson could barely control the rage inside him, waiting for Emory to get out of earshot. His blood charged and every muscle tightened. His hands wanted to clench into fists. He wouldn't display his anger because showing emotions put a man at a disadvantage. Even with his mother. A hard lesson learned.

Laughter from the party filtered through the trees. Everyone was having a great time. Except for him, and his brother. And now Emory.

How dare this woman attack Emory, his sister, and the woman he thought of as his mother? He needed to find out what Victoria Croft wanted and get her out of the party.

Out of Castle Ridge.

Out of his life.

He sent a glare that had scared grown men in the boardroom. "You were listening to a private conversation."

Victoria's expression appeared serene, but some

emotion flashed in her normally blank eyes. "I saw you sneak off from the party, and thought it would be the perfect time to talk to you alone."

He had left the party alone. To meet Emory. To pay off Emory.

Sparks ignited in his system. He'd known the girl for most of her life, why did he think she'd take a bribe? He'd need to come up with a different plan to keep her apart from Ryder.

Focus, Jackson. He needed to focus on the woman who'd given him birth, abandoned him and his brother after the divorce, and suddenly arrived out of nowhere. "You followed me and you eavesdropped."

Because Victoria had heard the comment about paying off and hadn't made herself known until several minutes later. Typical. She'd frequently listen at the door of Father's office, suspecting him of doing something wrong. Jackson should call security, except he didn't want the woman to make a scene.

"I was being considerate by not interrupting whatever this was." She waved a long, scrawny hand toward the place Emory had stood and his checkbook. "Emory? An unusual name."

His stomach roiled. If his mother figured out who Emory was, she'd make the girl's life miserable. A lowly servant's daughter making moves on his brother. Victoria might help his cause, except he'd didn't want her involved in the matter. In any matter. He had to stop the line of pursuit. "Leave."

"Can't I check in on my two sons?" Her saccharine-sweet grin made his teeth ache. She'd never checked in on them before.

"After almost fifteen years?" He couldn't hold in the skepticism.

"Where is Ryder? I didn't see him at the party."

Jackson wanted to hide his little brother away from this woman and the destruction she brought. Yet, a nibbling curiosity pecked at his brain. "Why? You didn't care about us after you took off for Europe when we were teenagers."

She'd taken the large divorce settlement and left the country without a word. No goodbyes, no contact, not even a birthday card. He'd waited every year on his birthday for at least a phone call. Anything to show she cared, to show she remembered he existed.

Her gray gaze narrowed into slits of shale. Her brow furrowed and her plump lips snarled. Would she throw one of her famous temper tantrums? He remembered those. The screaming and throwing things. The broken glass and broken hearts.

Internally, his stature shrunk, as if he was that young boy watching his parents fight. Outwardly, he stood taller and threw out his chest. He'd promised his father he'd protect the company and the family, and she would not destroy anything or anyone in his protection.

It was weird how he'd hated her and loved her at the same time. Relieved she'd left, yet sad she hadn't called or visited.

Her lips uncurled and lifted into a smile. The kind of smile she'd used to get her way. "While your reception might not be welcoming, I'm sure your brother's will be. Just like he welcomed that girl."

The words were modulated evenly. Too evenly. He

sensed a threat to both Emory and Ryder. Showing he cared would be tantamount to waving a red flag. His mother had been at the party longer than he'd thought.

"Ryder's sick. Call him and make your own arrangements. Off-premises." Jackson wouldn't show his worry about his mother influencing his brother. He couldn't exhibit any vulnerabilities. "Leave, or I'll toss you out."

"I'm going. I'm going." His mother's tone sounded defiant. "And I'll call Ryder later."

Good luck. He would be sleeping the entire night, and most of the day tomorrow. The muscle in Jackson's cheek spasmed. Sleeping and sick because of what he'd done. Plus, in his experience his brother never made appointments.

His mother whirled around with a swish of her dress, and headed toward the front of the house.

Following behind, he made sure she got in a car and drove away, while a jackhammer drilled through his lungs. The hairs on the back of his neck stood at attention. The sense of knowing when something wasn't right set off alarm bells. It had saved him several times in past business dealings.

Why had she come back now, when he was in the middle of the biggest deal of his life?

With anticipation thrumming through her veins, Emory knocked on Ryder's bedroom door the following morning. She'd kissed him while they'd danced last night, and he hadn't responded. Was he even interested in her? Or not interested because he knew she was Emory Barrington? The kiss had barely been a peck before Jackson had interrupted their dance. Maybe Ryder hadn't had time to respond?

That must be it.

Warmth combined with doubt, making her slightly sick. She'd responded instantly to Jackson's quick kiss. Only because of shock. She'd been completely surprised when his hard lips had caressed hers. When his mouth had moved and elicited sparks of...

No, no, no. His touch had elicited absolutely nothing.

Desperate to escape her doubts, she knocked a little louder. Still nothing. What if something was wrong? She'd been up early because of jet lag. The rest of the house was quiet. She really should check on him. Twisting the knob, she opened the door slightly, and peeked inside the room.

Ryder lay on his stomach, the blankets up to his broad, bare shoulders. The mound moved up and down slowly. He was sound asleep.

She'd never dared enter his bedroom when she'd been a kid. When she'd help her mother with cleaning, she'd assist in the kitchen or other living spaces. Never did she enter either one of the brother's bedrooms. She didn't now. But she did peek.

His bedroom was large. So much larger than hers or her mother's at the back of the house. A Bernhardt king-size sleigh bed centered the room, with dark blue covers. End tables matched a tall dresser filled with a selection of skiing trophies on top. The small seating area was littered with dirty clothes, and the closet was messy, too. A perfectly clean desk sat on the far side of the room. He obviously didn't use the normally-necessary piece of furniture.

Burying his head in the pillow, his long hair was plastered to his head. From her post by the doorway, she couldn't see any of the effects of the allergy poisoning. He looked so cute and cuddly. And contentedly asleep.

"Morning, Emory."

She jumped at Jackson's greeting behind her. Thinking about what had happened between them last night, her pulse zoomed. The kiss, the buy-off, his mother. Her zooming pulse incited waves of excitable shivers across her skin. Not because of the kiss. Because of the anger from him trying to pay her off.

Wheeling around, she forced her lips up in a pleasant smile. She wouldn't show him the tumult of emotions running inside her.

He took off the baseball cap he wore, and ran fingers through his dark hair, and she couldn't help wondering how his hair would feel between her fingers. He was dressed casually—for him—in nice khaki pants and a blue, button-down shirt. Not his daily uniform of suit and tie.

"Is Ryder awake?"

She tensed, hoping their truce about her dating Ryder wasn't over. "No."

Jackson snapped the bedroom door closed, and his gaze bored into her. He was trying to intimidate.

"I was checking to see if he was okay." She stood tall, demonstrating to him she had every right to be here. "You told me I could visit this morning."

"I did."

The silent hallway added awkwardness between them. His bedroom was only a door away. Her skin heated, wondering how his room appeared. Was his bed larger than his brother's?

Swallowing, she moved away from the door and sank into an empire style chair in the hallway, trying to decide what to do, or say. The wide-striped cushions surrounded her, giving a little protection. She ran her fingers over the smooth, glossy wood of the armrests.

He took the seat on the other side of the Bombe chest with marble top. "The doctor gave Ryder a strong medication, so he'll sleep through most of the day."

A hint to leave this part of the house? Besides the bedrooms, she'd had free rein of the home as a kid. Now she was back, maybe he expected her to stick to her mom's suite. "For an allergic reaction? That seems extreme."

Jackson's cheek ticked for a second. "The doctor wants to keep my brother comfortable, so he doesn't scratch, or do anything else to make the reaction worse."

"Oh." Sympathy flowed through her. There'd been shrimp appetizers at the reception last night. "Doesn't Ryder know to stay away from shellfish?"

"He does." Jackson defended his brother, but not quite. "It was an accident."

She loved eating shrimp and crab and lobster. Something she'd have to pass on while dating Ryder. Because she couldn't kiss him if she'd exposed herself to shellfish, and she wanted to kiss him. She'd always wanted to kiss him. Not the little peck she'd given him last night. Real kissing, like how Jackson had kissed her.

"Are you doing anything today?" His change of topic pressed against her, making her cornered and curious.

After visiting Ryder, she'd planned to visit with her mom and get going on her business plan. "I need to design business cards and work on a website."

Jackson beamed, resembling someone about to bestow a present, or because the edges of his mouth appeared rigid, like a person setting a trap. "Do you want your first client?"

She jumped for the second time. Had someone at the reception talked to him about needing a designer? "Who?"

"Me." His eyes went wide, trying to look innocent. Too innocent.

A ripple of unease went through her. She didn't trust him after last night, and yet he was now open to her dating his brother, and he placed a tempting offer in front of her.

She scanned the long hallway with its marble sculptures, Italian chandeliers, and perfectly-hung art. "This house doesn't need to be redecorated."

"I bought a penthouse years ago, and haven't done anything to it." His casual tone belied the intensity of his gaze.

"In Castle Ridge?" That didn't make much sense, when he lived in the mansion. Flames crawled up her cheeks. Unless he brought women to this penthouse.

She didn't know if she could decorate *Jackson's* love nest.

"Denver. We can leave right now, if you're available." He stood and placed the hat back on his head. The baseball cap made him appear younger and more relaxed. More relatable and real.

Having a place in Denver made more sense. If he had a late business meeting he could spend the night, instead of coming home to Castle Ridge.

"Going to Denver will take all day." She didn't want to be gone long from her mother and Ryder.

"I want to make up for my behavior last night. And I really need the help." Jackson's sincere expression soothed her nerves. This was business. "I have time today. We can fly down this morning, and be back this afternoon."

Getting a commission from Jackson Croft would go a long way toward building her reputation as an interior designer, especially after losing her internship. "What about Ryder?"

"He'll be sleeping most of the day. You can leave a note you were here and will stop by later." Jackson said the right things.

He was okay with her seeing his brother, and he wanted to give her a huge job. Her first job. A high-end design job, which would help her get more high-end clients. He'd said he was sorry about last night, and he'd defended her to his mean mother.

She weighed the options and opportunities. She couldn't say no. "Okay."

His slow smile spread through her chest. Because she'd agreed to his deal and made the right decision.

After leaving a note, saying goodbye to her mom, and grabbing the items she'd need for reviewing and estimating a job, she and Jackson drove to the small regional airport near Castle Ridge. The entire thirty minutes had been accomplished swiftly and efficiently, and she couldn't believe she sat in a private jet.

Jackson had barely said two words. He'd focused on driving, and now his computer. He couldn't be bothered to appreciate the luxury. She guessed he was used to it. She sat across from him, studying his expression, curious to know how his mind operated. He'd always been an enigma to her, and not around much when she'd come home during college. Running Croft Industries from the time he'd graduated college must've kept him busy.

Her mom always spoke highly of him. And her mom was a good judge of people.

His pupils darted back and forth, reading quickly. His brows would furrow together at times, as if thinking about certain points. His Roman nose reminded her of the marble sculptures she'd seen in European museums.

He was classically handsome. Gorgeous, really, with hard lines and sharp angles. His strong chin showed his determination to succeed. And his lips, which she admitted had been very kissable, were now flat. If he smiled and laughed more often, he'd be irresistible.

For someone else. She was only interested in Ryder.

"Looking for something?"

Her heart rattled at being caught staring at Jackson's mouth. She jerked her head up, and inspected those depthless gray eyes. "No, I, um…you have something on your lip."

"Do I?" He didn't wipe at his mouth, knowing she lied.

Her cheeks flushed, and she picked up a magazine from the seat pocket and buried her face inside until they'd taken off.

Once in the air, the attendant served orange juice and water. Emory unbuckled her seat belt and took out her camera, pointing the lens out the window.

The sun shone brightly for the early spring day. The bluebird sky was dotted with puffy white clouds. The tall mountain peaks were covered with snow, with the green tree line creating a division between beauty and majesty.

She sucked in an awe-inspired breath. "It's beautiful."

She'd missed this incredible slice of nature. Barcelona was beautiful in a different way. These snowcapped mountains and hills would always be home.

"Hmm?" He glanced up from his laptop.

"The scenery. It's beautiful." How could he not appreciate the natural beauty? "Do you ever look out the window?"

"No." He stared at her instead, making her uncomfortable.

If she was sophisticated, she'd be used to such sights. She refused to pretend, and wouldn't buy his blasé attitude. Doesn't matter how often you've seen something, beauty was beauty.

"What about when you travel to foreign cities? Don't you ever climb a monument, or go to a museum?" She was being impertinent, but if she was going to work with him, design his personal space, she needed to know about him.

She'd spend hours in the museums in Barcelona. For design inspiration, and for life inspiration.

"No time." He studied his screen with a blank face. "Too busy with work."

He must not pay attention to anything when he traveled, except business. A man who'd accomplished so much, and yet experienced so little.

"You're a billionaire, Jackson. How much more money do you need?"

He looked up from his computer again. His expression swooshed with irritation. He contemplated her. "It's not about the money."

Something about the way he spoke told her it was the truth. He didn't work hard for the money. He worked too much for some other reason.

Whatever that reason was, he needed to experience real life.

"Observe and enjoy." Without thinking, she placed her flat palm on his cheek, and angled his head toward the window.

Her skin blazed from the warmth of him. The roughness of his stubble scratched her palm. Sparks electrified up her arm. She should remove her hand now that he peered out the window.

He didn't shake her hand off, either. He didn't turn back toward his computer. He held his head stiffly, as if afraid to move.

Or maybe he enjoyed the contact as much as she did.

Chapter Five

An hour later, Jackson continued to feel Emory's palm on his cheek. Not because he was attracted to her, but because she'd pointed out the obvious.

He never peered out the window of his private jet. When he visited places, he went from plane to car to boardroom or meeting. He didn't tour monuments or museums. A waste of time and frivolous.

He'd also never regarded her.

Known for his ability to size up a person or a situation within seconds, he hadn't seen her coming. Or at least her impact. On him, and on his brother.

Her too-cute, short hair wasn't what he was normally attracted to. He enjoyed long and lithe, not short and petite. And opinionated. Because her command to enjoy the scenery had been profound and knowing. Her insight had shaken him.

How much more did she see? He wasn't used to people understanding him. Or even caring. He'd removed her hand a second after, realizing her touch's impression. If he'd listened to her advice and taken the time to do any of those things, he wouldn't have a successful business. He hadn't had a choice. He'd needed to stay focused on his goal.

And right now, his goal was to keep Emory away from his brother. Keep her busy with the penthouse project by setting unrealistic deadlines. Possibly spending time in Denver, and not in Castle Ridge. And, if needed, he had more ploys to keep her away.

"I haven't been here in a while." The private elevator whisked them to the top floor of the building he'd purchased in the lower downtown area of Denver. "It's a place to sleep when I'm in town."

The penthouse wasn't a home. More of a place to go after his business meetings and dinners were over for the day. Another place to work, and sleep. And, at one point in time, an escape.

The area had been up-and-coming when he'd purchased. Old manufacturing buildings being converted to stylish condominiums and loft apartments. Hip, experimental restaurants were popping up in the area. Trendy retail stores were becoming destination shopping. At the time, the artsy area had appealed to him. He'd purchased the entire building. Now, it was only an investment.

The elevator doors swished open, letting them into the main living space. A stale smell assaulted his senses.

"This is the living room and dining room combined space." This need to fill airtime and explain was new. He shouldn't be nervous around Emory.

She circled around the room, past the utilitarian couch and coffee table littered with reports and financial journals. He probably should've cleaned up the place before bringing her here. Except this had been a last-minute decision.

Working her way past an antique bureau he'd picked up in England on one of his earliest overseas trips, he noted the shape of her fine ass in tight, black capri pants. How could he not notice?

She stopped at an African mask he'd received as a business gift sitting on a round table at the end of the couch. The aesthetics of the mask had appealed. With her back to him, he focused on the skin peeking from the shoulder cut-outs of her long, shapeless blouse.

"Who painted these?" She bent behind the couch, sticking her butt in the air, distracting him from the question. "The name of the artist?"

"Artist?" He froze. His heart stopped pumping while his brain processed her question. He'd forgotten the paintings he'd left behind the couch. No one ever came here, and he went straight to the kitchen or bedroom whenever he arrived. The blood in his veins rushed forward, and so did he. "No one. Nothing."

The three surrealist paintings sat on the floor, leaning against the back of the couch. Never framed because they hadn't been worth the effort. The muted colors didn't do the objects justice. The haphazard arrangement messy.

He stepped in front of them. "Garbage."

Reaching around, she picked one canvas up and held it toward the light. She contemplated the painting. "Garbage?"

His sentiment exactly. "They're taking up space. I plan to get rid of them."

"Why?" Was that disgust? It must be.

"They're not by a professional. Not by anyone famous." With jerky-panicked motions, he flipped the third painting around.

"If you appreciate the art and see something you enjoy in a painting, it doesn't matter who the artist is." She set down the first and studied the second. "If the painting speaks to you in some way, or you enjoy them…that's all that matters."

He felt queasy. He spotted the amateurish brushstrokes, and the immature use of colors. Painted by a hobbyist who never learned the proper strokes.

"I worked on the design of a Spanish aristocrat's home, and he hung forgeries on the walls." She sounded amused.

Amused at his paintings. Anger flared, and he wanted to fling the paintings off the balcony. "Throw them out. I don't want them." He didn't want to be reminded of foolish dreams.

"These would make a great inspiration for the design of your—"

"I said, get rid of them." His skin chilled. There'd be no discussion. Grabbing her arm, he tugged her toward the floor-to-ceiling windows. "Look over here."

"Great view of the mountains." Her gaze veered toward the paintings as if drawn.

Drawn to what? Ugliness?

Forcing himself to contemplate the view, not her and not the paintings, he noted the haze in the distance. He usually arrived here after dark so didn't get the full effect of the majestic mountains. "I suppose."

"You suppose?" She pursed her lips with clear disapproval.

His disposition soured. She judged him for not having time to enjoy life. He wanted to rail into her and explain past circumstances. He didn't.

Twirling around, she said, "What a great space for parties. Do you, or do you plan to entertain?"

The small nook would be a great place to set up a bar. "I never thought about it."

This was his private space. When he entertained for business, they went out to a restaurant. When he dated, he preferred to go to the woman's place afterwards.

Nodding, she trailed her fingers on the leather couch. "I was hoping to find more of your personality, to get an idea of what you'd appreciate. There's not much here to work with. It's kind of a mish-mash of styles, between the utilitarian furniture and the exotic decorative pieces."

"Do what you want. What you'd enjoy. It's why I hired you."

She could use this place for her portfolio. He really didn't care.

Her eyebrows rose in skepticism. The professional she was, she didn't comment, just took out her notebook and started writing. "What type of style do you like?"

Getting down to business. Good. He could work with focused and efficient.

"I don't know." He gritted his teeth.

This was her job. She should be telling him what would be best. Decorating went along with sightseeing. Something he didn't have time for.

"You must have some idea of what you want."

What was she writing? Boring? Sparse? Totally uncoordinated? He could see it now. How the room would appear from her point of view. As if he didn't care. Which he didn't. Not normally.

Her lips quirked, curious about him and his penthouse. "I don't see you with a rustic style."

"Modern. Simple." He wondered what she'd think of the statement. The house in Castle Ridge was so different. Hadn't changed since his father died. "You probably think that's cold."

She took a small camera from her satchel, and took a few photos from different angles. Her moves were fluid and graceful, flying from one position to the next. Again, the image of a fairy entered his head.

She was light and airy and fluttery. "You can have a modern style and bring warmth to a home."

Her being here brought warmth to the room.

Shaking his head, he tried to get rid of the fanciful thoughts. She wasn't a fairy, and he wasn't interested in her warming his room or his bed. Cold and heartless and hard were his trademarks.

He tried to make his voice icy. "Are you saying I'm cold?"

Fear equated with respect. He'd needed to earn the other business professionals' respect, in order to protect his father's financial secret. In order to become a success.

She bit her lower lip and her expression seemed unsure. "I've heard some people find your negotiation tactics..."

A small pain in his chest expanded, twisting and

trembling. He kept silent, waiting to see what she'd say. He wanted to know what she thought, not what others thought. Not that it mattered. His internal denial was shy of the truth. He forced the recognition away.

"Ruthless." She moved into the kitchen, with its white-and-gray marble island taking up most of the space.

Ruthless was good. He needed to be the hard-ass to be successful. Following her, he asked, "What about you? Do *you* think I'm ruthless?"

Her violet gaze flashed with some emotion, making the orbs morph a deeper purple. A fairy in the light of day. She tilted her chin in a defiant angle. "Last night. Yes."

His body scorched, remembering their exchange. He'd been cruel, savage even. Stealing a kiss then, knowing he wanted another now. He should take her advice and live a little by kissing her again. He grabbed her arm and swung her around to face him.

The scent of apples, plus an exotic spice he couldn't place surrounded him. He didn't know if it was her perfume or her shampoo. She'd always smelled that way. The scent must've imprinted on his brain from when she was a teen. He remembered coming into a room in the house and smelling the heady scent, and wondering if Mrs. Barrington had baked apple pie.

Emory's eyes went wide, and her body petrified at his touch.

Did she find him repulsive, while yearning for his brother? Disgust at the sudden need to please her rampaged through his system. "I said I was sorry."

For the attempted buyout, not the kiss.

"You did." Her cheeks reddened.

Was she remembering the kiss, too? The tension stretched between them. The clock in the hallway ticked. He held his breath, waiting. Would she lean in or away?

He tugged her a little closer, bringing her within an inch of his chest. "What about today? Now?"

Did she think he was being beastly? He was. He planned to keep her busy, dazzle her with his forgotten charm, and keep her away from his brother.

Her cheeks became a deeper red, like the apples of her scent. Her lips flattened, as if wanting to speak and yet unsure of what to say. Pulling her arm free, she stepped away. "You gave me this amazing opportunity, so I should get to work."

His shoulders dropped. Not really an answer. And no kiss. He shouldn't want a kiss. Wooing her was not his goal. Charm would be his last, desperate measure.

Taking out a measuring tape, her movements became jerky but efficient. Work mode. He recognized it well. Work mode was his constant mode. Normally, he appreciated people who got straight to business. Her avoidance left him ill at ease. Decorating a penthouse wouldn't keep her away from Ryder long enough if she was too efficient.

"May I?" She pointed down the hall toward the bedrooms.

"I'm not planning to redecorate the bedrooms or the office. Only the main living space." Jackson waved his hand at the great room. Living room, dining room, possibly updates to the kitchen, if he needed more time. "At least at this second."

"I know. I thought it might help get a better idea of your style." She glided toward the first open door.

"Guest room." Moving in behind her, he checked out the room.

Queen bed with beige comforter. Long dresser. Comfy chair for reading. A couple of fake plants, and a boring scenery painting above the bed.

"Nice. Comfortable."

"Kind of resembles a hotel room."

"Yes, it does." She laughed, and the light breeziness slammed into him like a hurricane.

He whirled with the tinkling noise, it vibrated from his ears to his soul. Joyful and free. Stunned, it took him a second to realize she'd moved on.

She placed her hand on the doorknob and turned. "It's locked."

Rushing over, he took her hand off the knob. Nerves scattered the remembered sound of her laughter. "For storage. Nothing to see."

She angled her head, and studied him quizzically. The curious expression becoming familiar. She arched her brows, and pointed her gaze at him still holding her hand.

He dropped her hand, as if it was on fire. Because the heat, her heat, had ignited him. Between her discovery of the locked room, the lust flaring whenever she was near, and her laughter intruding on his dark thoughts, he couldn't keep his head in the game. Flustered was a new emotion.

"And back there?"

"The master bedroom."

"May I look?" She wouldn't find any secrets or even his personality in the master bedroom.

"Be my guest."

Because he was only a guest in this home. Maybe he'd only been a guest throughout life.

Hours later, Emory found herself sitting across the table from Jackson at an expensive restaurant. She'd thought they'd examine his penthouse and fly straight back to Castle Ridge. He'd wanted to talk about styles and budget and furniture shopping.

For a man who didn't care what she did, he wanted to talk about it quite a bit.

She pinched her arm under the table. She'd fallen into an alternate universe. Jackson taking time out of his busy schedule to have lunch with her? Him giving her an amazing opportunity to showcase her design skills? Jackson being more human than she'd ever seen him?

Most of the other restaurant customers were dressed in their Sunday best. She wore capris and a blouse. Professional, not expensive. When they'd arrived, she'd hurried to the table, hoping no one would notice. He'd noticed. He noticed everything.

He wore khakis and a golf shirt. The baseball cap was gone, and his hair stuck up in tiny tufts. So unusual for the normally perfectly coiffed man.

She'd taken photos, made notes, sketched the floor plan, and measured the entire penthouse, only occasionally thinking about the locked door down the hall. He'd worked on his laptop, or spoken on his phone.

Guess they both were working on a Sunday. And now they were at a business meeting. Her stomach twisted, reminding her this was a business meeting to discuss decorating, not a lunch date. Or any other kind of date.

The twisting braided tighter. It didn't help the man sitting across from her was gorgeous and personable and completely different from what she'd expected.

Opening her iPad, she presented various styles, fast-forwarding to the Mid-Century Modern, Industrial, and Scandinavian. "Since you lean toward modern, let's look at these."

She saw him as an Industrial type of person. Although, she hoped she could persuade him to Mid-Century Modern. The style was characterized by refined lines, minimalist silhouettes, and natural shapes.

"What style do you lean toward?"

The intensity of his voice and his expression had her quivering. Did he really want to know, or was this a test? Did he believe because she didn't appreciate his current sparse style, she couldn't decorate his place?

"My style doesn't really matter." She brushed his question and her insecurities off. "Once we determine a layout and the type of furniture you'll need, I'll go to the Denver Design Mart to pick out a few pieces."

"Can I come with?" He seemed eager. Too eager.

This man, whose only interest was Croft Industries, wanted to peruse furniture? He was too busy to look out his plane's window. Why would he want to walk the aisles of the Design Mart?

The quivering traveled through her system, making her tremble. He must not trust her. It's why he wanted to shop for furniture with her. "Well, you could come, but it takes time. I can have items delivered to your penthouse, and if you don't want the pieces they can be returned."

"That's a lot of effort. Why don't I come with you?" His nonplussed expression seemed too innocent. "We could go shopping early this week."

She startled. The design process didn't work that way. Yet, she needed him as a client. She bit her lower lip, trying to decide what to say. "I have to complete my designs first. Get your approval."

"I'm sure I'll love them."

His bulldozing—or bullshitting—plowed her under. Yet, to list Jackson Croft as a satisfied client would help her new business.

Bundling her anxiety, she moved the schedule forward. "I've got a few ideas I could sketch up."

"By tomorrow."

"Tomorrow?"

"I've got meetings in Denver all day. You can come by my office tomorrow evening and show me what you've got." He spoke as if everything was settled.

Which it wasn't.

The deadline was close to impossible. Plus…

"I'm not spending the night here." Her earlier challenges about why he was decorating at this moment struck her again. "I'm not prepared, and you said I could see Ryder tonight when we got home."

Jackson lifted his water glass and took a sip. "You can. I had an emergency come up this afternoon so I'm going to spend the night at the penthouse."

Her cheeks flamed. *He* was spending the night. Not her. "You're not flying home with me?"

"I'll send the plane back with you this afternoon. And you can drive my car down tomorrow. We can drive back together."

Her entire plan flipped upside down. She thought they'd fly back, he'd come home with her, and they'd stop by to visit Ryder together. She couldn't spend much time with him. She was too busy. She had to research and complete the designs for Jackson's penthouse. By tomorrow.

The waiter slapped the bill on the table between them.

Stiffening, she sucked in air. He was her client, so she'd be expected to pick up the lunch bill. She had no money for this expensive meal. "Um, I haven't figured out my own expense account yet."

"Don't worry. I've got this."

"But you're my client."

"And I pushed you into coming today, took you away from your mom, and insisted on lunch."

"Why?"

"Because I was hungry. You can get the next meal." He chuckled.

The sound fascinated. It was deep and rumbly, and totally uninhibited. His Adam's apple moved up and down, and there was a twinkle in his eye.

A twinkle she'd never seen before. The twinkle shone, bringing a glowing, relaxed expression.

Making him less formidable. And even though he laughed at her, she appreciated the vibration and his expression. "You should laugh more often."

"Why?" His head tilted at a curious angle, as if he really didn't understand how handsome he was when he was happy. "I want to be taken seriously."

"Taken seriously and being too serious all the time are different things. If you're always serious, how can you enjoy life?" She clapped her mouth closed. She shouldn't be talking to him in this way. Yet, designing someone's personal space made the link between client and designer closer.

Spaniards took siestas. They enjoyed their jobs with the understanding it was only a job. Life was to be lived. It was something her mom had always stressed when pointing out Mr. Croft. And now Jackson. Ryder had the opposite philosophy, goofing around and having fun. She was somewhere in the middle. She wanted her interior design business to be a success, knew she had to work hard, but she didn't want to lose the joy of life.

"Look at Ryder."

Jackson's expression darkened. "Ryder doesn't take anything seriously. He doesn't work. His life is a constant party."

The slight against the man she'd always loved cut into her. Except she understood Ryder, because she'd studied everything about him. He'd worked hard in school and in sports. He still skied hard, and donated his time to a kids' ski team. He was smart, something his brother never noticed.

She sent a challenging glare Jackson's way. "Maybe

if you didn't handle everything, if you actually asked Ryder for help, he'd show you what he could do."

"And if he messed up?" Jackson's lips twisted together in disbelief. "Some of us aren't allowed to mess up. We have responsibilities. People to take care of and provide for."

Sadness floated through her bloodstream like a slow-flowing river. He truly believed he needed to do it all, he was responsible for everything and everyone. He'd never learn how to enjoy life.

His lecture pressed on her heart, and she wanted to teach him how to be more free.

The waiter brought the check back, interrupting a conversation Jackson didn't want to have. He signed, digging the pen into the slip of paper.

Everything inside him callused. It was well and good for Emory to talk about taking time to appreciate life, to tour foreign cities, and to peer out windows. He had responsibilities. People who counted on him. He was tired of her believing she knew everything.

He took care of things. Business. People. The estate. His second mom's medical care. Emory's college. That was his job. Even now, he was taking care of his little brother. He hoped Ryder would realize it with time on his own, and not the gorgeous Emory distracting him.

Yes, he was interfering. Shey would be good for his brother, and the merger would be great for Croft Industries. And he believed Ryder loved Shey.

Jackson glanced at his watch. Too early to let her go home giving her time to work on the designs today while his brother slept, and then she could spend time with his brother tomorrow. Not going to happen.

A ton of work awaited him. Sunday was a great day to catch up on emails and financial journals. He needed to consider distracting Emory his work for now. She was part of the job to ensure the deal between Croft Industries and Webber Resorts was completed.

"It's a beautiful day. We should rent Segways and tour the neighborhood." Resolute, he set his napkin on the table and stood.

"You want to rent Segways?" She jerked back in her seat. "What about your financial research and spreadsheets?" She spoke as if they were dirty words.

He was more than spreadsheets, wasn't he?

"If you're starting a business, you're going to have to put together a business plan, which will include *spreadsheets*." He put a tease in his tone, trying to keep them on a friendly path, even though a darker emotion poured through his veins. "Aren't you the one who said I should experience life? See the places I visited? Why not start with my part-time hometown?"

"How can I say no when put that way?" Shrugging her sexy shoulders in a sensual droop, she stood and sent him a smile.

A smile that struck through his chest like red at the bottom of a financial statement.

"You can't." He held the door for her, while trying to catch his breath. She couldn't affect him this way. She was a task, a thing to check off on his list. A job.

"This way." He'd spotted the Segway rental place while walking to the restaurant, and thought it was something she might enjoy.

A group of mangy dogs sat out front of the storefront. Their leashes were tied together, by a water bowl sprinkled with loose hairs and dirt. He skirted around them.

Emory bent down and scratched first one dog and then another under their chins, so close to the sharp teeth. "Aren't you a cutie?"

His body tensed when the dog licked her chin. "You like dogs?"

"Don't you?" She sounded shocked anyone wouldn't love the mongrels at her feet.

"Of course, I do." His immediate agreement with her pissed him off. He didn't need to please her, just keep her away from his brother.

It's not that he didn't like dogs, he'd never really been around them. Victoria Croft had hated animals, and Lexi's mom had been allergic.

"Show this guy some love, then." She cocked her head to study him, cradling the dog's head between her hands.

The one dog took advantage and licked her face. Another dog rolled over at her feet, displaying his tummy and asking to be stroked. The third dog peered at her with adoring eyes, begging for attention.

"Love?" He recoiled. He understood the word. He loved his brother and Lexi and the second Mrs. Croft, but to be so besotted to beg? Not him. Never.

"You said you liked dogs." Something settled on her face.

A challenge? Disbelief?

"I like dogs." He enunciated each word trying not to show his true uncertainty. He liked dogs as a concept, man's best friend and all, yet having one lick your face with the same tongue that licked their behind?

"Do you?"

Scanning the area, he tried to think his way out of this. He spotted an old industrial building he'd recently purchased. He planned to turn the building into trendy housing, or restaurants and retail stores. "In fact, I like dogs so much I'm donating a building I purchased to become a no-kill dog shelter."

Regret slapped him on the side of the head. Another lie. Another attempt to please.

Her eyes went soft and she beamed. Not the sassy smile she'd given at the restaurant. An appreciative-grateful grin, making him want to believe the dog shelter was what he planned all along. That he was a good person.

"You're not as ruthless as people say."

"Don't tell anyone. You'll ruin my reputation." Another tease. Where were these coming from?

Her laughter tangled his insides into knots. He was ruthless. He'd try to buy her off. He brought her to Denver to get her away from his brother. He lied about the animal shelter to win her favor and to distract her from making him pet the mutts.

"Pet him." Her demand jolted him out of the gutter of guilt.

So much for distraction. He needed to prove he wasn't a total liar. He didn't hate dogs. The knots pulled tight. Bending down partway, he patted the top of the dog's head, similar to how you'd pat a small child who'd pleased you in some way.

"I said pet, not pat." The second demand irritated.

He crouched down closer, imitating her stance. He wouldn't be cowed by a dog. Clawing his fingers, he went low, scratching under the dog's mouth. His fingers stroked the fur beneath. The dog lifted its chin, enjoying the scratch. He stroked harder, enjoying the sensation, experiencing the love and appreciation from the animal.

The dog made a quick move, its tongue lapping out and reaching his face in a kiss. The devoted and immediate love the animal showed was more than many people gave him. The women he dated wanted to be seen out with him, and taken someplace nice. They never got to know him, care about him.

Something warm slid around his heart. The warmth spread, and he couldn't stop a smile. The dog was a cutie. Liked him, even though he was *ruthless*. The dog wouldn't care how much money he made, or where he lived, or how well he supported his family. As long as someone fed it and petted it, the animal would be happy.

He could use a little devotion in his life. Maybe a dog was the answer.

He frowned. His usually cold heart chilled. He was too busy to take care of a pet. He didn't even have time for a girlfriend.

Chapter Six

The following day, Emory sat on the wicker chair beside Ryder's bed, staring at the boy she'd loved since she was a child. Except with his stubbled cheeks and broad shoulders, he wasn't a boy anymore. He was a man.

A man so different from his older brother.

Although they both had strong chins and noses, chestnut hair, broad chests, and strong arms, Jackson was clean-shaven. His hair styled. He wore suits and confidence similar to a suit of armor. Ryder's long hair was always tousled. His cheeks were frequently unshaven. His preference for expensive, yet casual, clothes demonstrated his comfort with his place in life.

The rich playboy and the billionaire businessman.

Both attractive.

Both single.

Both demanding in their own way.

Jackson had demanded she drive to Denver this afternoon, to present her designs for his penthouse. She'd sketched on the lonely plane ride home while thinking about what she'd learned. He wasn't the mean, elusive billionaire he pretended. Beneath the tough surface, he was kind. Donating a building for a dog shelter, signing up to be her first client. And kind of a daredevil on the Segway.

That had been unexpected. And fun.

Last night when she'd arrived home, she'd scoured online catalogues and researched various decorating sites to find the perfect inspiration for her designs. The paintings from his penthouse kept flickering to the forefront of her mind. The images were powerful and emotional. Why would he want to get rid of them?

Since she couldn't use the paintings for inspiration, she'd spent most of the night sketching and thinking about him. Because he was her inspiration.

Energy electrified up her spine, heating her body.

The clean, lean lines of her design matched his lean, muscular body, with a few curves in the right places. Like his ass and his smile. The strong, broad furniture matched his broad chest and strong determination. In business and in life. The sparse accessories matched his communication style. Direct and to the point.

A few of the sketches included him standing in his newly-designed surroundings. Not her normal presentation style, but she couldn't help including him in the environment. Exuding power, he shaped the things around him. Looking out the floor-to-ceiling windows with a hand on his hip. Sitting behind a sleek wood desk she'd found on a website. Contemplating one of the paintings with intensity.

Ryder shifted and moaned in the bed, pulling her

out of her thoughts about Jackson. No, her thoughts about Jackson's designs.

She put her hand to Ryder's warm forehead. His lips were swollen and his cheeks puffy. A rash showed on his neck and shoulders.

"You're okay. Just sleep." She imitated a parent to a small child.

When she'd been eleven, she'd watched another moaning patient. Her mother had foot surgery, and Emory hadn't known what to do. Jackson had helped her mom take pain medication and sat on the couch all night, while Emory had fallen asleep. The following day he'd acted like nothing had happened, pretended to be colder, as if he wanted her to be afraid of him.

And she had been. Until now.

Now, she saw the generous man he pretended not to be. The protective man he'd become for his family. The man who appreciated art.

Ryder rolled onto his back, displaying his bare chest. "She—"

"Shh. I'm right here. It's Emory."

"Em."

She'd always hated the shortening of her name. Bending closer, she used her fingers to straighten his hair. The smoothing of strands should've been thrilling because of her teenage fantasies. It wasn't. "How're you feeling?"

"Tired. And itchy." His muffled voice came through, even though his mouth smashed against the pillow.

"You should know better than to touch shellfish."

He probably loathed the lecture. If Jackson

demanded tight deadlines, Ryder demanded fun and playfulness all the time. That could become tiring, too.

"I do know. I didn't..." His eyes closed and he gave a loud snore.

Everyone on staff knew of his allergies. The caterers were always so careful to keep the shellfish separate from other food items. Her mother had once fired a caterer for not adhering to the strict rules, so how could this have happened?

He snored away, unaware of her presence.

She'd wanted to talk to him, to say she was sorry he'd gotten sick and they couldn't finish their evening together, to tell him yes to a future date.

Except the tingles that wouldn't leave her while dancing with him had fizzled over the past day. Jackson's kiss and attempted bribery had angered her and dimmed her teenage dreams. His offer to become her first client had fired her hopes. Now, she was focused on her first decorating job, and very demanding client.

Her phone vibrated, and Jackson's number appeared. Palpitations pounded at her wrists. Thinking of him must've caused him to call. ESP? Or did they have some kind of weird connection?

After saying hello, he asked, "How's traffic down the mountain?"

"I'm not on the road yet." She'd wanted to talk to Ryder before driving to Denver. He hadn't been awake, so she'd waited.

"Where are you?" Jackson's demand rubbed her the wrong way.

She regarded the sleeping form. "Ryder's bedroom."

The other end of the line went silent. And awkward. The tension stretched across the miles.

Before she could explain, Jackson asked, "I'm not interrupting anything, am I?"

Her cheeks flamed and disgust curled in her stomach. His tone implied she was having sex. "Your brother is sleeping."

"Are you coming to present your designs?" The demanding voice was back. The voice saying he was in control of everything and everyone around him.

Even though he was her client and she lived in his home, he wasn't in control of her.

She need to make that clear when she arrived in Denver.

Jackson patrolled in front of the shiny mahogany desk in his office and stopped to stare at the large orange ball of the sun sinking behind the mountain range. Emory would say something poetic about life and the beauty of nature. To him, it was a sign the day was ending, and he hadn't accomplished everything he'd wanted.

Including keeping her away from his brother. Otherwise, she would be here. Had his charming brother woken up and persuaded her to stay home?

Someone knocked at the door and he jerked around, expecting Emory.

Instead, his assistant, Barbara, scurried in. "Is your date late?"

"Date? Why would you assume I had a date?" He hid his disappointment behind bluster. He should tell his assistant to mind her own business, except she knew everything about his business. And that's all this thing with Emory was.

Business.

Barbara considered him, her curious graying eyebrows arching. "Because late this afternoon, you asked me to get two tickets to the hottest musical in town, and dinner reservations at Chez Alphonse."

After the phone call with Emory, he'd been unable to focus on business. His plan to keep her away from his brother wasn't working. He needed to change his tactics. To impress her with what she could have with him. To make her forget about his brother and his silly romantic gestures. Jackson could be romantic, more romantic than his brother. He just needed to apply the business principles of a corporate takeover to a woman.

His assistant tapped the envelope she carried against her fingers, still considering the possibilities of a date.

He snatched the envelope from her hand, and used his grumpy voice instead of his worried one. "How much did this set me back?"

"You said to set up a date how Ryder would. Do you really want to know the cost?"

"No." Jackson stashed the tickets in his suit pocket. Pacing to his private bathroom, he squinted in the mirror and grimaced. He resembled the figure from The Scream masterpiece. His pale face needed a tan. His red eyes needed sleep, and less worry about work. He needed more time in the day.

He wheeled back to his assistant. "How do I look?"

Barbara's lips lifted in a sardonic smirk. "For a business meeting, or a date?"

"Business meeting." His harsh tone caused her to lean back. "Date."

The evening would start as a business meeting. Then, he'd invite Emory to dinner and a show, turning the meeting into a quasi-date. A date where she'd forget about his brother once she realized he had connections to other wealthy clients for her business. He had money to take her places and buy her nice things. He had charm.

Charm he'd use to win her over, and she'd forget about her crush on his brother. Ryder and Shey would get back together, and the deal would go through.

"Well, which is it?"

"Both," Jackson snarled. So much for his charm.

"You're combining business with pleasure?" Barbara's response scratched against his nerves. "Interesting."

His nerves morphed to irritation and he bristled. "Nothing interesting about it."

"If it's not interesting, I'm off for the night." She headed toward the open door and stopped. "I believe your appointment is here." His assistant waited for Emory to enter before closing the door behind her.

Emory wore high boots, and a pencil skirt covering her hips in a tight hug. Her brilliant-colored jacket with floppy lapels said business and artsy. The curls in her short hair sprung to attention. Her lips lifted in a short, uncertain smile.

His pulse thumped. "You're here."

"You ordered me, and you're my client." Her voice trembled.

Nervous about her designs, or about being with him? Why would she be nervous about being with him? To her this was only a client meeting, a business transaction.

It was a business transaction to him, too. Except he planned to transact with her heart. "You're late."

"You knew I left late, and I hit traffic coming over the pass." Her apple scent wafted toward him.

Sour apples.

"How is my brother?" He fisted his hands and carefully unclenched them. Part of his charade was to approve of her dating his brother. Her defenses against him would be down, and he'd swoop in with charm, surprises, and time spent together.

"He's sleeping so much. Has he been given too much of the prescription?"

Definitely. He'd told the doctor to keep him comfortable and out of it. Time to change the topic. "Did you have enough time to complete your designs?"

She tilted her head, displaying her long and elegant neck. "Did I have a choice?"

"No." The rush design job had been the original plan. He'd seen the flaw in the strategy when he'd talked to her this afternoon. But he needed the excuse. "I'm in a hurry."

"Why now?" Emory's languid tone belied the underlying curiosity. She analyzed and questioned Jackson's every move. It kept him on his toes. "You've owned the penthouse for years. Why the sudden need to decorate?"

Her questions hammered. No one put him on the spot anymore. His word was law. Taking a deep breath, he calmed himself. "Because I decided it was time."

His harshness wouldn't win him any points. *Remember, charm.*

Her eyes brightened and she grinned, not afraid of his harshness, even though she should be. "Is there a woman involved?"

Yes. His panic swooshed, similar to a newly-minted businessman caught in a trap. How had she guessed? Except she couldn't have guessed. She must think it involved a different woman, and he couldn't have her believing that. Not if his plan was going to work.

"No. No woman."

She perused his office making him antsy. "This is more what I expected in your penthouse."

"What do you mean?" His office had been redecorated to highlight his success. He'd gotten rid of his father's mementos and awards, and kept everything clean and sparse. His father's photos of family and staff, trinkets from company celebrations, and good luck charms had been stored away. He refused to fall into the same trap of sympathy his father had fallen into.

"Lofty. Clean. Kind of clinical."

Criticism of his character. His gaze narrowed, zeroing in on his target. Just because she declared the terms terrible, didn't mean they were. He wanted to be viewed as tough and clinical. Even if Jackson would've preferred his sister's wedding photo, or a sweet plaque his mother had given him, he refused to display any object that could be considered a sign of weakness.

She set her black portfolio case on the coffee table next to the couch and two chairs. Unzipping the case, she took out a tablet and a sketch book. "Well, these are quick sketches. You can get an idea of the direction I think would be best to go." When she bent over, he got a look at the creamy tops of her breasts peeking from her silky, button-down blouse.

His pants tightened between his legs. He swung around to get behind his desk and shut down his computer. "Wait until dinner to show me."

"Dinner?"

"We have reservations in ten minutes at Chez Alphonse. My treat."

She stood straight, covering the enticing globes and his body relaxed. "I thought we had a meeting."

Most women would jump at the chance to have a meal at the fancy French restaurant. Emory wasn't like most women, certainly not the ones he'd dated. The complexity of his confusion grew. He admitted he found her attractive, obviously by the way his body reacted. Hormones were a distraction. He didn't need distractions right now. He needed to close a deal, and to do that, he needed to spend time with this woman, create an attraction between them, without falling for her. He had to remember she was a tool.

"We did, but you're late. We'll discuss the designs during dinner. You have to eat." He wouldn't take no for an answer. In order to woo her, he had to spend time with her doing more than discussing decorating.

She tugged down her blouse, emphasizing the roundness beneath. Now he'd had a glimpse, he yearned to hold the tempting globes in his hand. To taste them.

"After dinner, I have tickets to a musical." He name-dropped the popular traveling Broadway show, impossible to get tickets to.

Her mouth rounded in a delectable O. "What? I thought we'd meet, go to your penthouse to see how my designs would fit, and drive home."

"Don't you want to see the show?" He rocked forward onto his toes waiting for her response.

"Everyone wants to see the show." She flayed her hands in an uneasy gesture. She was cute when she was dumbfounded. "I didn't..."

"You told me to appreciate life. Now, I've planned something fun and you're hesitating." He used a wounded tone, turning her earlier words against her again. The tone was fake. He didn't need to appreciate life. He was too busy.

She scanned the room, looking anywhere except at him, searching for an escape. "I...I..."

"We had fun on the Segways. This is a business meeting over dinner and a show." He suggested this was a normal situation. Lots of business people had dinner and went to a musical.

Maybe normal business people did. He never had. Something dark hit him in the pit of his stomach and snagged, trying to pull some emotion to the surface.

"Oh, all right."

Her agreement flashed through him in a green light. His plan was a go.

Within minutes, they'd left his office building, walked a block to the restaurant, and were settled in a private booth.

The exclusive restaurant was packed with diners, many probably attending the same musical after dinner. Men in suits and women in cocktail dresses. Emory didn't stick out, she glowed. He couldn't compliment her, because it was too soon in the scheme. She believed he was okay with her dating his brother.

He never noticed the intimidating atmosphere of the restaurant. The soft ambience in the dining room, compared to the harsh fluorescent lights near the entryway, resembling an interrogation room. Watching Emory's expressive and impressed face, he remembered his first time dining at this restaurant with fellow executives. How he'd felt young and unworthy of the restaurant and the company. He'd been nauseated, and tried to put on a stoic face. Now, he could own the room two times over.

That didn't mean he couldn't empathize with what Emory was experiencing. He reached across the table and massaged her arm. "You were born to eat in nice establishments."

Her pink lips twitched. Her gaze gleamed with appreciation. "Thanks, but I don't believe you. You're trying to make me feel better."

And he was.

Surprise thunked inside his head. He wanted her to be comfortable and enjoy the evening.

Because that was his goal. His business goal. Woo her, win her, and get her away from his brother.

He used his finger to trace a pattern on her arm, enjoying her smooth skin. "You look like you belong."

She laughed, a light tinkling chime. "I'm the housekeeper's daughter."

He leaned forward and his finger pressed into her skin. "Is that how you see yourself?"

Her gaze widened, and she shook her head. "No. Of course not." She lifted her arm, and his hand slid off and onto the table. Waving around the room, she tried to dismiss her words. "I've dined in nicer places than this."

"You have?" Here he'd been trying to impress her, which was ironic since he'd never tried to impress any other woman he'd dated. Either they liked him for him and his money, or they didn't. "Where?"

"In Barcelona." She clamped her mouth shut and focused on her lap, but not before he caught the gleam in her eyes dim.

As if she'd shared something she hadn't wanted to share. And even more bizarre, he wanted to know everything. He wanted to make the sad and haunted expression disappear from her face.

The waiter came, and they ordered their meals. Once their orders were given and the man was gone, Jackson continued, "Client dinners in restaurants nicer than Chez Alphonse?"

"Sort of." She raised her head. Her cheeks were flushed and her pupils darted. "I was only an intern."

She'd made an insulting reference to herself earlier. Couldn't she see how beautiful and talented she was? He'd recognized her intellect when her mother had talked about her high school grades. He'd seen her talent when he'd followed up on the college scholarship she'd been awarded. He could tell by the way she carried herself and communicated with others she was special.

Agitation prickled his skin. "Only an intern. Only the housekeeper's daughter. Why do you talk about yourself in a belittling way?"

Emory's insides dropped at Jackson's accusation. Her body went cold, and her face heated. His taunting words were a reminder of her treatment in Barcelona. She'd grown past the insults and accusations. Past the attacks on her professionalism. Past the feeling of being lowly or inadequate. Hadn't she?

"I don't." Her protest was a lie, because she had said both those things. Those labels didn't define her. Not anymore. She sat up in the button-tufted wall bench, forcing her spine straight. "I mean, those are truths. I am a housekeeper's daughter—"

"Nothing wrong with that." His bland expression told her he believed his statement and soothed her resentment.

"And I *was* an intern in Barcelona. A good one." She angled her chin to emphasize her point. He was her client. She needed to reassure him she could do the job. "Sometimes interns…were treated differently."

The muscles in his face tightened. He held his body still, expecting the worst. "Did they mistreat you?"

The question sounded threatening. Not toward her. Toward her previous employers.

His protection wrapped a cloak of warmth across

her shoulders. "No. Of course not. I wouldn't have stayed so long." She'd stayed because of Alejandro.

The name didn't cause pain any longer. Her heart didn't pitter-patter, or thump. She'd been over him for a while. It was how the break-up had transpired that caused the hurt to linger.

"Why did you leave?"

"The internship was almost complete. I'd learned everything I could. I was ready to come home." She'd needed to get away from the toxic atmosphere. From the belittling tactics and the thin vein of jealousy. She needed a place to recharge and restart. She'd missed her mother, and the mountains surrounding Castle Ridge.

Plates were put before them on the table. Her plate was filled with a shrimp and steak combination, and she took in the delightful smell.

"Have you ever been to Barcelona?" She cut a shrimp in half and placed it in her mouth.

She wanted to know more about Jackson. She'd known him since she was five, and yet never really knew or understood his varying layers. And there were layers. The reason for her curiosity. He was so different from how she'd always pictured him.

"Many times." His vague answer didn't satisfy.

"And?"

"And nothing."

"You seemed as if you were about to say more." Although why she thought she could read the unreadable Jackson Croft was a mystery. "What was your favorite thing about Barcelona?"

"Mandarin Oriental Hotel."

Her mouth dropped open. "Really? A hotel?"

"A five-star hotel." He loosened the tie around his neck.

Or maybe it was her questions making it difficult for him to breathe? "When there are so many amazing and inspiring sights? You pick a hotel?"

"I usually see the hotel I'm staying in, and the business offices of the people I'm meeting." He spoke casually, similar to how he spoke on the plane about the scenery.

This time, this time, something was different.

A yearning in the way he stretched the vowels? A spark of interest in his slate orbs? As if he was interested in seeing things and didn't want to admit it. She couldn't define it, but it was there, and she softened toward him.

"You're already traveling to these wonderful places. You should take advantage of it." She might be the housekeeper's daughter, yet he was the one deprived.

"What was your favorite thing about Barcelona?" His expression revealed his interest, and she perked up.

Maybe she could open his eyes to the world. They were going to a musical tonight because she'd said something about enjoying life. "*Parc Guell.*"

"No hesitation." The tease in his voice sent bubbles of pleasure through her bloodstream.

"Why would I hesitate?"

"You said Barcelona has so many amazing sights."

"*Parc Guell* features Gaudi's designs in a park setting. It's beautiful, inspirational, and fairytale-ish."

"Like you." He clamped his strong lips shut, and his high cheekbones became darker, redder.

She glowed from Jackson's compliment. What was going on with her? "Excuse me?"

Stroking his chin, he captured her gaze with his intense stare. "The other night at Lexi's reception, you reminded me of a fairy with your golden dress and sparkly hair. You appeared ethereal."

Everything inside her floated, as if he'd cast a spell on her. His compliment caused her to grin. He thought she was fairy-ish?

Confusion weighted her down. Did he find her pretty, or annoying like trolls and dwarves? Did it matter? She was supposed to be going on a date with his brother. He was her client and being nice. He couldn't be attracted to her.

Besides, she didn't think a man with a merciless reputation would want a woman who reminded him of a fairy. The women he'd dated in the past were tall, svelte, professional, hard-nosed businesswomen. Women who could match him in intelligence and ruthlessness. She wasn't even in the same league.

And yet, since returning to Castle Ridge—except for the first night—he hadn't acted beastly or merciless. He'd been open and kind. Fun and flirtatious. Interesting. At least to her.

Why, when he knew she was attracted to his brother? Wasn't she?

Images of the two of them teetered in her mind, tipping them in a different direction.

Chapter Seven

Jackson watched Emory fold her napkin precisely in half and set it on the table, signaling she wouldn't be distracted anymore. It was time to get down to business. She'd tried to change the discussion to design several times as they ate. He kept changing the conversation. If they didn't get to the conversation before the show tonight, they'd have to continue it in the morning.

She opened her portfolio, and took out a sketch book and passed it to him. She set her tablet on the table and faced it forward, being the consummate professional. She flipped open the sketchbook to a pencil sketch of his living room. Instead of his hodgepodge of furniture, the couch matched a chair and contrasted with a rug.

"Again, these are rough. You didn't give me much time." A small smile stirred on her lips, causing a stir in his midsection.

"You're a real artist." Unlike him.

"This one is Industrial Modern." Her nose wrinkled.

A charcoal pencil portrait would do the crinkle justice in a sketch. "It could work with some of what you have in your penthouse."

"Which isn't much."

"At first I thought..." she fiddled with the edge of the paper. "I thought this would fit your lifestyle, but..."

His nerves tightened, waiting for an insult. So much for impressing or wooing her.

"Never mind. This is Mid-Century Modern. It's modern with an eclectic feel. Things like the African mask, or those paintings—"

His blood pressure spiked. "Don't bring up the subject of the paintings." Ever. Again.

"Okay." She waved her hand at the design. "Mixing elements from other design styles helps to keep the look fresh."

The view took centerstage in her design. She'd made the mountains appear closer, resembling a canvas instead of a window. The furniture was characterized by refined lines and natural shapes. A couch, coffee table, loveseat, and a few selected accessories made the room fresh, clean, and inviting.

"Mid-Century Modern uses interesting materials. Molded plastics and aluminum. Its pieces are highly versatile."

She made the penthouse a home. A place you lived and not just slept. A place that tugged at your heart. He found himself leaning forward, and he spotted a shadowy figure staring out the window. A lonely figure, haunting.

He pointed at the image. "A ghost?"

Her head tilted and she studied him, trying to puzzle him out. "Do you believe in ghosts?"

His immediate response would normally be to dismiss the ridiculous notion. Something about her expression had him sitting back and considering. "Do you?"

"Not the supernatural kind." Her answer spooked him. Could she sense the ghosts in his life?

He tapped his finger on the drawing trying to direct the conversation. "Who's by the window?"

A blush reddened her cheeks, and she glanced at the table before raising her head. "It's you, looking out your window, surveying your world."

Did she think he believed he owned all of Denver? "I live in Castle Ridge."

"You travel the world." Her voice held an envious yearning, except he understood she'd do more than go from plane to meeting.

Nothing to be envious about, when you didn't see the world you traveled around. "So have you."

"Yes, I traveled while doing my internship. You travel constantly."

"For business." His gut soured. "As you pointed out, I travel but I don't see."

The words he spoke couldn't be more true. Seeing the world didn't matter. What mattered was sealing the business deal with Webber Resorts. Then, maybe, he'd take time off to travel, unless some other important deal came up. He never wanted to be in the position his father had been put in where the deals faltered or slipped away, where investments went south.

Her sharp gaze drilled into him, trying to read his thoughts. As if she understood he'd never do something so reckless to his career and to his company. "Maybe you should take the time to actually see."

Her passion deepened. He imagined her passion directed toward him, and lust squeezed his balls. The entire dinner he'd been thinking about exactly that. When she sipped her water, he'd fantasized about her sipping on his lips. When she'd laughed, he thought about laughing in bed with her. Her crush on his brother came between them. A silly crush not worthy of her intelligence. He'd turn her head and destroy the crush.

"Maybe I should." He might need to get out of the vicinity once he'd tricked her and she realized the extent of his deceit. Or, he'd need to get her out of Colorado.

The restaurant noise faded into the background. His head spun. Did he mean the words he spoke, or was he only trying to say what Emory wanted to hear? He focused, stopping the spinning. The latter, of course. He wasn't interested in a love affair or anything permanent. He'd stick with women who knew pleasuring each other was as far as the relationship would go.

Shocked at the direction of his thoughts, he tried to clear his head. Never before had he thought about travel and sex during a business meeting. She was already opening his eyes.

"Can I bring you anything else?" The waiter broke the silence between them, and the confusion between his ears.

He had to stay on point. "No, thank you. We're done."

She snapped her tablet closed. "Now that you've decided on a style, I'll have to go to the Denver Design Mart to pick out the actual furniture, and order from the catalogues. That's where I got these photos." She picked at one of the fabric scraps.

"When should we go?" Anything to keep her from Castle Ridge.

Her mouth gaped open. "I need to call. Set up appointments."

"Soon?" Standing, Jackson held the back of her chair, helping her stand.

Nodding, her scent of apples tickled his nose, and he found himself hungry for dessert. Not apple pie. Her.

She started to gather the various pieces and put them in the black portfolio.

He could use this unwanted attraction to his advantage. "Let me know when."

Her hands froze. "You want to come with? Aren't you busy?"

Yes, he was busy. Yes, he had a million things to do for work. Yes, he already feared the unusual thoughts and yearnings she triggered inside him. Even so, he needed to keep her busy and away from Ryder.

"I'll make the time."

Why had Jackson's words hinted at a threat?

Emory had wondered the entire time she'd watched the Broadway musical. Sitting so close to her, he'd been an ominous presence with his clean, crisp scent. She'd studied his silhouette and seen the sharp angles of his nose and chin. Chiseled. Imitating a statue carved from stone. Or marble, with his wealth.

I'll make the time.

As if decorating his penthouse was the most important thing to him at this moment. Sparing his precious time and no expense. During dinner, for a second, she'd thought he'd been toying with her. But when he'd readily agreed to her first choice of design style instead of arguing or becoming difficult or demanding, she'd realized he only wanted the job done. And quickly. Why would she expect differently from him?

She was happy he was leaning toward the Mid-Century Modern. It suited him. A serviceable base with room for adjustments. Clean lines with whimsy.

Similar to him.

He acted all business, and then he'd throw in sweetness like making sure she felt comfortable at the restaurant, and tickets to the most popular musical. He enjoyed touches of interesting art, like the African mask and the paintings.

The surrealist paintings she'd found behind the couch had intrigued. The painter's depth of emotion had welled within the confines of the art. She couldn't believe he'd actually thrown them away.

"What did you think of the musical?" He flung his arm around her shoulders in a casual hold as they left the theater.

She stiffened. Not businesslike at all. He'd put his arm around her before. One time when they were teens strolling back from the tennis courts at the back of the house. He'd beat her soundly in a game, and she'd been upset. The arm around her was meant to console, but she remembered other feelings. Tingly feelings. One of the things that had scared her and caused her to avoid him.

Those same sensations returned now. Stronger tingles. More direct. Shooting toward her womanly apex.

"Good." And it had been good, she'd just been too preoccupied with her companion, throwing her off-kilter.

"It's too late to drive back to Castle Ridge tonight." He dropped his arm from around her, and she chilled.

From his pronouncement, not the loss of touch.

"What?" Alarm rang in her head shaking her entire body.

"It's late. I'm tired. You must be tired."

"But…" She couldn't string two words together.

"We both had wine with dinner, and at intermission." He mimicked a lawyer pleading a case.

He'd poured more wine, saying they were walking to the theater. She figured by the end of the show he'd be alert and awake enough to drive home. He was a night owl. She knew, because when she'd been up studying in high school, his bedroom light had been on as late, if not later.

She hadn't expected to spend tonight in Denver. She hadn't planned on dinner and a show, either. He'd swept her along with his plans, taking control of her and the situation. "I'll need to find a hotel room."

"You can stay at my place." He tossed the invitation casually, not sexually.

Yet, shivers cascaded down her body to pool between her thighs. Tonight hadn't even been a date. "Excuse me?"

His lips quirked in a teasing grin. "You know I have three bedrooms. Two beds."

Only her mind had dived into the gutter. And analyzing herself, she could acknowledge a pinch of disappointment. Sleeping with Jackson Croft would be tempting and intimidating. And what about Ryder? She was supposed to be in love with him. Time to get her mind back on the professional track.

"Not much else." Shuffling forward, she forced a tease into her tone about his current décor, to prove to him she wasn't affected by what she'd thought was his sexual advance.

"Which you will be remedying." He strode beside her, slowing his long strides to match hers.

His hip bumped against her, and her mind flashed to a different kind of bumping. A more intimate kind. A naked kind. Her entire body ignited, and she unbuttoned her coat, trying to cool her desire.

They continued to walk the few blocks to his building. To his penthouse. To his bed.

Two beds.

He had two beds. One for her and one for him. There'd be no sleeping together. He hadn't even sounded interested. He knew she liked his brother. They were professionals. It would be similar to staying in a hotel with a colleague. Separate bedrooms. Three bedrooms.

What was in the third bedroom, if not a bed? He'd told her the room wasn't part of her project. Wouldn't even let her in the room. What was stored there?

"Here we are." He punched in a code, and waited for her to step inside.

"Good evening, Mr. Croft." The doorman welcomed them.

Her face flushed, thinking the doorman probably thought they were going to sleep together, yet he hadn't indicated anything. Very discreet, or was he used to Jackson bringing women to his penthouse?

Growing colder, she narrowed her gaze until the edges went green. How often did he bring women to sleep over? Not that she was jealous. Just curious, like she was curious about the third bedroom.

"How're you, Peter?" Jackson asked, as he stepped toward the elevator, in a sexy-as-sin way. The way his body moved spoke of hard muscles and languid caresses.

He wasn't trying to be sexy for her. It was in her mind. He'd mentioned staying together, and she'd jumped to a certain conclusion, and now she couldn't stop thinking about it. He'd planted the sex seed, and she couldn't stop the roots from taking hold.

"Can't complain," the doorman said.

Jackson held the elevator door open for her. "This is Ms. Barrington. She's my interior designer, and she'll be coming and going from my place."

Emory straightened and gave Peter a smile, now he understood she and Jackson weren't sleeping together. She squirmed because she wasn't averse to the suggestion.

"I'll be giving her a set of my keys." He jingled his own set, before the elevator doors closed.

Nerves swooshed in her belly, rising with the flight of the elevator. The attraction toward Jackson was only because they'd been spending so much time together. Once she spent time with Ryder, her attraction would go back in the right place. She wanted someone light and fun. She didn't want Jackson.

She didn't.

The doors slid open, and Jackson let her step out first, like a date. No, this wasn't a date, and she needed to stop thinking and comparing.

The large living space seemed more bereft than before. He flicked on the lights and took off his coat, revealing the impeccable clothes he always wore. How would he look without clothes?

Her legs jittered, and she moved toward the other side of the couch. "What happened to the paintings?" The artwork had been the one clue to his true likes and dislikes.

"I got rid of them." His gruffness tried to hide something.

She couldn't figure out what. "They were beautiful."

"Amateurish, by an unknown."

"I admired them."

Shifting toward her, his gray orbs intensified, and she found it hard to turn away. Time stretched in front of them, weaving their gazes and their bodies, pulling them closer. She found herself tilting forward, and almost fell.

Twirling around, away from temptation, she moved toward the floor-to-ceiling window. She had to escape. "A sofa table will look amazing here."

"You look amazing here." His deep voice rumbled through her chest, and surrounded her heart like a fluffy cloud.

"What?" Her throat so dry she barely got the single word out.

He cleared his throat. Quiet steps moved toward her, pounding in time with her pulse. "Sorry. The way the moonlight caught your hair, you glowed, appearing to be a magical fairy princess."

His compliment flipped a switch inside her. An attraction switch. "You compared me to a fairy before. Is that a compliment?"

"Yes."

Pivoting, she found him standing right behind her. An internal tug moved her forward, toward him. She ran a wet tongue along her dry lips. She wanted a kiss. He blinked and she remembered when he'd kissed her in the garden. An assault and an attempted bribe.

Everything inside her hardened, and she took a step back, knowing she couldn't fall for his charm. He was her client, not her master. "I should get to bed. To sleep."

She was not going to bed with him. She was not going to kiss him. She needed to get back to Castle Ridge and Ryder.

"Of course." Jackson stepped back and used his formal voice. "This way."

He led the way down the hall to the second bedroom, and opened the door. "There's an en suite bathroom, and it should have a toothbrush, toothpaste, face soap, everything you need."

She paused at the door of the generic bedroom.

He'd covered the basics, and she didn't need make-up to drive home in the morning. "What about pajamas?"

Their bodies were close. So close she smelled the crisp scent clinging to him, even this late at night, and saw the way his pupils shifted from her lips to her eyes. She could become lost in his gray eyes. How they changed from midnight to slate with his mood, resembling an alpine lake high in the mountains.

"I can give you a T-shirt. I sleep naked."

The image burned in her brain. The broad shoulders leading to a muscular chest, possibly with hair. The trim waist and the ridges of his abs. The slender hips leading to... She swallowed. Heat scorched her skin. His heat.

"Good to know."

His mouth moved closer. Or was she moving closer?

"Emory?" His lips brushed against hers as he asked.

Asked for permission.

Except it was too late. How could she not return the kiss, when it flared between them like an open-hearth fire?

When Emory's lips pressed against his, Jackson's entire body vibrated. He hadn't expected a response, only meaning to tempt. When he'd admitted he slept naked her violet gaze had changed to a deeper purple. Desire. The tension between them had turned into a magnetized connection, each of them leaning closer toward the other. He'd planned to kiss her lightly, teasingly. He hadn't expected her to return the kiss.

The shock had him standing motionless, letting her mouth caress his, letting her take control. The kiss was different from the one he'd stolen at the wedding reception. She'd responded to that kiss out of shock. But this kiss, she was the one initiating.

The single thought spurred him on. He pushed her up against the doorframe and got fully involved. Sliding his tongue over the seam of her lips, he coaxed her mouth open and dove inside. He tasted the wine she'd drank with dinner, and a lighter, fresher taste.

Her distinct taste.

He thrust his hands in her short locks, gripping her head with his fingers, trying to find the perfect angle to make the kiss go deeper. Her hands landed on his back and imprinted in a brand. Her tongue tangled with his, dancing to their own beat.

He hadn't danced with her at the wedding. His brother had.

His passion shut down, filled with green envy. He was a replacement for his brother. A shallow stand-in. Second choice. Instinctively, he broke off the kiss. The kiss didn't mean anything to her. How could it, when she'd kissed his brother, too?

He scrutinized her expression. Closed eyes. Expression dazed by lust. Soft lips, plump from their kiss. Slightly upturned nose, making her appear innocent.

"Jackson?" Her eyelids fluttered open, and her hazy gaze betrayed her confusion.

He wanted her, and he shouldn't. If she could be this easily swayed from one Croft brother to the other, her feelings weren't very deep. He needed to use her attraction toward him, not fall under her magic. That would only spell disaster.

He released her hair, and let his arms drop to his sides. Clenching his fists, he controlled his baser instincts. "Goodnight."

Reeling around before she could respond, he headed down the hall to his bedroom and clicked the door closed. Closing off the temptation that was Emory.

He needed to stay all-business with her.

All business, all the time. His slogan.

Why did the decision leave an empty and unsatisfied swirl in his gut?

Chapter Eight

Holding back his breathing, Jackson listened at the closed bedroom door. Sleep had eluded him, as he lay in his bed, picturing Emory sleeping on the other side of the wall in her bed, probably naked. He ground his fist into his other palm. Becoming attracted to her wasn't part of the plan.

And now, he stood outside her bedroom door, listening. Hearing nothing. No snoring. No restless scratch of the sheets. She must be deep asleep, undisturbed by the passionate kiss they'd shared. He could picture her tiny, lithe frame under the covers, barely taking up any space in the queen-sized bed. Her short hair would press against the pillow, her eyes would be closed, her expression sweet.

Moving away, he paced toward the locked third bedroom door, reached above the transom, and fished out the key. Inserting the key into the lock, he steeled himself before entering. He hadn't been in this room for at least two years. After struggling in secret for three years to stabilize Croft Industries, he'd purchased the penthouse in celebration, and in hopes of gifting himself time. He'd been twenty-six.

He'd work hard all day at business, and come here to paint all night. Dreams of being an artist had haunted him, then.

His shoulders dropped, and a weight pressed on him. He'd thought he was good, in college and just after. Believed in his spare time he could dabble with his hobby. Except he didn't have any spare time to be creative. The original reason he'd bought the penthouse was so he wouldn't have to commute back and forth to Castle Ridge after meetings in Denver. Instead of working on his hobby with the time saved, he'd only worked more. He put his right-brain efforts into the business. Maybe that's why his plans were successful, because his creativity went into scheming and plotting.

Now his artistic dreams were dead.

The door creaked open, and he stepped inside, closing the door behind him. The punch of the paint smell hit him first. Oils and acrylics. Paint thinner. At one time, the mixed scents had been perfume, heady and creative. Now, the smell made his stomach turn.

Several easels were placed around the room, holding unfinished canvases. Unfinished dreams. Finished paintings were stacked against the walls. Tarps laid on the wood floor for protection. Small tables holding a can of brushes, tubes of paint, palettes.

He picked up a brush, and ran his fingers over the bristles. The bristles poked and prodded him into remembering. Remembering dreams of sharing the responsibilities of the business with his brother, and becoming a part-time artist. Those dreams had collapsed when Ryder graduated college and wasn't interested in Croft Industries. Wasn't interested in much of anything.

Jackson's painting at night and on weekends had become not painting at all. Ever.

Because he'd worked late, and didn't have time.

Because he'd been tired.

Because he'd lost his imagination.

Now, his imagination tried to take flight. His fingers itched, and his brain flickered images of colors and textures, and techniques and faces.

Who was he kidding?

Only one face.

Emory's.

Her delicate alabaster skin. Her skeptical dark eyebrows. Her silky, black hair. Her expressive, violet gaze, whether angry or curious or passion-filled. And her lips...apple-red and sumptuous.

Kissable.

His blood raced, remembering. Remembering their kiss, how she'd responded. How he hadn't wanted to stop.

How getting involved with Emory wasn't part of his plan.

Emory sat in the car beside Jackson early the next morning. They were both early risers, so after a quick cup of coffee, they were on the road headed to Castle Ridge. He'd barely spoken to her, only grunting the bare minimum. He'd been on the phone since they'd gotten in the car, taking one business call after another. He'd never mentioned the kiss.

While she'd lain awake for hours, thinking about nothing else.

Her body warmed at the memory. When she'd grazed his lips, she'd lost her mind. The only way to explain what had happened. She'd forgotten about Ryder. Forgotten Jackson was a client. Forgotten the lessons she'd learned about mixing business with pleasure.

Because it had been pleasure.

Sparks had ignited when their lips touched. The demanding power he'd displayed had morphed her to mush. Her body and her brain. The kiss had started slow and gentle, inquisitive, in a way. As if he was unsure if he should be kissing her. And then, she'd kissed him back, responded, welcomed him. Passion had erupted between them, on both sides, and she'd been spiraling to heaven. Suddenly, he'd broken their connection, ended the kiss, said a curt goodnight, and left her alone.

An ache expanded in her lungs. She stole a glance at his hard profile as he drove. His tone vibrated with power, but she remembered the gentle way he'd said her name. Now, his eyes glinted like steel. Last night, they'd been soft clay, ready to be molded. And the hard shape of his lips had been pliant against her mouth. Pliant and tender.

Squeezing her fingers together, she pursed her lips, trying to hold in her frustration and confusion. Was he never going to mention the kiss? Was he not going to talk to her the entire drive? Business, business, and more business.

Last night, she'd seen the type of man he could be. The type of man she was attracted to. Her heart boomed, echoing throughout her ribcage. What about Ryder? He was the one who'd asked her to go dancing. He was the one she'd crushed on since she was a kid.

Turning her head away, she blindly stared out the window. She needed space. Away from Jackson's clean, crisp scent pervading the car. Away from his rumbling voice, causing an answering rumble in her midsection. A few minutes to pull herself together. "I need to use the bathroom."

He tossed her a nasty scowl that said, *how dare she interrupt his conference call?* He pulled the car off the freeway toward a rest area and scenic overlook. He never paused his phone conversation.

She wanted to give him a nasty word.

Once parked, she got out of the car, and slammed the door. Hard. After taking care of business, she pressed her palms against the white porcelain sink, and slowly breathed in and out. "He's a client. I can't be rude."

She wiped away the mist forming on the dirty bathroom mirror. "We shouldn't have kissed." She should've learned the lesson while in Spain. "It won't happen again."

After making the vow, she straightened yesterday's outfit with dignity, and continued her internal lecture. She was a professional. She was starting an interior design business. She needed him as a client. Her first client.

With a clear head, she marched out of the bathroom, with her head held high. She forced a brilliant smile on her face, and reached for the car door handle and yanked.

It was locked.

Her stomach dropped. He wouldn't lock her out of the car, would he?

"Emory." Jackson leaned casually against the short rock wall guarding the scenic view. His normally perfect hair blew slightly in the wind. His suit jacket was open, and his tie was gone. The cell phone's earpiece was missing from his ear. He appeared completely different.

Back to the man she found attractive. The one who could learn to enjoy life.

She took the steps slowly, unsure what to expect. "You're off the phone."

"I am." He beamed, causing a ba-bump in her chest.

"Did you lose the connection?" The only reason he'd stopped talking business. "What're you doing out here?"

"I completed the call." Wheeling around, he faced the deep valley giving way to snowcapped mountains. "Taking in the view. It's spectacular."

Why this sudden change? He'd gone from super executive without a minute to talk to her on the long drive, to entranced tourist. Shaking her head, she looked out.

The gorge in front of them dropped to a dizzying low, with a river rushing over rocks and downed trees. The smell of evergreens wafted in the air. The snowmelt had happened quickly this spring. The mountains rose from the valley, with only the tops covered in white. The craggy boulders jutted out, making everything more dramatic.

Resembling an excited schoolboy instead of the business executive, he pointed at something in the distance. "Look at the mountain goats."

"How many times have you driven this road?"

"Hundreds, possibly thousands. I go back and forth to Denver a lot."

Birds chirped in the blue sky, adding to the noise of the river flowing below. Adding to the confusion in her head.

"And you've never stopped to look?"

"No." His sheepish tone and expression was adorable.

"Colorado has amazing scenery." The natural music sang in her bloodstream. This was home. The mountains, the rivers and streams, the small town of Castle Ridge. Getting away from Spain had been good for so many reasons.

"I know." His serious expression said he was talking about more than the scenery. He understood how much she appreciated her home.

"But do you see and appreciate and become mindful of the moment?" She shifted sideways, to watch him taking in the view.

His gaze widened to encompass everything. His lips lifted in a grateful smile. His entranced expression signified his appreciation of the view, understood the significance of the beauty, and was honored to be present.

She tilted toward him, her arm brushing his, and sparks flamed. Watching him taking in the scenery, she was entranced. Her pulse bolted, sending a rush of blood to her heart.

This was the real Jackson. The Jackson he hid behind his business shell.

The rest of the drive Jackson ignored his phone, because he had every right to enjoy a few stolen moments. He could take a few hours off and not lose his company.

He'd been ignoring Emory out of cowardice. Ignoring her initially sunny expression, ignoring her cheerful apple scent, ignoring the memories of the passionate kiss they'd shared.

Except he wasn't a coward, and he'd devised a way to use this unwanted attraction to his advantage. For the ploy. The charm offensive would continue, and he'd count on her attraction toward him.

He'd gotten out of the car to prove he was interested in the scenery, interested in seeing the world, interested in her.

The scenery at the overlook had come alive. The babbling river, the tweeting birds, and the wind whistling through the trees had turned into a song. The colors had become more vibrant. He could see how dabbing with a brush could allude to the texture of the trees, and a swirly motion could represent the floaty-ness of the clouds. A fine brush could etch in the goats. His fingers tingled with the urge to paint something besides Emory.

They'd gotten in the car, and competed to point out significant or unusual scenery. An old miner's quarry. A raft in the river winding beside the road. A ski run.

"Tell me about Spain. What you did. What you saw." He wanted to know everything about her.

No. That couldn't be it. A few eye-opening moments at a rest stop and an idyllic kiss wouldn't change his goals. He wouldn't fall for her charm. It was supposed to be the other way around. Learning about her would help him find her weak points, to steer her away from his brother. The only reason he needed to know everything.

"I was mostly in Barcelona, where my internship was located." Her enthusiasm exhibited love for her career. He wished he could bottle her enthusiasm and use it in his everyday work environment. "We had some high-profile clients, accounts I worked on and got to assist with design."

"Sounds exciting." Much more exciting than his *beloved* spreadsheets. "Your mother mentioned they asked you to stay on as a full-time designer. Why didn't you?"

He'd politely enquired about Emory over the years. After investing in her college education, he'd wanted to know what she was doing with her degree. He wasn't a stalker, just an interested investor. Plus, her mother loved to talk.

"I was ready to come home." Enthusiasm dipped in her voice, and filled with strength, determination, and something else. Something he couldn't define. "I wanted to start my own design firm. Be in charge."

Open-book Emory was hiding something. His

intuition when working with colleagues and competitors had sharpened this skill. He knew.

He knew, because he hid things, too. Things about his past, the way he did business when he first started, the fact he'd lied about getting his college degree. He'd always assumed what you saw was what you got with Emory. There was more here, deeper stories between the lines and chapters. And he wanted to discover them.

Nerves wobbled in his gut, because he realized learning her deeper truth was not about business and keeping her away from his brother. It wasn't about the ploy. It smacked of personal interest, something he couldn't afford.

"There's the top of Castle Ridge Ski Resort." She waved her hand toward the mountain.

They were almost home. It was around lunchtime, and Ryder would probably be awake.

Jackson sucked in a sharp breath, his mind clicking for options. "Let's stop for lunch."

"My mom prepared lunch, knowing we'd be back."

Lunch at home meant his brother sitting at the table asking questions, and Emory eating in the kitchen with her mom, also probably asking questions.

"And *I* have lots of work to do. For you," she continued.

"Do you want me to drop you off by the back of the house? Your private entrance?"

She could go straight to her suite of rooms and not bump into his brother.

Her body stilled. He sensed the tenseness in the air. What had he said? He glanced at her sideways. Her lips were flat, angry. Her gaze was narrow, glaring straight ahead.

"What's wrong, Emory?"

Her cheeks reddened, and she kept her head facing forward. "Are you embarrassed to pull up to the front of the house with me?"

He'd been trying to keep her hidden, but not for the reasons she thought. "No. Of course not."

"Are you sure?" She twisted in the seat to face him, to confront him. Her angry eyes flared. "You don't want me dating your brother, and you tried to buy me off."

His Emory didn't back down from a fight. *His Emory?* No, his problem. She had become his problem. And yet, he respected her challenge. Most people did what he demanded. "I thought we'd straightened that out. A misunderstanding."

"And the kiss? What about the kiss?" If it was possible, her body stiffened more. She held her back straight, and didn't drop her challenging stare. She must've been thinking about their kiss the entire drive.

As had he.

Trying to buy time, he pulled into the long, steep driveway leading to the house. What would she respect? *The truth.* He couldn't tell her the truth. A partial truth, then.

"I'm sorry. I got carried away last night."

She curled her fingers into a tiny fist. "If you think hiring me for a design job is another way to buy me off, you're wrong."

He'd realized that last night. Hence, the dinner and

Broadway musical. And the kiss. He couldn't forget the kiss. Because he'd planned a light brush of lips, he hadn't expected her response.

Driving around the circular drive to a spot in front of the steps leading to the front door, he noted the strange car parked farther up. Maybe Ryder had a visitor. Not Shey, though. Jackson put his car in park.

"I need a designer. You're good." And smart. Smart enough to realize his scheme.

"How do you know I'm good?"

Why couldn't Emory take a compliment and run? He couldn't tell her he'd followed her progress in college, and had researched her internship when she'd gotten the offer. He'd wanted to make sure she would learn, and be appreciated for her skills.

Maybe a little more honesty would help. She could paint in the rest of the picture, and be wary of the situation. He angled to face her, placing his arm along the back of her seat.

"The thing is…" He took in her innocence. Had she even had a serious relationship before? "The thing is, I don't want to see you get hurt." And he truly didn't, and yet he knew playing this dangerous game would hurt her. "My brother is about to get engaged."

She crossed her arms and her eyebrows shot up in doubting arches. "They broke up."

And Emory had had a silly crush on Ryder since she was an impressionable kid. She was willing to take a risk on a heartbroken man.

What about a heartless one?

His non-existent heart dropped, and he slumped in the car seat. Where had that thought come from? He didn't want her to take a chance on him. This wasn't about him.

"Hello! Jackson!" The irritating, high-pitched trill carried through the car windows.

Victoria Croft, wearing high, high heels and a short, short skirt strutted toward them from the other car.

His head pounded, knowing the woman didn't bring good news. He might act too old, while his mother dressed too young. "What is she doing here?"

Emory turned her head toward the window. "Your mother."

"Yes. My mother." He poured his disdain and dislike into his response. He needed to get rid of the woman, and tell her to quit riling up rumors. He got out of the car, and slammed the door. "I thought I told you to stay off the property."

The Castle Ridge home had never needed extra security. Locked doors and an alarm had been the most they'd ever used. Maybe it was time to change the relaxed security protocol.

"It was my home at one time." Victoria's fake-innocent expression didn't fool him. "I was visiting Ryder. It's his home, too. Or do you try to control everyone, like your father?"

Jackson cringed. He hated being compared to his father. A man everyone believed was brilliant and kind. The businesspeople he'd worked with had compared the two of them, and Jackson had always come up short. "I'm not my father."

His father had been nice, and he wasn't. His father slacked off on his duties and ruined the company, so he never would. His father didn't work schemes, poison people, or charm a woman for nefarious purposes.

His father was dead, so the man couldn't judge him.

Emory got out of the car and stood by the front of the car. He really didn't want her witnessing this exchange.

"And you hate your mother." Victoria's hands waved around dramatically and she flipped what must be a fake ponytail. "You really should see a psychiatrist about your mommy and daddy issues."

A wave of heat, chased by chills raced across his body. Emory heard every lie this woman spouted. He clenched his fists, wanting to toss the woman who'd given him birth.

"Emory, isn't it?" His mother moved toward another victim, an innocent victim. "You and Jackson together again. Is this a romance, or a tryst?" Her garishly-painted lips twisted into a vile smirk. "Or something different? An upstairs-downstairs affair?"

The woman's accusations were slashes from a hot poker, prodding him to defend Emory. He took a menacing step forward.

"What *is* going on between you and Emory?" Ryder stood on the top step.

Jackson's heart clobbered his ribs with its gigantic boom. He hadn't noticed his brother standing there, and he didn't know what to say. He hadn't wanted his brother to witness his attempts to lure Emory away.

It would only make the forbidden more attractive.

Chapter Nine

Emory teetered between two polar opposites, and she felt a chill from both directions.

Ryder stood on the top step in a bathrobe and slippers. His relaxed stance appeared too casual. His hair was mussed, as if he'd just woken up, so Victoria Croft was lying about her visit. The swelling on his face had gone down, and he looked adorable as always. Jackson loomed on the driveway, a lower position geographically, yet standing taller and straighter. His handsome face oozed power. And was that a bit of fear?

She sensed it in the way his gaze darted between her and his brother and his mother. He was unsure who to deal with first. She'd never seen Jackson unsure before. He always plowed through any obstacles.

"Em?" Ryder held out a helping, welcoming hand. "What're you doing with my brother? I thought we made plans to go dancing? To go on a date."

Ignoring the nickname, she shuffled toward him. She had promised him they'd go out—a teenage fantasy come true. After the way her last relationship ended, she needed fun and uncomplicated. Not dark and brooding.

Taking one step at a time, she peered at Jackson and caught something more than power or fear flash on his face. Could it be hurt? She sucked in air. He shuttered his expression before she could fully analyze and faced his mother, effectively dismissing her. Couldn't have been distress. Not when he didn't care she was sidling toward his brother. Not when he said it was okay for her to date Ryder.

Yet, something tugged her toward Jackson. Except, she'd made a promise to go on a date with Ryder, and she needed to talk to him without an audience. She realized she didn't want to dance with him anymore.

"Yes. We did make plans." She watched Jackson, wondering how he felt now about her dating his brother. After their kisses, after their conversations.

"What do you want?" He demanded of his mother.

The meanness with his mother sent a shiver down Emory's spine. He always took a hard line. If you crossed him, you were cut off, making it impossible to count on a relationship.

Her confused thoughts brewed in her head. Which brother did she really want? And did what she want matter? Jackson could be toying with her, and Ryder was recovering from more than an allergic reaction. Plus, she wasn't interested in the mean, buttoned-up Jackson. And yet, she'd seen hints of a gentler, different man. Could she save him from himself?

Moving beside Ryder, she didn't take his hand. "How're you feeling?"

"Much better. I have no clue how I was exposed to shellfish." His grin was self-effacing and infectious.

"Even I knew of your allergy. The entire staff did." She glanced at Jackson again, to see the small tic in his cheek working overtime. "Jackson?"

"What?" The single word cut into her, chasing thoughts of fear and hurt completely away.

This man didn't fear anything, and nothing could dent his armor. Certainly, not her. Why should she give up her teenage dream of dating Ryder because Jackson had kissed her? What if he really had no interest in her, and the kiss had been because of the evening and the mood?

"Do you know how Ryder was exposed?" Jackson oversaw everything, including his sister's reception. He'd spoken to his brother right before he became ill.

"No. Of course not. Why would you ask me?" He spoke fast. Too fast.

A chill combined with the slight breeze.

Victoria tapped a finger against her chin displaying interest, not concern. "Even I remember Ryder's allergy. My poor boy."

"Mother." Both sons spoke at the same time, in completely different tones. Jackson's was more chastisement, while Ryder's betrayed embarrassment.

The two sons flung hostile daggers at each other. Each one obviously feeling different about their biological mother. Jackson wasn't one to forgive, while Ryder was more understanding and open.

"We should talk about our date. When are you available?" Ryder snatched her hand, and raised it to his mouth.

The graze of his lips didn't leave even a tingle. But this was supposed to be her dream. She needed fun and uncomplicated, not a commitment. Not drama and heartache. She and Ryder were both at the same place in their lives. Recently single, and looking for fun.

Jackson stood in the same spot, eavesdropping on her answer. The draw toward him was a riptide pulling her under, and she found it difficult to breathe. Fear she was in over her head with him crushed her lungs and made her chest ache. She'd end up damaged, even more than when she'd broken up with Alejandro.

If Jackson was attracted to her, really attracted, why had he cut the kiss short? She should jump at the chance to go dancing with his brother. She'd been so excited Saturday night, until she and Ryder had been interrupted.

"Em?" Ryder squeezed her hand, bringing her attention back to him. "How about tonight?"

"Tonight?" She flinched from the strike of Jackson's glare.

"Five minutes, Mother. That's all the time I can give you." His harsh tone would've sliced through a lesser woman than his mother.

The tone would *slice* through Emory. Is that how he treated women? Once he got what he wanted, a business contract or a penthouse design or a night in his bed, he'd brush them off or toss them to the side.

Like he did with his mother.

He might've said he wouldn't interfere with her dating his brother, but he wasn't happy about it. And now he was an important client. An unhappy important client. And why would he kiss her if he was okay with her dating his brother? Did the two brothers share women, not caring how it affected people? Questions bombarded her brain, making her head throb. These brothers might be too much trouble. She needed to focus on her career, on the job Jackson was paying her to complete.

"Em?" Ryder interrupted her confused thoughts.

"I can't tonight. I have a ton of work to do." She slipped her hand from his.

"Work?"

"For your brother."

His relaxed expression tightened. His gaze calculated. He wasn't as laid back as he pretended. "Oh, really?"

He believed there was more than work involved. And while he was wrong, he was sort of right. She'd kissed Jackson. She was attracted to him. It had to end there.

Grounding her feet, she strove for determination. "Yes. He hired me to decorate his penthouse in Denver. That's where we were."

"All night?" Ryder didn't sound jealous, and yet there was a hard edge to his tone. Did he understand what was going on more than she did?

"I took him the designs last night. It got late. We spent the night." She needed to explain. "Not together. I mean, at his penthouse but not together, together." Her cheeks scorched, remembering the kiss.

She needed to forget about the kiss. Jackson certainly had.

"I believe you." Ryder's earnestness had the contents of her stomach swishing back and forth. "And I understand you're busy. When can we go out?"

Jackson gripped his mother's upper arm and thundered toward the gazebo. He didn't want to hear Emory say yes to a date with his brother. Didn't want to hear the joy in her voice. And then, didn't want to hear her disappointment in the future because Ryder had feelings for Shey. Deep feelings.

Shey made Ryder happy, and less destructive in his partying ways. She made him want to be a better man. She was the best thing that ever happened to his brother.

And to Croft Industries.

Jackson's plan for Emory was failing. He needed to increase the pressure and step up his game. She might get hurt losing Ryder, but she wouldn't be devastated because she didn't really love him. How could she, when she didn't even know him anymore? It was a childish infatuation. Nothing more.

If she did truly love him, how could she kiss Jackson with such passion? His mouth tingled at the memory, and his fingers dug into his mother's arm.

"Ouch." Victoria yanked her arm away. "Don't manhandle me."

One problem at a time. "Why are you here?"

The flowery scents from the night he met Emory in the garden faded. He only smelled dirt and deceit. Victoria wouldn't return to Castle Ridge without a good reason. She'd always hated the town and the people.

"I came to see how your brother was doing after his incident." The lie snaked around her gray eyes.

The same eyes that peered back at him in the mirror. Flat, cold, heartless.

"Why are you back in Castle Ridge? Why now?" He'd learned to do without her. To manage on his own. And once his dad died, to manage the family on his own.

"Now's as good a time as any." Her airy excuse blew away in the slight wind. "You and your brother seem to be having…issues."

Adrenalized anger lunged through his veins. Her statement was clearly fishing. He'd learned to recognize a tactic.

"Ryder and I are fine." Jackson pinched his lips together, controlling his reply. Or most of his reply. "As if you cared."

He couldn't stop the sentiment from falling out of his mouth. Couldn't completely stop himself from expressing the agony she'd inflicted.

"I care when my two sons are fighting over the housekeeper's daughter." His mother spoke as if Emory was a wishbone they both coveted.

She wasn't a wishbone, although she might get torn apart in their tug-of-war.

"Do you think Emory isn't good enough for either of us?" His mood darkened. She was too good for him. Fun and full of life, creative, persistent.

"I don't care who you sleep with, as long as you marry appropriately. Wealthily. You might need it in the future." His mother had done her research. She knew who Emory was. "From what I've heard, Ryder is going to marry Shey Webber."

"You lost any right to interfere in our lives when you left. Leave our love lives out of this." Leave Emory out of their sordid family battles. "Leave Ryder alone, too. I'm handling it."

While Jackson wanted his brother to grow up and get serious, he never wanted him to lose his innocence and his sense of fun. The last thing Ryder needed was another person interfering in his life. Irony struck, digging a hole deep in Jackson's conscience. He and George were interfering.

"You weren't handling it back there." Waving in the direction of the front steps, the subtle threat wasn't as much in Victoria's words as her tone. "Ryder's smitten with the girl."

"I've got a plan for Emory, and it doesn't involve Ryder." Jackson refused to let them get involved. He'd protected his brother from the truth about the business when their father died. He'd protected him from hangers-on who only surrounded Ryder because of the money. And Jackson would protect his brother from Emory's innocent flirtation.

A glint of avarice and interest flashed in Victoria's gaze. "So Ryder will marry Shey, and the merger will go on as planned."

"Once we're family with the Webbers, they can't back out." Jackson realized his mistake. He shouldn't have said anything about the merger plans. "How do you know about the merger?"

"I have business connections. I hear things." The

evasiveness didn't work, because greed gleamed in her eyes, hinting at something more.

She couldn't know anything. She was fishing again.

"Your five minutes is running out." He tapped his foot on the brick paving stones.

"All right." Crossing her tanned arms, she scraped a long nail against the exposed skin. She might look silly, but she wasn't dumb. "I want to talk about our business."

"*Our* business?" The darkness inside him rolled into thunder.

"Croft Industries."

The thunder rumbled in his head. "My business."

"Ryder's too." Her too-innocent expression hinted of a slyness beneath. "The family business."

Her compromising tone struck like lightning. A flame burned in Jackson's lungs. She was scheming and conniving and…similar to him. No, not similar to him, at all. He was scheming to get Emory out of the way to help the family business, not personal gain.

While his mother was only about herself.

"I think the way you're handling the merger—"

"You have no right to discuss or suggest anything to do with Croft Industries." The flame ignited into a firestorm. How dare she even make a suggestion? The nerve, the audacity. "You gave up that right when you and Dad got divorced."

Her smugness struck a nerve. "I received stock in the divorce settlement."

"Not enough to have a say in what I do." *Stay calm. Stay calm. Stay calm.* "I'm surprised you didn't cash out the second you'd vested."

"Why would I cash out a few worthless pieces of paper?" Smug changed to devious satisfaction.

"Croft stock isn't worthless." Jackson held his breath waiting, waiting…

"It was back then."

Her statement sucker-punched. He reeled back, the torment digging in his gut and his brain. His mother understood the financial position of the company when Dad had died. Knew of the mess and the legal discrepancies.

She patted him on the shoulder in a patronizing way. "You've done a wonderful job with the company."

He didn't respond. Didn't whack her hand off his arm. Didn't attack.

Because he couldn't.

His chest ached, remembering the situation, remembering the struggle and the defeat. Of how the merciless mask he wore had been a prison. A prison where he still was captive. Eventually, he'd won. He'd saved the company and his dad's reputation.

"Which is why I've kept quiet until now."

He didn't want to give her more ammunition. "No one knows about the problems when we were a private company."

Those bright-red lips turned upward, imitating an evil clown's. "I know. In fact, I kept a few of the documents proving your financial straits."

His thunderous storm dissipated into rain. The anger fell into puddles, drowning him in worry. He didn't want his father's legacy tarnished. He couldn't let people find out about the shady deals he'd made to save the company. His mother must keep the secret.

"Go ahead. Take it to the financial journals. It's history." He bluffed with every acting skill he possessed. "Time for you to go."

He started stomping back up the brick path toward the driveway.

She sauntered next to him, patted him on the cheek, and slipped into the driver's seat. "Did you ever wonder who bought your precious stock when it was low? Who helped keep the doors open? Who's been buying up Croft stock since you went public?"

Chapter Ten

"Emory, come and eat dinner." Her mother called from the living area of their suite of rooms. "You've spent the entire afternoon in your room."

"I'm working." She slapped down another photo of an Eames lounge chair made of black leather and sleek wood. Focused, she'd spent the entire afternoon concentrating on Jackson's penthouse.

Colorful swatches lay on her bed, printouts of pieces of furniture, sketches. A design program was open on her laptop. She tried to fit things into place like doing a jigsaw puzzle. Similar to her feelings for Jackson. Lust and liking versus flirtation and fear. Her emotions juxtaposed against each other, rubbing each other raw.

"You need to eat. Mr. Jackson would not expect you to starve in order to get your designs completed so fast." Mom didn't know Jackson Croft that well.

She served him. She didn't socialize with him. She'd never kissed him.

Emory's lips sparked with heat. She hoped her mother had never kissed Jackson or Ryder. Giggling, she flopped back on the bed scattering the small pieces of paper. She was certifiably insane, thinking about one brother while promising a date with the other.

"Emory. I'm not asking again." Her mother used the I'm-your-mother voice. Which she was. Still, Emory was twenty-four and had lived on her own for years, getting her own dinner and making sure she got enough sleep.

Picking up a photo of a Noguchi table, she studied the freeform-shaped glass laying across two perfectly balanced pieces of wood. This wouldn't work for Jackson. It didn't fit his personality. Everything needed to suit him, make him comfortable at his place. Her design and her furniture decisions needed to be perfect.

Why? Because she wanted to please her first client, or because she wanted to please Jackson? Both, actually. She wanted him to be pleased with the design on several levels. Mostly, she wanted him to be pleased with her.

She ran fingers through her short hair. Continuing to search online catalogues wasn't going to help her make decisions. "Coming." She picked up two swatches before heading to the small kitchen table.

"Sit, sit." Smiling, her mother pulled a blue casserole dish from the oven. Her mom loved to cook and take care of people. Some people might look down on her for being a housekeeper, but it was what she loved.

She'd never looked down on her mother, although she'd been embarrassed as a teen. Most kids were embarrassed of their parents. Jackson had recognized her shame at dinner last night. He understood her and really listened.

Her mom's small kitchen had every modern appliance, a scaled down version of the large kitchen in the main home. The ceiling featured white-painted, tongue-and-groove boards to reflect light captured by the window above the sink. The window looked out over the rose garden. Light, blue-gray cabinets contrasted with the limestone floor.

Emory had helped pick out the flooring and cabinets when she'd been in high school, and the experience had confirmed her calling to be an interior designer.

"Something smells delicious." She settled into a chair. Her chair. It was the chair she always sat in when she was home, and the warmth of welcome hit her again. This is why she'd come home. To spend time with her mom. To start her business. To start the next phase of her life.

How did Ryder and Jackson fit into those plans? She'd seen dancing with Ryder a teenage fantasy come true. Fun, flirty, and nothing serious. Jackson she hadn't seen coming at all. His offer for her to design his penthouse had come out of nowhere. This attraction had blindsided.

"Your favorite. Hungarian goulash."

The thick soup with big, fat noodles had her mouth salivating. Her frustration with the design project lessened. She couldn't stress about making Jackson's penthouse perfect. Things would fall into place if she relaxed.

"Thanks Mom. You didn't have to go to this much trouble."

Wearing comfy jeans and a light sweater, Mom took the seat across the table and settled in for a long talk. Normally, Emory loved talking to her mom for hours, except not when she had a deadline. "Mr. Jackson likes my goulash, too."

"Jackson?" Emory wanted to be sure they were talking about the same man. She found it hard to picture him liking the ethnic, home-styled, comfort food. "I didn't realize you made this dish for the Crofts."

Their fare was normally more elegant, with rich sauces and fine cuts of meat. She took a bite of the goulash, which had the consistency between a soup and a stew. Spices of paprika and bay leaves twirled around her tongue.

"I don't." Mom leaned in conspiratorially. "I was lonely when you went away to school. He must've sensed it, because he dropped by after dinner. I'd made goulash, and he sat and ate with me." Mom's smile grew wide, and her eyes twinkled. "He might act a big, bad businessman, but inside he's a sweetheart."

Emory shook her head, trying to picture his large body sitting in the small kitchen, keeping her lonely mother company. "Did you know he donated a building for a no-kill dog shelter in downtown Denver?"

"He's done a lot of charitable things. Some for publicity and others in secret." Mom's gaze softened for a second, as if thinking of something more specific. "I haven't heard anything about a dog shelter."

Shrugging, Emory took another bite. Her mom heard a lot between the kitchen and the dining room.

"How's Ryder feeling?" And through the same rumor mill, her mom would know the answer to the question. Except Mom wanted the answer from Emory.

"Better. I saw him when I got home this afternoon." Guilt swirled, and the delicious goulash sat heavy in her belly. He'd tried to get her to commit to a date, and she'd put him off. A date hadn't seemed right. She didn't know if it was the sadness in his eyes, or the misgiving shredding her stomach, or the final glare shot at her by Jackson.

Or the kiss she'd responded to.

A few days ago, she would've jumped at the chance and gone on a date with Ryder at the first opportunity. Now, she felt pressed by work and by Jackson's kiss. Why had he kissed her last night? Had it been a spur-of-the-moment thing, or something more? And why had she kissed him back? The questions were a whirlpool in her head.

Her mother frowned. "I don't understand how Ryder was exposed to shellfish. Everyone in the kitchen is so careful."

"I know, right?" The image of the tic in Jackson's expression when she'd asked this morning came back to her. Could Jackson know something?

He loved his brother, had been protective toward him when talking about the break-up. Mom had talked about how he wasn't a ruthless businessman as everyone believed.

"I saw Mr. Webber arriving to meet with Jackson after dinner."

"Mr. Webber?" Emory tried to remember how she knew the name. Being back in Castle Ridge was like passing through a yearbook. So many familiar names and faces, yet none she'd known well. She hadn't kept in touch with the few friends she'd had in high school.

"Shey's father. I'm wondering if Ryder and Shey are back together."

"No. Ryder asked me out for tonight."

Mom sat back, her expression tightening. "You had your dance with him. I hope you told him no."

What was wrong with her dating Ryder? Either Croft, for that matter? "I told him no. For tonight." The scrap of green fabric reminded her why she'd put it off. She was busy. Had work to do. "We might go out another time."

"Emory."

She knew what her mom was going to say. The Crofts were her mother's employer, they were older and more sophisticated, they lived in a different world. And Emory herself was now working for Jackson. She didn't want to hear her mom's concern, because those same thoughts had run through her head. In Barcelona, she'd put those common-sense thoughts aside, and dated someone in a higher station and a client. And the relationship had ended badly.

She held up the fabric scraps needing a distraction. "What do you think of these?"

"What's this for?"

"Jackson's penthouse in downtown Denver." She'd

told her mom earlier about the job, and why they'd spent the night there.

"I never pictured Jackson with so much color." Her mother tilted her head to study the swatches. "I like them both."

"Me, too." She wavered between the forest green and the Cambridge blue. Both would look good in the living room. Both would go well with his eyes. "I want to pick the perfect color palette for him."

Mom froze and continued to study her. It was the same expression she'd given when she knew Emory was lying or hiding something.

Emory's feet fidgeted. "What?"

"Nothing." The tone meant something.

"What?"

"I love both Ryder and Jackson, but one is dealing with a broken heart, and the other has a reputation for not having a heart. Although I don't know if I believe everything I've heard."

Standing, Emory picked up her plate, not wanting an inquisition. "I'll clean up after dinner. Go watch your television program. Thanks for dinner. It was wonderful."

Her mom hugged her. "You're wonderful. Just be careful with those two boys. Both of them have the capability to break your heart."

Break it, by pulling it in two different directions.

"What an unexpected visit, George." Jackson held out a glass of bourbon after leading the way to his home office.

Unexpected. Unwanted. Unprepared.

He hated being unprepared. George had ambushed him, by arriving after dinner without an invite. Jackson was normally the one making unexpected visits or challenges. He was the one in the driver's seat. He'd had everything organized and arranged, from the merger paperwork to helping his brother pick out an engagement ring. And then Shey broke up with Ryder, Emory came back to town, distracting both Croft brothers, and George's behavior became more erratic.

Jackson was losing control, and he hated it.

The man snatched the drink and downed the brown liquid in one gulp. "Who the hell do you think you're playing with? First, your brother is flirting with the hussy."

The insult lacerated Jackson's chest. "Emory's not a hussy."

Who even used that word anymore? Old people like George. And apparently, Jackson himself.

George helped himself to another two fingers of brown spirits. "And then, your mother accosts me at my office."

The liquid in Jackson's glass sloshed over the edge. He set the glass on the desk with a quiet thunk. His mother was becoming a nuisance.

The man took a swig from his second drink. "I didn't even know you had a mother."

People thought he was so cold and heartless they didn't believe he had a mother? Not that he cared. He should be pleased by the description. But for some reason the reputation sat flat in his stomach.

"You think the devil spawned me?" He tried to pass it off as a joke.

"Of course not. I did my research. Heard about your father's divorce and second marriage." George ambled across the room to stare out the window leading to the side yard, the nasty scent of cigar smoke trailing behind. The same yard Jackson's mother had stood in, threatening. Guess her threats had been real. "I assumed your mother was no longer in the picture. Or the business."

The woman's taunt about who had helped keep the doors of Croft Industries open stabbed in his head. "She isn't involved."

"The woman owns stock."

"A small percentage." Or so he'd thought, until he researched her this afternoon. "Nothing significant."

The lie slipped from his lips, but not easily. If he'd uncovered the truth, other people could, too. He needed to stay calm and not hint at any shadiness.

George tugged on his old-style tie. "Are you sure? Because she waved around threats the way most women wave around Tiffany diamonds."

Everything inside Jackson hardened. His bones. His muscles. His determination. "I've got my mother under control."

Except he didn't. He didn't know much about her, or her dealings during the past decade. He didn't have his brother under control. He'd heard Ryder ask Emory out and heard her positive response. He didn't have Emory under control, either.

His family, his business, his life was churning into chaos.

Acid roiled, tangling his emotions in a tight wad. He had to hold his emotions in check. He couldn't give in to the rampant anger, and protectiveness, and desire.

He had to take back the reins. Uncover what his mother was up to. Force his brother to propose to Shey. And wrap Emory around his finger.

Jackson fisted his fingers around the brush. The smell of stale paint infiltrated the room, even with the windows open. Standing in front of an easel, he examined his pathetic efforts. His hands couldn't imitate what he saw in his head. A dark-haired fairy with a twinkle in her purple eyes, and magic floating around her delectable body. He stretched his fingers and tried to focus.

He'd had to escape the Castle Ridge house. Frustration over George's strange behavior, and his mother's unknown schemes, had Jackson wandering the big, empty mansion. Ryder had gone to meet friends after dinner. Emory was down the hall in the suite of rooms with her mother.

Jackson had strolled by the door, and heard the television and the mingling of female laughter. The tinkling sound had touched him, and he'd wanted to join them. Which would be awkward. He only visited Mrs. Barrington occasionally, and if he knocked on their door now, Emory would wonder why.

Swirling his brush, he mixed a little white paint with the black, trying to show the way the moonlight had highlighted the dark hair, making it shine. The paint was thick and harder to manipulate than ever before. Or was it his unpracticed talent? He hadn't painted in years, but since unlocking the door the other night, he couldn't get the room out of his mind.

Unlocking the room one time had unlocked his soul.

The room and his vision of a fairy Emory had etched into his mind. She was frequently in his thoughts, and the blank canvas had called to him at odd moments of the day. Because he couldn't caress her soft skin, his fingers had itched to capture it on canvas. He'd admit to himself his attraction. It was more than lust, more than he'd felt for any other woman. He'd learned if he had an itch, he needed to scratch it. Hence, the painting, and the plans to lure Emory.

One itch he could scratch.

When he'd arrived at the penthouse tonight with no real plans, he'd unlocked the door again, and stepped back in time.

To a time when he could paint whenever and wherever.

To a time when he believed he had potential.

To a time when his *time* wasn't taken up by business.

He scowled at the canvas. He didn't need glory or fame. He just wanted to recapture the joy of art. The pleasure he found in painting. How he could forget the world existed outside the canvas. Forget his troubles for a while.

Croft Industries was part of his heritage, and in his blood. He'd never sell and walk away from the company. Having downtime to paint would lessen the strangle of responsibility.

Mixing white with red, he tried to duplicate the exact shade of Emory's lips when she'd kissed him. He squeezed the brush tighter, knowing this fascination with the woman was not good. She'd made him feel things he hadn't experienced in years. Made him want to paint and to see the world, not just travel for work. This constant dissatisfaction with his life was her fault.

Standing back, he studied what he'd painted so far. The colors weren't cohesive. The shapes were disjointed. The art didn't flow. He tossed the brush at the almost-blank canvas. A red line squiggled down his attempt, ruining whatever he'd envisioned. Ruining the silhouette.

Picking up the painter's knife, he slashed through the center of the canvas. Why was he even trying? He couldn't go backwards. He couldn't become a good painter. He was trapped in an office, wearing a three-piece designer suit. And Emory wasn't a magical fairy princess come to set him free.

Emory's heart walloped, when Jackson strolled into the Design Mart lobby. His overpowering presence in a custom business suit with crisp creases in the pant legs, silk shirt, and designer tie made him appear out of place, and yet he commanded the room. The suit fit his trim, athletic build.

His wariness shifted when he focused on her, and the connection went straight to her soul. His lips lifted in a slight grin, causing her pulse to pick up pace.

Standing, she moved toward him, watching the interested glances of the other designers and showroom personnel. Even though she'd told him about the appointments, with his meetings and deadlines and *speadsheets*, she hadn't expected him. "I'm surprised you came."

"As I said when I replied to your email, since it is my furniture you're picking out, I thought I should be here to express my opinion." He took both her hands in his and his gaze ran up her body. "Hello to you, too."

She'd chosen her outfit of professional slim skirt and boots to make a good impression on the Design Mart employees, not for his benefit.

"Hi." She slipped her hands out of his, because the greeting wasn't professional. He was her client, and she would be working with the people at the Design Mart for other clients in the future.

Pulling herself together, she went to the couch and picked up her portfolio case and bag. She moved to the counter and he followed. "Karen, this is Mr. Croft. Karen is the sales manager who will be helping us today."

"Call me Jackson." He shook hands with the sales manager.

"Did you say you were her client?" Had Karen held onto his hand longer than was necessary?

Emory's skin tightened. The woman wasn't flirting with Jackson, and yet something in the way she spoke said she wanted to. It wasn't her business. She had no right to be jealous after only one kiss. A kiss she'd initiated.

He smiled in the serious-businessman way of his, and his head tilted to the side. "What does the word client actually mean?"

He zeroed in on Emory, and his lips looped upwards. A flirtatious smile, letting the other woman know he wasn't interested.

Emory quivered. He was flirting with her. Why now? When he'd put an end to their kiss.

The last thing she needed was for people she'd be working with professionally to believe she was having an affair with a client. She didn't want a bad reputation.

"Yes. He's a client." She swatted his arm in a playful way, and jerked her hand back. The friendly swat did not resemble a client-designer relationship, either. Nor like a lover. It would appear personal, though. She fisted her hand to keep her fingers from touching him again, not wanting false rumors being spread about how she treated her clients. "We've known each other since we were kids."

His eyebrows arched in a calculating way, figuring her out.

"Ah." Karen gave them both a knowing leer. "We'll be starting with furniture. Come with me."

Karen sauntered beside Jackson pointing out items of interest as they went through the lobby toward the individual showrooms. Emory followed behind, resembling a servant or a second-class citizen.

Granted, she wasn't familiar with the layout of the mart. She'd made a quick run through the place when she'd arrived late this morning to see the various showrooms. Even picked out a couple of things she wanted to present to Jackson. She'd done her homework.

Karen sunk into a VIG Chesterfield sofa and patted the place beside her. "Feel this, Jackson. Smooth. Soft. Sexy."

Emory choked, before realizing the woman was talking about the leather. The woman was upselling furniture, not herself.

Not taking a seat, he stroked the arm of the couch. "What do you think, Emory?"

Rising above any jealous thoughts, Emory guided him toward a Bugatti sofa. "Feel this. It might be more suited to your needs. The clean lines are more the style we're going for."

"Good point." His gaze flashed with amusement. "I have to defer to Miss Barrington's opinion. She's the expert."

Straightening her shoulders, she realized he defended her choices. He was on her side, and trusted her judgement. He *got* her. He'd helped her as a kid, too. One time she'd been window shopping on Main Street, and some older girls had given her a hard time about not being able to afford anything from an expensive boutique. He'd told the girls he was going to buy her whatever she wanted. The girls had scattered, and Emory had been so confused and afraid she'd run in the other direction. She'd forgotten about that until now.

She softened. "Thanks."

"You're welcome."

"Of course." Standing, the woman nodded, and led them toward a different section. "Let's move on to a few of the items Emory has selected for you." The woman became only their guide, and the rest of the time went smoothly.

Hours passed as if minutes. He wanted to see everything she might think appropriate. They'd end up agreeing on the final choice. They were in sync with each other. If she liked a chair, he liked the same chair. If he hated a color or a style, she agreed, and had been silently relieved he hadn't chosen something not fitting her design direction.

"That was a lot of fun." He held the showroom door open.

"And work." Emory collapsed onto the couch in the lobby. They'd gotten the bulk of the ordering done for the big furniture pieces. "We only have the accent pieces left."

"Enough work to make a man hungry. How about a bite to eat?"

"You don't have a dinner meeting?" Her tease bought her time. She wanted to say yes, knowing she shouldn't. She should go home, work the pieces they bought into the design, talk to Ryder.

"You know, you're not the only one to give me the same advice about enjoying life." Jackson's leading statement had her leaning forward.

He had taken her advice to enjoy life with the Segways, and the dinner and musical.

A shadow crossed his expression. "My mom told me something similar on her death bed."

"Your mom?"

"Lexi's mom."

"How does your real mother feel about you calling

the second Mrs. Croft mom?" Emory bit her lip. The intrusive question had come out of her mouth because she wanted to know. Was curious about him.

His real mother wouldn't like it. She'd called Lexi's mom a harlot.

"For a discussion about my biological mom, we need a drink. Come on." He held out his hand to help Emory stand.

She held her breath. She was tempted. By his offer. By his hand. By his invitation for a drink. She wanted to learn more about this adult Jackson. He'd changed so much since she'd gone away to college, and yet she saw glimpses of the younger man.

Putting her hand in his, she came to a stand. "Okay, a drink."

His large hand engulfed hers. "And dinner."

"Only if I choose the restaurant." No fancy places where they wipe the crumbs off the tablecloth in between courses. She knew the perfect place. Stepping outside in front of him, a large white flake hit her cheek. "It's snowing."

A few inches already covered the green grass. Tree branches swayed with the weight of the snow. The sidewalks and roads were only wet, because the pavement temperature melted the snow on contact.

"They predicted a big spring snowstorm." He took her hand again, to help her step over a puddle.

The gentlemanly gesture lifted her spirits, before disappointment tricked in like the spring melt. "We should skip dinner and head back to Castle Ridge before the roads get bad."

"The worst part won't hit until after midnight."

A slight uneasiness slid through her. Most late-spring storms didn't stick. Only a couple of inches had fallen. Maybe if they waited, had drinks and dinner, the storm would pass. The uneasiness rolled through her gut. The temperature would drop, possibly forming ice. Slippery ice. Black ice.

But she couldn't stop the skid of her heart. She wanted to spend more time with Jackson, and a possible snowstorm wasn't going to stop her. She was taking a risk with the weather and her heart.

Chapter Eleven

Jackson had never noticed the small, brick building stuck between a shoe repair shop and a bank. The dark door led to a narrow stairway. With Emory leading the way down the steps, he questioned the wisdom of letting her pick the restaurant. Basement dining wasn't something he'd acquired a taste for. He kept his doubts to himself, not wanting her to change her mind. She'd agreed to a drink and dinner and he'd follow her anywhere, as long as they stayed inside.

When they hit the bottom step, noise filtered toward them. A lot of noise. Talking, music, glasses clanking. And the smells…

Warm toast, roasted malt, and yeast.

"What is this place?"

"Craft brewery." She pushed open a glass door, and the scents and sounds surrounded him.

People gathered around long picnic tables, or sat at high cocktail tables. The concrete floor sported stains and pocked-marked holes. A large bar filled up one entire side of the wall. On the exact opposite was a stage and small dance floor. A band was setting up.

Interesting. Popular. Totally not his kind of place.

Picking a tall table, she grabbed a couple of menus from a passing waiter. Her relaxed smile proved her comfort in the environment. She was less tense compared to when he'd picked the restaurant.

She'd never fit into his current lifestyle. Like he didn't fit into his current lifestyle. Not naturally. The thought jumbled. He'd had to learn his ruthless persona.

Of course, she didn't need to fit in because this, whatever this was, wasn't permanent.

He perused the menu. "There's no food."

How was he going to make the evening last, if they had to go someplace else for dinner? If the storm picked up early as it was supposed to, she'd notice, and insist on driving back to Castle Ridge.

She sent him a sly grin. "Pick a beer." She ordered a pint of some strange brew.

He scanned the menu, and picked a featured flight of different beers. That would take him awhile to drink, since it seemed they wouldn't be eating anything except pretzels.

"Are you trying to get me drunk on an empty stomach so you can take advantage of me?" The tease came naturally. Something fluttered in his chest. He wanted the statement to be true.

Only because it would help him in his quest, but the internal lie didn't sit well.

A light, tinkly laugh bubbled out of her, causing him to tumble a little deeper.

"Follow me." She hopped off the tall chair and sauntered toward the back of the brewery.

Her tiny butt swayed back and forth in the tight skirt she wore. The lower part of her thigh peeked through the slit in the back. Lust pulsed through him. He'd follow her anywhere.

Only because she was leading where he wanted to go. The two of them together, flirting and having fun. Her crush on his brother completely squashed. Them taking this attraction to the next logical step when they got stranded in Denver overnight. He wouldn't take complete advantage of her, but his plan was back in his control.

She led them out another set of doors and into the bottom floor of a parking garage. Trucks were circled around, resembling Western chuck wagons. People stood in line by the different trucks.

He crinkled his nose, trying not to display disgust. "Food trucks?"

"Gourmet food trucks." She rotated toward him and frowned. "You're not a fan."

He didn't want to ruin the evening. He'd risk food poisoning to continue with his plan. "They're food trucks." Greasy, rat-infested trucks that serviced several industrial parks.

"Award-winning food trucks. A couple of these have even been on television."

A Hawaiian food truck decorated in pineapples and leis featured roasted pig and poi. A truck sporting the French flag served crepes. There was a truck with gourmet hamburgers and one with crockpot meals.

He'd never realized the variety of food they served. "What do you like?"

"I like them all." Her smile went wide, showing her perfect, white teeth. She'd worn braces in middle school, and had always hid her mouth. He thought she'd been cute then, and beautiful now. "Tonight, I'm going to eat in the Philippines. What about you?"

A frigid, brisk wind blew through the parking garage.

He needed to get her back inside, so she'd be unaware of the changing weather outside. He planned to use the changing forecast to his advantage. "I'll have the same."

After getting lumpias, meat skewers, and crabby-cheese wontons, they headed back to the table. Her pint and his flight of beer waited at their table.

She put one of the wontons in her mouth. "These crabby-cheese wontons are the best."

"Do you love all shellfish, or only crab?" He pointed out what he hoped was obvious. She wouldn't be able to eat those, if she was on a date with Ryder. The selfishness smacked.

Frowning, her brows furrowed, understanding exactly why Jackson had asked the question. "Yes. I could forgo them if needed." Her stiff voice showed she wasn't pleased with the turn of conversation. "So, tell me about your mother."

Groaning, he used a plastic fork to take a bite of lumpia. "I'll talk, if you tell me something about yourself next."

"Like what?"

"I'll have to think about it." He put a threatening-teasing tone, pretending to think about a question for later. Except he knew exactly what he wanted to ask. "You were around during my parents' divorce. It was terrible."

Darkness enveloped him at the memory of the shouting and the fights. The frigid silence between them had been the worst.

"I remember the atmosphere was always tense. My mom would come back to our rooms after dinner and be upset."

"You were only seven. You probably don't remember much."

"You were only eleven or twelve."

His darkness went pitch black. "Yet, I remember everything."

She reached across the table and put her hand over his. He put his other hand on hers and stroked her soft skin.

The comforting connection dispelled the darkness. He'd gotten through those *getting divorced* months by painting. Holed up in his bedroom, or in the art studio at school, he painted away the pain. He let the vibrant paint colors bring light into his life, and poured his emotions of loss and abandonment into his creations.

Because his mother had abandoned him and his brother.

With Emory holding his hand, the anguish was more bearable. He never discussed or thought about those dark times, because it brought back the torture. But right now, he wanted to share his past.

"My mother was a shopper." A shopaholic with a

desire for expensive items. "My dad might've had money." *Might've* being the honest word. "He didn't spend it crazily."

"Your house alone is amazing." Emory's expression was appreciative, not filled with avarice.

With her education, she understood the value of each Louis IVX or Chippendale piece. Knew how much the furniture in the Castle Ridge house cost, and its current value. And yet, today she hadn't pushed him to buy the most expensive leather couch or a designer lamp he wouldn't appreciate. She wanted him to get what was right for his penthouse. To her, designing wasn't about getting the most expensive item so she'd get the highest commission. It was about finding the right piece of furniture for him.

The experience had been refreshing. Most of the women in his past were about expensive and excessive.

"My dad believed in living comfortably. Mother leaned toward excessive." And once Jackson understood their finances, he understood the fighting so much more.

Dad had not been honest with his mother about the company's problems. He hadn't been honest with anyone. Maybe he'd been embarrassed about the state of his financial affairs, how he'd run the company to the ground. Maybe his pride dictated not exposing the truth. Whatever it was, he'd tried to control spending at home and his mother had rebelled.

His father had been weak, something no one would ever accuse Jackson of.

Which didn't excuse his mother's behavior after the

divorce, especially since she'd learned the state of the finances.

"Is that what the divorce was about? Money?" Emory shuddered and pushed her paper plate to the side.

"I think my mother thought she could get more from him in a divorce than married."

Maybe she'd been right. She'd gotten a huge settlement because his dad wouldn't reveal the financial truth. At that point, the family had personal money. The financial situation had gotten worse and worse, up until his father's death.

"Money was important to my mother." Still was, from what he'd gathered from various sources.

"Your mother disappeared after the divorce." Emory's innocent tone shoved a spike in his heart.

Disappeared and never communicated. Dad had paid her off with money scraped together from personal holdings, and what he thought were worthless stocks. Even when Dad died, she'd never communicated any kind of sympathy or remorse.

What the hell was Jackson doing? Sharing so much of his past, of his personal pain? Something about Emory made him babble on about things he never discussed.

"Probably for the best." He kept his response short.

"Having a mother around is important." Emory's soft expression filled with sympathy.

She'd grown up without a father. The man had died when she was a toddler, and her mother never remarried. She understood the loneliness, if not the torment, of being a child of divorce.

"Not my mother." He didn't want to discuss the woman any more.

"She's back now."

The solemn words hit him in the solar plexus. Pain radiated outward in waves of warning. "Yes, she's back."

And up to no good.

Emory finished the last of the wontons and lumpia. She didn't remember much from that period of living at the Croft home, her mom had protected her from the scenes and the gossip. She did remember the frowns on her mother's face, and how Ryder's normal joy had dimmed.

Jackson had spent more time in his bedroom. He'd become quieter. More of a loner. A boy who needed love, but was afraid to ask. In a way, he still acted that way.

Right now, he nursed his flight of beer. The five short glasses changed in color from golden to amber to dark brown. Similar to how he changed in her mind. He'd shared more of himself with her during the past few days. She knew him better than a client or even a friend.

He set the small glass down on the wood table with a clink. "My turn."

The band started playing a song with a deep beat, similar to movie music before a cliffhanger.

Nerves eddied in her stomach. She didn't have anything to hide. She only hoped he didn't ask about her feelings for his brother. Right now, she was completely confused. "Okay."

"What happened in Spain?" Not how was Spain? Or why did you leave Spain? Did he know something had happened?

She thought she'd freeze with the horrible memories rushing back. "Nothing. I wanted to come home. Be with my mother. Start my own firm."

He studied her, his gaze never leaving her face.

Squirming in her seat, she picked up her glass and tried to take a sip of beer. Her empty beer. The reasons she gave were true. They just weren't the entire story. She ran her finger along the outside of the condensed glass.

"You were offered a permanent position."

She flopped back in her chair. "How do you know?"

"Your mom enjoys talking." The tic in his cheek spasmed, a now-familiar reaction.

Her gaze narrowed, watching the tiny tell. Lying or covering up? Her mom never talked about his parents' divorce, or about his and Ryder's personal life. Why did Mom talk about her daughter's life?

"Proud mother." Jackson must've sensed Emory's disbelief.

Her mother was proud of her accomplishments. And she'd never told her mom the full details about her relationship with Alejandro. What should she tell Jackson?

"What's the real reason you didn't stay in Barcelona?"

The squirming moved to her insides, and burned in her chest. Her mind fought against the memory and emotions. The pounding pain didn't come. She was over the Spanish Casanova, even though the shame continued to strike a blow. She'd been naïve and stupid, and blown away by his wealth and his title.

Jackson knew there was a deeper reason. He'd shared parts of his ugly past. She could trust him with her secrets. "I dated a client."

Would he think she was only after the Croft money? Her colleagues had accused her of something similar with Alejandro. Except now she wasn't even sure she wanted to date Ryder. When she closed her eyes, she didn't picture the younger brother's face, she saw Jackson's stronger expression. Her confusion ran circles around in her head. She'd crushed on Ryder since she was a teen, except she wasn't a teen anymore. She was a woman with experience, and different wants and needs.

Jackson's gaze flared wide and softened. Curious, but not filled with sordid gossipy interest like her boss and coworkers. His chin tilted at an angle ready to defend her. Just as he'd defended her this afternoon.

Her spine firmed, deciding she'd tell him everything.

"Was it serious?"

She harrumphed and her lips twisted into an ironic smirk. "I thought it was."

"You're smiling, so you must be doing okay." He took her hand and lifted it off the table. His fingers trailed from her thumb to her wrist, sending a shiver through her.

"Time heals all wounds." While Ryder made her remember she was an attractive woman when she'd arrived in Castle Ridge, he'd quickly faded from her mind. To be replaced with the man sitting across from her.

"So they say." Obviously, Jackson's wounds hadn't healed.

"Alejandro was a client and a Vizconde." At Jackson's puzzled expression, she went on. "It's similar to a Viscount, a minor royal."

Jackson's finger paused. "Royal."

She shrugged wanting to brush the topic off, because Alejandro didn't matter. "A royal ass."

His fingers dug into her arm. "What did he do?"

To you? She heard it in his voice.

The immediate defense of her spread a lightness through her. "Nothing terrible. He was royal, rich, and…a womanizer." Her heart ached with a shadow of remembered anguish.

She'd thought she'd been in love with Alejandro, foolishly in love. And he'd seen her as a challenge. The same way he'd seen her colleagues. The man ran through the entire female population of the design firm. Including one of her bosses. He'd been so fun and friendly. One of her colleagues had warned her. She'd foolishly believed the woman was jealous.

"We actually ended up friends." Once she'd seen through his flirtatious ways, and taken him at face value.

"Good to know you weren't permanently scarred." Jackson stroked her skin again, and her body hummed. "What made you decide on interior design?"

His switch in topics eased her worry. He was really interested in her. Not her one indiscretion.

"It's creative and practical. I lived in your glorious

house for most of my life so I was exposed to style. I love putting together different colors and textures and materials."

"It's like painting in three-dimensions." His insight blew her away.

"Yes."

"Must be nice to have a choice."

She almost missed his murmur. "What do you mean? You didn't want to take over your father's business?"

"Not at age twenty-two." His hard tone edged with sourness. His expression stayed the same, except for the bleakness in his eyes. A hurt.

Tonight, she'd learned about his childhood sorrows, and why he'd become more serious and alone. And to find out he'd been thrust into the role of president and chairman of the board at such a young age. All that responsibility. All that pressure. It explained so much about him.

"You studied business in college." The fact stuck in her mind. She couldn't remember what Ryder had studied.

"I had two majors." Jackson spat and the tic in his cheek went wild. He held out his hand. "Do you want to dance?"

Her pulse knocked. Guess they were done with the conversation and moving on to...dancing. "Um, sure."

Standing, she put her hand in his. His crisp scent overwhelmed the beer smell.

What was she doing? He was a client. Her first client in her very own firm. She couldn't repeat the same mistakes, and yet Jackson didn't feel like a mistake. He felt right.

He led her toward the small dance floor. A slow song was playing. And he took her into his arms.

His light embrace had her not caring about much of anything. Her body melted from his warmth. Electrified spirals circled her, urging her to drape herself around his strong frame. The attraction she held for him was palpable. How would it look if she suddenly changed her affections from Ryder to Jackson? She'd appear a silly girl, or a gold digger.

She wasn't either of those things. His strong arms held her at the waist. His fingers branded her body. His breath scorched her neck. Their bodies meshed, moving to the music together.

Dancing with Ryder, she'd been giddy. Living her teenage self's dream. Dancing with Jackson was a real-life fantasy.

"Jackson?" A woman interrupted.

Emory's body stiffened. She didn't want anyone intruding.

He leaned back from the embrace. "Shey. What're you doing in Denver?"

His facial muscles tightened, peering between the two women. He looked guilty. Why? It was Ryder who'd had a relationship with Shey.

The woman's chestnut hair flowed into a long bob. Her expertly-applied make-up appeared fresh. Her slightly upturned lips expressed friendliness and curiosity.

Emory's face heated, and she regarded the ground.

Why did she feel guilty? Maybe because Jackson hadn't introduced her.

"Business for Webber Resorts. What else?" Ryder's ex-girlfriend's laugh was brittle.

"Totally understand."

The woman's gaze slid between the two of them. "Hi. I'm Shey Webber." Her friendly voice had Emory relaxing.

The woman seemed nice, and didn't deserve to see Ryder date someone else so soon. Although Shey was the one who broke up with him. Maybe only he was heartbroken.

"Hi." Emory flashed a short, non-committal smile. She didn't know how she should react to the woman. "I'm Emory Barrington." She held out her hand.

Shey's expression faltered. She took a step back, not even noticing the outstretched hand. "I thought… never mind." The shock on her face cleared, and her lips lifted into a deep, real smile. "Nice to meet you."

They shook hands.

"Nice to meet you."

"How's Ryder feeling?" Concern filled her tone.

If she'd heard about his allergic reaction, had she also heard about his flirtation? With Emory? Not really a flirtation. They'd danced. He'd asked her out. She'd said…maybe.

And now she was dancing with Jackson.

"Much better. You should give him a call." He sent her a concerned glance.

He must be worried she'd be upset about Ryder's ex-girlfriend calling him, which was nice of Jackson, seeing as he never wanted them to date in the first place.

Shey studied Emory for a second. "Maybe I will."

The answer made her feel absolutely nothing. She wasn't upset or worried or jealous. She hoped the couple could work things out. Her head whirled with the change. Her heart pumped with acknowledgement.

She didn't want Ryder. She wanted Jackson.

Chapter Twelve

The silence in the elevator added to Jackson's nervousness and frayed the tight rein he had on his lust. He shoved his hands in his coat pockets, while the elevator whisked him and Emory up to the penthouse. His scheme was working, and he hoped he had the guts to see it through.

But not *all the way* through.

When they'd finally left the restaurant, the snowstorm had changed into a late-spring blizzard. Just as the forecasters had predicted, except the timeline had changed. He'd checked the road conditions, and shown Emory the pass was closed. No way to get home tonight.

He'd prepared for this occurrence.

Champagne chilling in the fridge, candles by the fireplace, breakfast items in the pantry. The almost-seduction scene was set.

Almost, because he wouldn't take complete advantage of her. His goal was to woo her with kisses and distract her from his brother. He wouldn't bed her. Once she realized she didn't have real feelings for Ryder, once Ryder got his head on straight and went back to Shey, then Jackson would *un-woo* Emory.

Was that even a word? Un-woo?

Was un-wooing even possible?

She stood beside him, staring straight ahead at the metal elevator doors. The snow had made her short hair wet, and the edges had started to curl. Her mouth pursed, as if she were trying to control wild thoughts.

"Quite the storm." She twisted her gloved hands together, the fingers weaving in and out of each other.

"Yes." The storm outside matched his turmoil inside.

She was beautiful and attractive and vibrating with desire. While dancing, he'd held her in his arms and attraction had woven between them. Her gaze shimmered, alluding to her wants. If she'd been any other woman, he wouldn't hold himself back. Guilt gnawed in his stomach. He genuinely liked Emory, always had. He felt responsible for her. Responsible for giving her a chance at a successful career, not responsible for her love life. She would get over Ryder, and over Jackson's deceit, and find some nice guy to settle down with, get married, have babies.

An image of babies with dark hair and gray eyes flashed. Babies resembling both of them. A tenderness opened for those babies and sizzled through him. In order to make those beautiful babies, they'd have to have sex.

Lust yanked his chain. His cock sprung and his perspiring hands itched. Holding her close while dancing had ignited a simmer in his bloodstream. The heat of her body against his. The touch of her hand on his shoulder. The silkiness of her hair tickling his face.

An attraction was all this could be. He wouldn't have sex with her and then break her heart. When this ended, she'd be angry enough with him for leading her on. That would be the *un*-wooing.

"I thought the storm was supposed to hit later, in the middle of the night."

"Early forecasts said that." Not the later ones.

After Shey left, he'd convinced Emory to dance through several more songs. He'd been trying to lengthen the evening before going outside, wanting to make sure the blizzard had hit, not because he wanted to hold her longer in his arms. They'd not talked. The silence between them compatible, and yet, filled with a sexual tension, leaving him wanting more.

More he couldn't have, wouldn't have. This plan of his had already taken too much time. Time away from his business dealings.

The elevator doors swished open.

Neither of them moved.

He cleared his throat. "Here we are."

"Here we are." Her voice came out hushed, as if she knew, or at least believed, where tonight would end.

In his arms. In his bed.

She was wrong. He could control himself. He was known for his steely determination.

Marching into the room, he took off his gloves and coat, laid them across the chair.

"Let me help you with your coat." He helped remove the heavy white wool, and noticed the darker spot. "How did you get your coat dirty?"

"Ryder did it." Her lips twitched, sending a chill through Jackson.

Why would she be happy about his brother staining the coat? Was she totally besotted? He wouldn't ask those questions. He did not want to talk about his brother tonight. The idea was to make her forget his brother.

After putting her coat and gloves on the chair, he used the remote to turn on the fireplace and music he'd set to a love-song channel. "Champagne?"

Her violet gaze shot to his before glancing toward the kitchen. "Are we celebrating?"

"No." Although having her here made his cock celebrate. "We're living life to the fullest."

Her expression went soft and dreamy. "Really?"

As if she believed he was taking her advice. And his mom's. He popped open the champagne and poured two glasses. His blood fizzed, imitating the liquid.

She took a glass and sipped. "I had fun tonight."

The truth of her statement jolted. He'd had fun. He hadn't focused on the task at hand. He'd relaxed and enjoyed himself. With her. "Me, too."

Her violet eyes darkened to an amethyst hue, darkened with desire. He leaned forward wanting to taste those lips. She leaned in. Their lips met in the middle.

The sweet and gentle kiss became deeper. More meaningful. They both set the glasses down. Her mouth clung to his, and he answered by sweeping his tongue in her mouth. She tasted of the dark beer she drank earlier, champagne, and something mysterious.

Her apple scent mixed with the taste. Her palms landed on his chest and slid to his waist. She untucked his shirt and skirted her hands underneath. Her fingers caressing his skin. Burning, branding, bewitching.

His heart thumped. Things were going too fast. He wouldn't be able to stop himself. She was too passionate. He stiffened and pulled back. "Sorry. I shouldn't have."

"I wanted to kiss you, too." By the way she ogled him and the way she touched him, she wanted to do a hell of a lot more.

So, did he. Except that wasn't part of his plan. He needed to keep repeating the fact.

"It's just…" He couldn't sleep with her, not when he planned to send her on her way. She really didn't care for him. She didn't know the real him. The cold, calculating businessman. She saw him as a hero, and a man who needed to be saved.

He frowned. Maybe he did need to be saved.

But not by her, and not right now.

After his brother was engaged, his penthouse was finished, and he returned to his regularly scheduled life, she'd forget this attraction. And move on with her life with a nice boost for her design business.

His lungs shrank, and he couldn't breathe. He needed a distraction. "I need to tell you something."

Something honest to catch her off guard.

Her furrowed brow and wide-eyed confusion were adorable. The haze of lust filtered in her gaze in a fine mist.

He took her hand, led her to the couch and sat down. "Dancing tonight was a distraction."

Her luscious lips frowned. "You didn't want to dance with me?"

"I did. I do." He hated seeing her sad. "Isn't it you who said I needed to appreciate the little things?"

He appreciated this moment. With her. Sharing himself. Shock reverberated down his spine, sending zingers of truth. He'd been showing small parts of his real self all night.

"Yes."

"The band was playing. They were good. You're beautiful." He shrugged. Why did he start this mad confession?

"But?"

Because if he shared some of his secrets, maybe he wouldn't feel so guilty about what he was going to do. He'd tell her one of his biggest secrets ever. "I wanted to end our discussion."

She tilted her head in that way of hers.

"I didn't want to talk about my college education." He still didn't.

"You were such a good student. Why wouldn't you want to talk about it?"

He sucked in a big breath, trying to clear his lungs. "Because I never graduated."

"You mean you never went through graduation ceremonies." She ran a hand down his arm trying to comfort. "I remember, because Lexi's mom was upset about not seeing you walk across the stage."

"Mom was upset because she knew. She was the only one who knew I didn't graduate."

His second mother had been disappointed in him. She hadn't understood the gravity of Croft Industries' situation. She never would. Neither would Ryder, or anyone else in the business world. It was his secret to bear alone, because he'd promised his father to maintain the illusion.

"But you were in your last year when—"

"When my father died." Fresh grief struck at the thought of the loss of his father. The death had hit him emotionally—he'd lost his dad. And physically, because he'd had to quit school and go to work. And psychologically, because he'd learned his father hadn't been as smart as Jackson believed. "And I had to take charge of the business."

There'd been no one else his father had trusted to keep his secrets and secure the legacy.

Emory leaned into him and placed her hand on his upper arm. "I thought your university had given you special consideration."

Warmth traveled up his cheeks. "The school is prestigious. Even with good grades, they wouldn't let anyone skip the last few months of classes and exams."

Unless he'd given them a large donation. They'd asked. Bitterness tasted on his tongue. At the time, he'd been unable to do so. And later, it hadn't been worth his time.

Tucking in her chin, her mouth rounded in an *O*. "Why didn't you go back? Finish?"

"I was busy with Croft Industries. Most people believed I'd gotten the degree, so I let them." His cheeks burned hotter. He'd needed the weight of the degree behind him when he'd pulled deals out of his ass. When he'd made up shit to get the financial investment or a loan payment delayed. "I worked hard to prove myself. To prove I didn't need a piece of paper to be successful."

Her fingers stroked his arm up and down and up and down. The action mesmerized. "You could go back now."

His arm muscles tightened. His earlier guilt and anguish reared rushing through his veins. "Ridiculous. What could a professor teach me about business?"

Except maybe ethics.

"That's not the point." Her finger stopped stroking and started poking. "Not having your degree has obviously bothered you for years."

It had. First, he'd been too busy rescuing Croft Industries to have the time to go back. Then, since everyone assumed he'd graduated, he used it in his negotiations. Now, it was too late.

She grabbed his chin and forced him to regard her. "Tell me you'll consider going back."

It was as if she could see deep into his black soul. Past his lies and machinations. Past his sketchy deals and maneuverings. She could see the man he used to be, deep down still wanted to be. Yet knew he couldn't be anymore.

His shoulders slumped. It was too late for him, wasn't it? The effort to really change, to become a better version of himself might not be worth it in the end.

And yet, when he stared into her eyes, when he saw her trying to help him, he couldn't resist. He wanted to be that better person. "Yes."

And he really meant it in the moment.

She angled into him, draping her body across. Her legs tangled with his. Her chest rubbed against his chest. Her mouth moved closer and closer.

He didn't move. He couldn't stop her if his life depended on it. This need to tell her things, to give her what she wanted, to be loved by her, held him in paralysis.

Her eyelids closed. Her fresh, apple scent infiltrated his nose. Her lips puckered.

And there was magic. Real magic. She kissed him from the heart because she did everything from the heart. And he felt not like a victor after brokering a major deal, but something more powerful and more profound.

He responded, kissing her back. Kissing her as he'd never kissed anyone before, as if she would be his first and his last and his everything. His mouth opened, and her tongue entered, teasing and tantalizing. Sparks ignited inside, scorching from his tongue to his toes. He wrapped his arms around her and lifted her more comfortably, or uncomfortably, on his lap. He wanted to make contact with every inch of her.

Her hands roamed across his shoulders and back, tugged on his hair. Tingles swooshed from the top of his head to the bottom of his toes. His entire body thrummed and vibrated. His cock ached with the need for release.

A release he wouldn't get.

This kiss wasn't about the strategy he'd concocted. This was about a man and a woman, with attraction sizzling between them.

"Jackson." She hummed against his lips. "Let's go to your room."

Her tone shot a streak of lust to his balls. His entire body flamed, short-circuiting his brain. He wanted more. Needed more.

But he couldn't take more.

Holding in a groan of frustration, he tried to bring his brain back online. Where was the famous control and determination he was known for? He fisted his hands behind her head, fighting his lust, fighting his body, fighting her power over him.

"Emory." He wrested his mouth from hers. "We can't."

Her tantalizing lips were only an inch away. Her lungs heaved with long pulls of air. "Why not?"

In desperation, he tossed out his first thought. "I'm your client, and I thought after your last experience…"

He saw when the unfinished sentence finished in her head. Her soft eyes went sharp. Her pouty lips thinned. She shoved against his chest. "This is not the same in any way."

"Isn't it?" He hated being mean to her, except he needed to put this on pause.

"I'm not gullible."

Wasn't she? His ploy had worked from the start.

"I've known you since I was seven."

Amusement slipped into a smile. "Not helping your argument."

Her fierce frown highlighted she wasn't amused. "We're not children anymore. We are both consenting adults. I know you're not a womanizer, and you aren't seeing anyone else."

All true facts. "How do you know?"

Her gaze went to half mast, sensual and alluring. Her mouth lifted upwards in a sexy and light fairy grin. Her pink tongue darted out and licked her lips.

"Because we've spent practically the last four days together." Her voice dropped, and she leaned forward, planting a kiss at the corner of his mouth.

He held in a groan and fought the lust.

"You've made no secretive phone calls or hidden texting." She kissed him on the other side of his mouth.

He wanted to give in, to do whatever she wanted.

"You haven't hidden me from your office, or your assistant, or from going out." She kissed him straight up, using her tongue to moisten the seam of his mouth.

His lips opened for her, welcoming her tongue.

"We danced together for most of the night and even ran into Shey, one of your business associates." Emory's tongue stroked, fondled, tangoed. "You're a man of your word. Of honor. You wouldn't be with me in this way if there was someone else."

His steel spine melted under the assault. He wrapped his arms around her and dug his fingers in her short curls, pressing her body against his. Heat raged between them, flickering and burning. Igniting the heat into passion. Her tongue swirled with his, mimicking a more intimate dance.

Keeping her lips pressed against his, she asked, "I want you. I want this. Do you?"

If he was a man of honor, he never would've concocted this ploy. He wouldn't be with her now. So, since he wasn't a man of honor maybe he could…

Chapter Thirteen

Yes or no?

Emory's words tick-tocked in her brain, waiting. She'd offered herself to Jackson and now she waited an answer.

Yes or no?

Her libido screamed for him to say yes. It had been several months since she'd had sex. She wanted Jackson. She liked him. Okay, she more than liked him. She might even be falling…

Yes or no?

The decision was taking too long. His answer had to be no. Common sense said no. Yet, he'd set the scene for romance.

His dark gaze hooded. His brow furrowed. He seemed to be having an internal debate with himself. Which she understood, because she continued to question her sanity.

She might've known him her entire life, but they'd just started getting to really know each other as adults.

They weren't even dating. Only days ago, she'd proclaimed she wanted to date his brother. Jackson was her client, which he'd pointed out.

She started to perspire. Why had she asked? Why had she put herself out there? She'd suffered the consequences of dating a client before. Her shoulders dropped, and she started to slide off his lap.

His strong hands stopped her. "Yes."

Shock transferred to tantalizing tingles traveling across her skin and ending in a shiver. A shiver rocking her womanly core. She didn't care what common sense said. Her body sparked from his touch. Her lips burned from his kiss. She wanted him like she'd never wanted Alejandro. And Ryder had been a silly teenage crush.

Jackson whisked her into his arms and carried her down the hall, past the bedroom she'd slept in alone last time, past the bedroom with the locked door, and into his room.

When she'd been measuring, she'd peeked in the master bedroom. This time, she saw it from a different perspective, noticing the small touches that had jarred her last time, but now fit with the man she'd come to know.

Whimsical items. A large abalone shell sitting on the dresser, and a collection of pocket watches displayed in a thick frame, didn't fit. And yet, they did. An old-fashioned model airplane hung from a corner of the ceiling.

He eased his arm from under her legs and she slid down his body to a standing position. The friction from the slow slide set off tantalizing spirals between them. His body froze, and his other arm slipped from around her. Had he changed his mind?

She wouldn't let him. Getting on her tiptoes, she kissed him, slow and steady.

"Emory." He spoke against her kiss.

She used her tongue to silence him, increasing the speed of the kiss with reckless passion. She wanted this. Sliding her hands under his shirt, she reveled in the texture of Jackson. Strong muscles bunched beneath her fingers. She tugged the rest of his shirt out from his pants. His trim waist tightened at her touch and his arms came around her. The palms of his hands kneading her back.

His hands wrapped in her short hair, his fingers digging into her head. The electrifying pressure encouraged.

Keeping her mouth on his, she ran a hand down to his crotch, pawing the hard length of him. He might be denying he wanted her, but the proof was right there. The thought sent a thrill through her body, hastening her movements.

Her hands went to the top button of his shirt, and she undid it. She kissed him there, on the spot of his chest now uncovered. A firm, hairy spot. She undid the second button and kissed him there.

"Emory?" Half-moan, half-plea, she understood the question. He wasn't sure about making love.

She returned her lips to his mouth, pressed hard against him, opened the seam so he couldn't talk. Only kiss. Only feel.

His fingers massaged from her head to her sensitive neck to her lower back. He pressed her body against his, as if he couldn't get close enough. Her hands continued their progress, undoing one shirt button after the next, hurrying so he couldn't change his mind. Once his shirt was unbuttoned, she pushed the material from his shoulders and let the shirt drop to the floor. She was going to stay in control and do what she had to do to keep kissing, keep caressing, keep turning him on.

Power pounded through her bloodstream. Female power. It had never been this way with Alejandro. He'd been her first, and she'd been shy and unsure.

Jackson made her empowered. Maybe because she'd known him forever. Maybe because this didn't start as a flirtation. Maybe because she had always been her real self with him.

Her hands went for the belt buckle and undid the clasp. The tiny click sent her heart into overdrive. He moaned against her lips.

She released him from the kiss to trail smaller, lighter pecks down his chest and to his waist. Her hands gripped his hips, and her teeth settled on his zipper tab.

"Emory?" He sounded unsure.

Peeking up at him, she couldn't stop a grin. His eyes appeared glazed and his chin stuck out, seeming to be fighting with himself.

She enjoyed him being unsure about her. He always was so confident. Power zoomed stronger. Bet he'd never expected her to be the aggressor. Her teeth closed around the zipper tab, and slowly, oh so slowly, pulled the tab down. His cock twitched beneath her mouth.

She ran her tongue across the thin material covering his throbbing length. Tugging down his pants and underwear, she ran a fingertip over his moist tip.

"If you keep touching me, I'm going to explode." He spoke through gritted teeth.

Wetness pooled between her thighs. He was losing control, and she relished it.

"I don't want you changing your mind." She flicked her finger again.

He dug his hands in her hair and tried to tug her head up. "I won't."

"Do you promise?" She ran her tongue along the tip, tasting his manhood and savoring having the upper hand. Anticipating the time when both of them would lose themselves.

"I promise." His voice strained, and she knew she had him where she wanted.

In his bed, and in her heart.

Jackson yanked Emory's hair harder, trying to get her away from his sex. He'd lost all thought except one. He needed to be inside her. Feeling her, pleasuring her. Pressing his naked body against hers, he tried to cool his ardor, tried to bring back some semblance of control.

"I think one of us is overdressed." He meant it to be a tease, even though it came out a growl. An impatient, staking-out-territory growl.

"Must be me, because you resemble a Greek statue." She giggled and the bubbly sound soothed his wounded pride.

Emory had manipulated him with sex. That was supposed to be his tactic. Except for the actual sex part. But now, he'd said yes. He couldn't think about what might happen later. He didn't want to think.

So he felt.

Yanking her to her feet, he undid the buttons of her blouse and pushed the garment off. Her pure-white bra with Victorian-style lace made him even more horny. She sighed, and the modulation went straight through his ribcage.

He nuzzled against her breasts, kissing the fair skin between the delicate mounds. "You're beautiful."

"And overdressed." The irony in her tone caused his fingers to work faster.

He worked the hook and zipper of her skirt. The zipper sliding down was the sexiest noise, sending his nerve-endings into a buzz. The skirt fell from her body, revealing just-as-Victorian white undies. His cock pulsed harder.

She shimmied in front of him, and a sexy-sly smile landed on her face.

The come-on sent him over the edge. "I can't wait."

He wrapped his arms around her butt, picked her up, and dropped her onto the bed. His fingers twisted into the small piece of white silk at her hips and yanked. Her panties ripped, and her female secrets were exposed.

"Hey! Those were good underwear." Her joking made him respond in kind.

"I'll buy you a new pair. I'll buy you a hundred new pairs." As long as he was the only one taking them off.

The thought struck at his center, and he paused above her lying on the bed.

"Like what you see?"

Her tease brought him back to the present. She was a present. A gift he'd unwrapped carelessly. He took a moment to peruse her. One muscular leg was bent, hiding her womanly treasure. Curvy hips that teased and welcomed. A small waist leading to luscious breasts he couldn't wait to covet. Enticing neck with spots he wanted to kiss and explore. Enchanting pixie face, with a tiny, upturned nose and misty violet eyes.

Mine.

The word tattooed in his brain. He immediately rejected it. She couldn't be his forever, yet she could be his for right now.

"Love what I see." His voice trembled. "I want to pleasure you, but I can't wait."

"I don't want you to wait." Her breathy answer had him tumbling on top of her. His fingers found the apex of her pleasure, and she was already warm and wet. Ready.

She bucked on the bed, wantonly exhibiting her need. "Jackson."

The command was his undoing. His body tightened, and then flew into motion. He scrambled to the bedside table and opened the top drawer. Fumbling with his hands, he located the foil packet and tore it open. Sliding the latex on his cock, he poised above her. Anticipation thrummed through his veins. He needed to tell her, to let her know, even though he'd resisted. "I want you."

"I want you, too." The longing in her tone had him

slowing down, taking her in his arms, holding her close, touching her, caressing her.

Just being with her.

"Jackson?" Her need shattered through him, and he couldn't wait another second.

He slipped inside. Her eyes closed, and her mouth opened on a moan.

Her heat and wetness surrounded him, enticed him, made him lose complete control. There'd be no long, drawn-out strokes. There'd be no finesse. He rocked up and down, and up and down. The temperature increased. He couldn't think anymore. He reacted, let his body take him on a flight of fantasy.

He felt her intimate hug to his core. Felt her wetness. Felt her clenching around him.

"Emory!" His body strained, his muscles tightened. He was so close, about to take off. He wanted her to go with him. "Fly, Emory, fly."

She threw her head back and screamed. Her body went rigid. Her core clenched around his cock. "I'm flying, flying, flying..."

And they both flew. Flew together.

Jackson couldn't sleep. Making love to Emory should've tired him out, except his brain wouldn't shut down. His mind whirled, sending messages of guilt that gnawed at his stomach. He hadn't planned on taking things so far. Dancing, a couple of kisses, sure. Sex, a definite no.

Except, she'd changed his definite no into a definite yes. Connived and convinced and persuaded. Man, how she persuaded. His body went hot, thinking about how she'd stripped him naked. He was used to being in charge with other women. With her, he lost control.

A tremor jolted him. He'd never lost himself so completely before, never needed to be close to someone with such desperation.

Even now, she cuddled into him as if she belonged. Which she didn't. She couldn't. He wasn't worthy.

Shifting away from her in bed, he'd forced his mind to think about other things for an hour after she'd fallen asleep. He couldn't think about the sexy woman lying next to him, not how they'd pleasured each other, not how he wanted to do it again. Not how he never should've had sex with her in the first place. His cock throbbed. He needed to get away.

She was sleeping soundly and wouldn't wake up. Sneaking out of the bedroom, he paced down the hall, pausing at the locked door. His body tensed and pulled.

Pulled him toward the room.

Resisting, he headed toward the kitchen and poured himself a glass of water. What he needed was perspective. A chance to think about the changes sex would make to his scheme. Except her scent lingered on his skin, prodding his thoughts in the wrong direction. He needed to do something with his hands.

The paint smell would take his mind off her scent. His fingers itched to hold a brush. He never should've opened the door the other day. He'd had flashes of images he wanted to create. Colors at work or in the furniture showroom jumping out at him, telling him to replicate. And while he couldn't paint last night, inspiration struck him from the long length of her shoulder, to the slight row of freckles dancing across her cheeks, to her soft skin. He wanted to capture the image on canvas.

He tiptoed toward the door, and took the key from the top of the doorframe. Unlocking the door, he stepped inside and took a deep breath, trying to clear her scent from his senses.

Oil and acrylic paint inhaled through his nose, and lit an energy inside him. The smell was stuck in his sensory memories. Pleasant memories. Creative memories. As troubles at the company had mounted, the time he spent painting became smaller and smaller. Days and weeks would pass, and he wouldn't paint. Realizing a true artist never became distracted, he became angry with himself and locked the door. He wasn't a true artist. He was a fraud. He didn't crave to paint.

Until now.

He picked a tube of purple paint and unscrewed the lid. The violet paint bubbled at the top, reminding him of Emory's shining eyes. Her eyes when she was happy, or confused, or orgasming.

The slashed canvas from the night before sat against the wall. The attempt at painting had been a disaster. Tonight, he felt different. His fingers practically sparked, and his emotions swirled inside, needing an outlet.

Squeezing paint onto a palette, he picked up a brush, and swirled the color around. If he added a little ecru and a little gray, he'd have exactly the right color. Some black indicating the specks in her orbs and he could match the color, texture, and tone perfectly.

He stroked a bold, curved line of purple on the canvas. For the sensation of it. His muscles prickled with memory. A good memory. Mixing in the gray, he curved the line more. He tapped the brush with a tiny bit of black. The shape of her eyes was rounder. He corrected the image, and added the ecru to show the highlights when she was in a sensual haze.

His passion and guilt played out in the dance of his brush. He knew he couldn't keep Emory. She deserved someone light and loving. Someone willing to go out and experience life with her.

He dipped his brush in black and stippled the tip, jabbing onto the canvas. He was dark, black paint. Hard. Unlovable.

He swooshed another stroke of black, making the gigantic eye darker, more stormy or scared.

He'd slept with Emory. He never should've had sex. Yet, he'd loved every moment. She'd been fun and spontaneous and sensual. He loved every minute with her, whether it was picking out furniture, or dancing in her arms, or driving together.

His ravaged emotions poured out of him and onto the canvas—a free-flowing outburst in colors. Love of his brother and his family. Hate for the tactics he'd taken in the business world. Shame for not having his degree. And guilt for fooling Emory.

Because he'd tricked her. Even though she'd made the first moves, he'd tricked her into bed.

The next morning, Emory wrapped the large robe around her tightly after showering in Jackson's luxurious bathroom. There wasn't a thing she'd change about this room, with its walk-in shower and the rainfall head. The mixture of marble and glass tile. The sleek faucets. The room was perfect. Except it would've been more perfect, if he'd showered with her.

After making love, she'd fallen into a deep sleep, and didn't wake up until nine this morning. She didn't remember him waking up and showering. If he'd woken her, she wouldn't have let him out of bed. Which surprised her. She wasn't known for being a tigress when it came to the bedroom. Yet, she'd wanted him last night, and had gotten her way. She wanted him again, today.

Not just sexually, though. Desire and confusion mixed in an unknown blender of new relationships. She wanted to know him, understand everything about him. Like why did he hesitate before finally agreeing to make love? What did the tic in his cheek mean? When had he left the bed?

Heading down the hall, she passed the locked bedroom. Her gaze strayed to the handle. What did he keep in the room? More Jackson secrets she'd need to unveil. Passing the guest bedroom, she headed for the kitchen.

Jackson stood by the stove, fully dressed in a suit and tie, cooking eggs. His face was freshly shaven, his hair combed and in place. Quick disappointment looped through her, because he was already dressed. It was a weekday, and he probably had meetings. Or *spreadsheets* to complete.

The ironic thought didn't stop nervous jitters. Did he enjoy last night? She'd practically begged him to sleep with her. Maybe he regretted it.

Did the man regret anything? His deft movements displayed his confidence cooking. He dominated in the kitchen, as she imagined he did in the boardroom, and knew he did in the bedroom.

Biting her lower lip, she stepped farther into the kitchen. She'd be casual, and see his reaction. "Where did you learn to cook?"

He lifted his head, and his gaze roved across her body, setting off tingles inside. "Picked it up here and there."

Not very forthcoming. Or welcoming. Certainly, not a declaration of love.

She hadn't expected that. She *had* expected a good-morning kiss.

She noted a half-drank cup of coffee next to a cutting board. The board was covered in chopped mushrooms, red peppers, and cheese. She couldn't detect his clean, crisp scent in the midst of the smell of coffee and eggs, and she missed it.

Already missed him holding her and kissing her and making love to her.

"Hungry?" His smile made her hungry for him. Obviously, he wasn't on the menu, because he was fully dressed and ready for the day,

Forcing her childish thoughts aside, she took a seat on the raised side of the marble island. She wouldn't obsess about why he hadn't kissed her good morning. "Starving."

To distract her wild, emotional thoughts, she scanned the kitchen. The changes she'd make here would be minimal. Update a couple of appliances and add decorative pieces to bring warmth to the room and make it more him. Except she'd needed to figure out who the real Jackson was. She'd learned so much about him last night, talking, dancing, and making love. Still, she didn't know everything.

"I've whipped up veggie omelets." He slid a perfect omelet onto a white glass plate.

"You didn't have this much food the last time I spent the night." She remembered peeking in the cabinets—for design purposes, not curiosity—and seeing nothing.

Staring down, he slid another omelet on a second plate. "Since we're redecorating, I figured we'd—" He shot a glance at her and then inspected the plate. "—I'd be spending more time here."

His change of pronouns burned, making her less hungry. It made sense, though. He couldn't have predicted last night would happen. And yet, it had. He couldn't pretend they hadn't made love. Could he?

He set the plates on the counter, and pivoted to the expensive espresso machine. "Coffee?"

"Yes." Definitely wouldn't be changing that appliance. After getting home late, and being up—and active—most of the night, she'd need maximum quantities of caffeine.

He poured a full cup. The great billionaire Jackson Croft was serving her breakfast, and was completely comfortable doing so. Her stomach rumbled with anxiety, not hunger. Yes, it was a little awkward for her. She'd get over it. She could be sophisticated about their growing relationship. They didn't need to declare their love right away. These things took time. He might've set the romantic mood last night with dancing, the music, and champagne, but she'd initiated making love.

And now, he hadn't kissed her good morning.

He wheeled toward her, and took a seat at the island. His movement appeared stiff and uncompromising. Maybe the morning after was awkward on his side, too. Maybe he didn't know how to act, because he'd made love to her and they'd known each other since children.

She studied his severe profile. Determined chin, sharp nose, serious gray eyes. A small purple spot stood out on his nose.

"What's on your nose?" She'd never seen him less than perfect and put together, except for last night. Her lips twitched. She'd made him lose his cool control. Images of their bodies wrapped around each other to the point where she hadn't known where her limbs ended and his began flashed in her mind, scorching her from the inside.

"What?" He wiped at his face.

"Right there." She pointed at the tip of his nose. "It's purple."

"Purple." His hand froze. His entire body stiffened. He scratched at the spot. "What're your plans for the day?"

He hadn't kissed her yet. The thought drummed, and alarms rang through her head. That wasn't normal for two people who'd just had the greatest sex in their life. At least in her life. Maybe he always had great sex with any woman.

She pushed the negative thought away. "Since I'm in Denver…" She tossed him a teasing-sideways smirk because it was his fault she was still in Denver. "I think I'll go to the design center and check a few accent pieces." Her chin dropped to the bathrobe she wore. "Except I only have the one outfit, and no underwear."

Satisfaction swam through her. She didn't care about the ruined undergarments. She was remembering how they became ruined, and the pleasure that followed. She licked her lips, wanting another taste of him. Rotating on the stool, she shifted toward him, and quirked her head, waiting for a kiss.

None came.

Her body drooped.

"I thought about your clothes situation." He was so businesslike, while she'd been thinking about making love.

Her smile fell, and she tilted back. "So early in the morning?"

She hadn't been thinking about logistics. She'd been thinking about him, and why she was in this no-clothes predicament.

Her earlier satisfaction morphed to shame, and her body chilled under the heavy robe. She couldn't go back to the Design Mart wearing the same clothes she'd had on yesterday. The sales manager would think she'd had a one-night stand. Sex with her client.

And the woman would be right.

"I've taken care of it." His voice changed to smug,

and she didn't enjoy the modulation. Had he been in the same dilemma before, and knew how to handle things?

She knew she wasn't his first, but she hoped she'd been special. She didn't want this to be a one-night stand, although she had no one to blame but herself. She'd pushed him. Was she willing to push him again?

"No wonder you're successful. You barely need any sleep after such an—" facing him, she slid a hand down his chest, wanting him to be as heated at the memory as she was "—active night. And you're already formulating plans and answers."

He leaned sideways on his bar stool and gave her a chaste kiss on the lips. "I am."

She frowned. Too chaste. If she didn't want to be a one-night stand, then she needed to be more forward. Needed him to understand what last night had meant to her. "I'm hoping some of those plans include the two of us. Together."

If having sex with a client developed into a relationship, then there was nothing wrong with it. With Alejandro, she'd finally come to understand what they had wasn't a loving relationship. For him it had been one of many flings.

"Most definitely." Jackson's expression changed from uptight to heated. Liquid eyes and a wry tug of his lips. He cupped the back of her neck and gave her a slow, lingering kiss. "I want to make you fly again."

He almost did with his words.

She tilted in for another kiss, needing to know he cared. His hands moved through her damp hair, and his fingers trailed around the collar of the bathrobe and beneath the terry cloth. When his hand slipped under the robe and tweaked her nipple, sparks shot to her core. She arched toward him, wanting to feel his flames. Except he was fully dressed, and sitting on a kitchen stool.

He caressed first one breast, and then the other. Spirals of ecstasy swirled through her body and centered at her core. The robe gaped open, and the belt came undone. His fingers moved between her soft folds, tweaking and manipulating and making her melt. Everything tingled and tensed and tingled again. He stroked and palpitated. The thrills started where his clever fingers played, and then pulsed through her core. With her legs splayed open, she laid her head against his chest. Her hands twisted in his tie. Her entire body tensed and tightened. Tension curled into tight coils of bliss.

"Jackson!"

Spasms rocked her body, one after the other. She shattered. Her arms fell to her sides, and he was the only thing holding her upright on the chair. She was a wet noodle leaning against his broad chest.

"Good?"

"Yes, good." She could barely talk. Her hands went to his belt. "My turn."

His laugh tumbled inside her. "I thought you just had your turn."

She angled her head so she could see his face. "My turn to make you fly."

His laughter stopped, and his expression closed. The muscles in his cheek tightened, and his lips flattened. "I've got a meeting."

"Oh." Disappointment drowned out the satisfaction. An unequal-ness about the situation spoiled her mood. Making love should be a mutual thing, each partner pleasuring each other as they'd done last night. And even though she was fulfilled sexually, she wanted more.

"Eat your breakfast." He tugged the robe across her shoulders.

Did he think she was a distraction? After last night, he now had better things to do? Her anger brewed, and she shoveled a bite of omelet into her mouth. If he'd let her pleasure him this morning, she knew she could have him begging for more. Except she didn't want their entire relationship to be about sex. She wanted more.

More of what, she wasn't sure. She didn't want to be one of many like she'd been with Alejandro. She didn't want to be a simple crush like she'd had for Ryder. And she didn't want to be a rebound fling like she might've been to Ryder, either.

The repetitive thought triggered a tremor through her body. A foreboding clouded her head and her judgement. What if this was it? Or what if this was only while she was designing Jackson's penthouse, and after, they went their separate ways? A breath strangled in her lungs. If she wanted to see where this was going, she'd need to make the moves. He needed her to show him how to enjoy life. They were good together, and could only get better.

He picked up his empty plate and took it to the sink. If she didn't say something now she'd be wondering all day.

"Speaking of flying—" she'd given this some thought in the shower "—we should take a trip somewhere."

"A trip." He did not sound enthusiastic, and her panic caused the strangling sensation to grow.

Was she hanging out to dry any future they might have by being pushy?

"Yes. The two of us. We could visit the area by the university you're *considering* going back to." She'd thought about that, too. Not graduating had affected his outlook on life. She wanted to help him in more ways than sexually.

His brows gathered together, resembling a thundercloud. His frown appeared to carve into his face. He was not pleased with her suggestion.

Maybe she shouldn't push so hard so soon. Their relationship wasn't even defined yet. "Or Barcelona. I'd love to show you some great local places."

She spouted the first place she thought of. She'd been happy there, had learned a lot of local customs, and would love to demonstrate their relaxed attitude on life. Siestas and tapas. Long and late dinners. Dark espresso in the morning after dark nights.

His shoulders relaxed and his mouth loosened, liking her second suggestion better.

The intercom buzzer went off, and she jumped.

"Must be the delivery I'm expecting." He moved into the living room, as if trying to get away from her and her demands.

Doubts cracked through her. The suggestion of a trip had been a risk. Heck, sleeping with him had been a risk. A risk to her heart, and her soul. If he dumped her at this very moment, after only sleeping together once, she'd be beyond hurt. Beyond what she felt for anyone ever before.

And if they continued on and he dumped her later? What then? How would she feel?

Hearing Jackson saying thanks and something rustling as he walked back toward the kitchen, she straightened the robe and plastered on a happy face. She didn't want him guessing where her romantic and tragic thoughts had traveled.

He rounded the corner, carrying an assortment of shopping bags with the logo of an exclusive department store. Mischief shone in his gaze, and he gave her a pleased grin. "Here you go."

"What is this?" Nothing they'd ordered from the Design Mart would come this soon, or be in packages this small.

"I told you I'd replace the panties I'd ruined."

She scrutinized the shopping bags, like snakes waiting to bite. "There's more than one pair of panties in those bags."

"I bought you several."

The hissing snakes went through her system, reminding her she didn't want him buying her anything. She wasn't for sale, as he'd believed at the party.

"And what else?" Her voice hardened with a warning.

"The underwear." He unzipped a garment bag, and held out a multi-colored, stylish dress. "And you can't stroll out of here in the same outfit you wore yesterday. Or go to the Design Mart."

She had last time she'd spent the night, when they

hadn't slept together. Buying her panties was one thing. This was over the top.

Taking a shoe box out of another bag, he flipped off the lid. "Shoes. I thought yours from last night might be wet." He ripped open another bag, resembling a big kid at Christmas, except none of the items were for him. "A suit jacket, to go with the dress." He held up the black jacket. "What do you think?"

Her gaze widened, taking in the beautiful clothes and shoes. Had he picked them out, or some random salesperson at the store? And had he done this for other women in his past?

"I can't accept this from you." She yearned to run her fingers across the material of the dress and to try on the kid-leather shoes, except she didn't want him getting the wrong impression.

"It's my fault you had to spend the night."

His words hit in her midsection. He couldn't control the weather. "Your fault?"

Had their coming together only been because of a snowstorm? She'd believed it had been fate. Well, fate, with a little push from her.

Guilt was written on his face, with worried lines around his eyes and the small tic in his cheek. "My fault because I thought the snow would hit later. My fault because I brought you here and we—"

"There's no fault in what happened last night." She refused to let him blame himself. They were two responsible adults, and she'd initiated. "It was beautiful."

And she'd insisted even when he'd tried to stop.

The realization was a cold slap. She'd pushed him

into having sex. They both enjoyed themselves, and now he was doing what he could to make her feel better. She pulled back her shoulders. He was a client, and she couldn't go off the rails, at least until she could figure out where she stood. She wasn't willing to give up, yet.

"When did you have time to buy this stuff?"

"I searched for clothes online, and had my assistant talk to the store manager to get everything here first thing this morning."

The fact he'd known her sizes and styles lifted her spirits.

"In the early morning?" She peered at the clock and noted it was almost ten. "The stores aren't even open yet."

His earlier smugness returned. "They are when you spend this kind of money."

The clothes might be expensive, but she felt cheap. Her spirits went into a dive. In a way, a payoff. Scum stuck to her skin, even after the shower. Did he think she was easy and cheap?

He had experience procuring women's clothes when the stores were closed. How often did he invite women to spend the night? He might not have a flirtatious reputation like his brother, but he wasn't a monk. He knew how to please a woman.

Stupid, stupid, stupid.

He'd acted so odd this morning. Sterile and stiff. Why had she believed she was different? Special?

Chapter Fourteen

Jackson was early picking Emory up at the design center. Worry about the status of their faux relationship had bothered him all day. While he'd confirmed Shey had called his brother, while he'd worked with accountants on formalizing plans to buy Webber Resorts, and while he'd scheduled a meeting with his mother to find out what the hell was going on.

Frowning, he thought back to his short conversation with his mother two days ago. A discussion filled with innuendoes, hitting a little too close to the truth. About the business and about Emory.

He could admit he'd wanted her. And he allowed himself sexual escapades before, like any healthy adult male. He'd slept with plenty of women. Except they understood the arrangement wouldn't lead to anything permanent, because he didn't have time for a relationship.

He hadn't spelled that out to Emory.

This morning, he'd seen the hurt on her face when she'd suggested a trip, and it had shredded him apart inside. No number of presents would make it better. And he knew how much worse it was going to be when he let her go. Because he would let her go. He wasn't the right man for her. She needed someone who could spend time with her and cherish her. Someone who could help and guide in her business venture. Someone who loved her the way he didn't know how to love.

She'd think her heart was broken for a while. His Emory was strong. He spooked at another possessive pronoun. She wasn't his, and he needed to make that clear to both of them. She'd realize they weren't meant for each other. An SOB like him didn't deserve someone as special. And she'd go on with her life.

She and the same woman from yesterday strolled toward the lobby where he waited. Emory wore the outfit he'd purchased, including the sexy panties. His lust bellowed, remembering how she'd said she wanted to make him fly. Maybe that's why he'd cleared his calendar and arrived early.

She hadn't been happy about the gifts. He could tell by the confused-sour expression, as if she was expecting the dress and shoes to bite. He could read her so well. He could read everyone so well, which was one of the reasons he'd been good at business. With her, it was something deeper. Convincing her to wear the clothes had taken time. Time he'd rather have spent taking off her clothes.

Finally, she'd agreed, if she could pay him back. He'd agreed, only to get her moving. He didn't want people at the Design Mart to think poorly of her. She had a professional reputation, and would need to work with these people for her future clients. He wouldn't jeopardize her career.

No one would learn of their indiscretion.

"Hello, Mr. Croft." The woman held out her hand in a professional handshake. "Good to see you again. We were just finishing up."

Emory's mouth dipped, and a wariness came into her eyes. "I've picked out several different accessories for you. Since you're early, do you have time to tell me what you like?"

He didn't want to spend the time he had in a design showroom with other people around. He wanted to spend time with her.

"Pick whatever you like." Would that seem as if he didn't care? And if he didn't care, then why was he having the penthouse furnished? He wanted people to know he had complete trust in her. "I know I'll love your choices."

His penthouse would be the first thing in her portfolio, and he wanted her to love the finished product. Something she'd be proud of for years to come. His mind dazed, imagining the items she'd picked out, surrounding him for years. And then they'd part ways, and the couch and rugs and accessories would besiege him and suffocate him and taunt him. Each piece a constant reminder of her smile, her creativity, and her love of life.

"I can pick out what I think will work best, and if you don't like it we can send it back."

He'd pay for the furniture, keep it for a while, and then rip it out.

"Great." He rubbed his hands together, anxious to get out of there. "Let's go."

Once in the car, he put his arm on her headrest. He wanted to put it around her shoulders and pull her in tight, except by her stiff posture and her gaze staring straight ahead he knew the actions wouldn't go over well.

He shifted in his seat to study her, wanting to set the tone for the drive to Castle Ridge. Wanting to make things right. "Things didn't end this morning the way they should have."

This morning, after he'd bargained with her about the clothes, he'd gotten a call and she'd gone to get dressed. She'd wanted to rebel, and he heard her muttering something. He hadn't been able to ask, because he'd been on the call when they'd driven to the design center and dropped her off. She hadn't even kissed him goodbye.

He remembered the distraught feeling in the pit of his stomach.

"End?" Her voice cracked and her chin trembled. "Don't worry. I understand." She sniffed and twisted to face him, so brave. "I hope this won't affect our professional relationship."

Her words sounded formal and practiced. He couldn't stop his fingers from reaching out and stroking her cheek. So brave, and yet so soft.

"I don't mean end-end." He wanted to smack himself. He resembled a teenager in an argument with his girlfriend. "What I mean is, I don't want us to end."

Not yet anyhow.

Her brow crinkled. "You didn't want to have sex last night. You tried to stop."

She said sex as if they'd done something dirty, when it had been wonderful. In recent years, he hadn't thought of sex as magnificent. Only a function he'd needed. Yet, last night had been beautiful. From the woman, to the bold way she'd metamorphized into a colorful butterfly, to the way she'd built on his desire and he'd been unable to say no.

"If I hadn't wanted to, would I have?" He tried to inject humor.

She crossed her arms and looked straight ahead. "I don't know what you want. One minute I feel as if you really like me, and the next I feel as if you're playing a game of chess and I'm the pawn."

Her accurate observation knocked the wind out of him. She was smart, and he needed to play the game more carefully, become less guarded. Which would, in turn, make him more vulnerable.

With her, he was already vulnerable. He could tell by the way he thought of her in odd moments, the urge to paint her porcelain skin, the desire to share his desires and dreams.

He tugged her hand loose, and thumbed the soft skin. "Emory. Look at me."

She turned her head, and he examined the violet pools of her orbs. Her gaze tugged at his soul, his real soul. He wanted to get lost and become the person she believed he was.

"I wanted to make love last night, and I want to do it again." Completely true statement. Even now, instead of driving to Castle Ridge, he wanted to go straight to his penthouse. "I like you and respect you, and the only reason I hesitated was because I didn't want to take advantage of you." Also true. "I'm not very good or very practiced at relationships."

Another hard truth.

Uncertainty edged around her eyes. She licked her lips, and he wanted to kiss her. "Is that what this is? A relationship?"

His fingers stopped mid-caress. Shock numbed his movements. A relationship. The word thudded between his ribs.

Not a real relationship. A pretend one on his side. He didn't want to lie again. And he didn't want to scare her away. Scare her back to his brother. "Do we need to put a definition on this special thing we have?"

She snatched her hand away. "I want to know. Is it a fling? An affair? You said it wasn't a one-night stand. So, what is it?"

Her demands pounded and throbbed in his head. She didn't take things at face value. She always challenged him. Which was good, and bad.

He had to answer her. She wouldn't accept a brush-off. "Well, we're definitely seeing each other." He'd seen all of her and she all of him. "Except we haven't actually gone on a date."

"Dinner and a musical isn't a date?"

"I didn't ask. I insisted."

And yet they'd had sex, and talked about going away on a trip together. They were doing everything out of order. Confusion made him dizzy. After last night, the ploy had changed, becoming a lot more complicated.

"Are you asking me on a date?" Again, the demanding tone. The tone he admired and feared.

He swallowed the lump in his throat. "Yes. Of course."

She smiled, a smile blazing like sunshine. "I accept."

So, now they were dating. He'd become caught in a trap of his own making.

"Glad you're finally home." Emory's mom walked into her bedroom, carrying a basket of laundry. "Where did you get the outfit?"

The expensive designer dress became too tight, strangling her. "Um, I had nothing to wear today, so Jackson bought it for me, but I'm going to pay him back."

She had no idea what to tell her mom about what was going on between her and Jackson. Mom didn't want her dating either of the Croft boys. For now, Emory would keep it to herself. She didn't want the dreamy-hopefulness she'd had the entire drive home to be tainted by her mom's concerns.

They'd had a lovely drive, filled with laughter and conversation. The weather had cleared, and the snow on the roads had been plowed or melted. Why had she ever believed he was trying to buy her off with clothes and shoes? He cared about her and wanted to date. To see where this dating could take them.

She held the inner squeal inside. This deeper and longer squeal was so different from the one she'd had when Ryder had asked her to the party. This squeal filled her chest and warmed her soul. This relationship with Jackson was different. More real, built on substance and not image. Sure, there were things she didn't know or understand about him, but she was seeing the part of him he hid behind the business façade.

"That was nice of him." Her mom put away clothes in the dresser, totally clueless she'd slept with Jackson. Mom wouldn't be saying he was nice if she knew. "It's beautiful."

And expensive. Emory had looked up the clothes online.

Nodding, Mom stopped and stared. "Good thinking on his part to spend the night in Denver with the spring storm."

Emory squirmed. "Um, yes."

"I'm glad he texted me to let me know." Lecture voice again.

She hadn't texted. She wasn't used to living under the same roof as her mother. And her lover. "Sorry."

"Did you two go out?"

She froze. They'd done more than go out. She wasn't ready to confess to her mom. "Out?"

"I assume he fed you last night." Her mom gave her an aren't-you-silly expression.

Except it wasn't silly to her, it was guilt.

"Oh, sure. We went to a craft brewery place. It was fun."

Her mom slipped a piece of paper from her pocket. "Alejandro called. I thought you broke up." Handing her the paper, her mom studied her more intently.

"We did. I have no idea why he's calling." He'd never bothered to call her when she broke things off.

At the time, she'd been distressed, wondering how could he be so cruel. They'd sort of made up, and come to an agreement after a forced meeting. Now, she didn't care and wished him the best.

"He said he's in Denver."

She crumpled the paper in her fist. "Oh."

She had no clue why he'd travel to Colorado, unless it was to see her.

"Alejandro wanted your cell phone number. I didn't give it to him."

Emory was thankful for her protective mother. She'd gotten a new cell phone when she moved back to the States, and really didn't want him bothering her. "Thanks."

Her mom squeezed her shoulder. "I know he hurt you, but if he came this far to talk, aren't you curious what he has to say?"

"Not really." She spoke with complete confidence. She'd never felt for Alejandro what she felt for Jackson, and they'd just started dating.

"You need to return Alejandro's call and see what he wants." Her mom's advice echoed in her head.

Similar to how she needed to tell Ryder she could never date him. Not when she'd slept with his brother.

Guilt pushed Emory forward, out of her room and into the main house. Her pulse pounded a slow beat of doom. She needed to find Ryder and talk to him. Her pulse charged forward, racing her anxiety. She didn't want him to see her and Jackson together, or hear rumors of their relationship.

She found Ryder in the billiards room, shooting pool. A beer sat on the green felt, the condensation dripping from the cold bottle. His back was to her as he bent to take a shot. He had the perfect male body. Long and lean, muscular without being too buff. She could appreciate his attractiveness without being attracted.

Her feelings toward the two brothers had changed like night and day. Jackson was the darker, broodier of the brothers, yet she was drawn to him. Being with him, she could bring light into his world.

"Good to see you up and about, Ryder." Entering the room, she twisted her hands together.

The patio doors were open to the cool spring day, blowing in the scent of evergreen and early blooming flowers.

"Good to see you home." He straightened and glared. "And not with Jackson." The tone wasn't accusatory, it was knowing.

"He is a client." She sounded defensive. How was she going to explain to Ryder that her crush on him was nothing compared to what she felt for his brother?

"Shey told me she saw you and Jackson dancing together." Ryder dropped the pool cue, and grabbed her around the waist. "I thought we were going to go dancing."

She squealed, not expecting him to move so quick. "You are feeling better."

"Physically, but emotionally..." He slapped his palm on his chest. "You wound me."

Laughing at his dramatics, she shook her head. "You're being ridiculous."

He took hold of her hand and swung her around. "Is my older brother Jackson a good dancer?"

Her body flared with heat. They'd done more than dance. Her stomach performed a two-step of its own. Could Ryder tell she'd slept with his brother? Her expression was always so transparent.

"Well, about that… I think it's best…" She didn't know what to say or how to explain. "I think maybe we—"

"What's going to happen between us?" He reeled her toward the patio doors leading to the front courtyard.

Shaking her head, she let him dance her outside, not knowing what to say.

His frown communicated how he sensed he'd lost her. "I'm beginning to think we weren't meant to dance together."

He was right. She was meant for Jackson.

Jackson paused at the entrance to the billiards room and sucked in a sharp breath. Emory was in his brother's arms, and they were laughing. The sharp breath must've had spikes in it, because jagged pain of anger and jealousy stabbed through the thin membranes of his lungs. She laughed at what his brother said similar to how she laughed at his own teases.

Maybe she was a tease. Playing them both off each other.

No, that couldn't be true. He knew her. They'd had a fun drive home, talking the entire way, stopping for lunch at a cute café in a small mountain town. She'd slept with him.

But she'd always loved Ryder.

Jackson had believed it was a crush. What if he was wrong?

The stabbing pains continued because he deserved the torture. He'd tricked her. Dazzled her with his pretend charm and nobleness. Lied to her about the dog shelter and his plans to remodel. Used his past to soften her up. Kissed her into a desirous haze. Used her own sexuality to keep her wanting him.

She laughed again, and the noise twisted around his heart and pulled tight, cutting off the blood flow and the flow of any emotions he'd developed for her.

Ryder waltzed her out through the patio doors. Seething, Jackson was paralyzed. His plot had been going better than expected, or so he'd thought. But as soon as his brother crooked his finger, she went running back.

His mouth flattened into a hard line. Maybe it was time to tell his brother whose arms she spent the night in. Warn his brother off. Tell him to stay away.

The territorial-ness of his thoughts had him cringing. It was only because he'd thought he'd been successful in wooing her away, only to find out that wasn't true. He needed to do more, become more militant, make demands.

"Mr. Jackson?" Mrs. Barrington approached him with a concerned expression. "Are you feeling okay?"

"Yes, of course." *Of course not.* His stomach was nauseous, and his head ached.

"You had such a strange expression on your face." She angled her head similar to how her daughter did, except the mother let the issue go. She must not have seen Emory and Ryder together. "Mr. Webber and his son are here to see you. I showed them to your office."

"Thank you, Mrs. Barrington." Would she thank Jackson, when she learned what he'd done to her daughter?

Stomping to the office, he tried to control his anger at his brother and Emory. He'd thought they'd settled everything in the car. They were going to go on a real date.

Except it wasn't a real date. He needed to remember that.

"Gentlemen." He entered his office to find George Webber staring blankly out the window, and his son slouching in a chair.

Jackson had met Chance Webber before he'd moved to California to strike out on his own. The guy had been able to make his own choice and not join the family business. Sourness tasted on his tongue.

George swung around and waved his hands toward the outside. "I saw Ryder talking with that girl. What're they doing together?"

"Dad, she's a beautiful woman not a girl." Chance's defense of Emory put Jackson on edge. With his too-casual clothes and scruffy beard, he resembled a mountain man. The guy had made himself at home, and noticed Emory was beautiful.

Jackson bit his lip to stop a jealous response. "I explained before she's a friend."

The father's gaze narrowed, drilling into him. "A beautiful *woman* living under the same roof. I understand temptation."

The son glowered, obviously hearing the lame excuse before.

"She won't be here long." Jackson made up his mind, and his plan solidified in his head. She couldn't be trusted near his brother again. "She's going on a trip. To Barcelona."

She'd suggested the destination herself. He'd take her to Barcelona, make sure she was comfortable for a long vacation, and come back to sign the merger papers, never returning to her side. That would be best for both of them.

"Good. I don't want anyone screwing up this deal."

Neither did he. The effort going in to making this happen had been and would continue to be monumental. It had taken away his time and his ethics. He'd thrown morality away. Was it worth it?

"Dad. A business deal shouldn't be contingent on a marriage. That's so eighteenth century." Chance spoke in a slow, laid-back voice.

"You and your modern technology. That's why you lost your shirt, and apparently your suits, in California." George's derogatory tone about how his son was dressed seemed to be a constant contention between them.

"And my tie." The son grabbed the collar of his T-shirt. "Don't forget my tie."

The tie around Jackson's own throat tightened. The

business accessory was uncomfortable. It had taken him months to learn how to tie one properly, and he always thought it a noose. Many of the younger businessmen, men around his own age, didn't wear a full three-piece suit anymore. Not even for board meetings. Yet Jackson had donned the costume of the successful businessman to keep up appearances.

He loosened the tie.

"This is my son, Chance." The late and repetitive introduction sent an odd vibe through Jackson.

George had been acting odd lately, almost senile. Not Jackson's concern.

He shook hands with the man. The tech start-up Chance had been involved with must've failed, because he was back home taking his father's shit again.

Maybe that would lessen Jackson's load.

George thumped his son on the back. "He's back from fooling around, and will become vice president."

"Considering it." Chance shoved his hands in the pockets of his holey jeans.

"What about Shey?" Jackson knew how much she loved her position.

"Once Shey marries Ryder and starts giving me grandbabies, she's not going to continue to work."

Jackson tried not to actually reel back. The future grandfather appeared to still be living in the nineteen-fifties.

"You don't know for sure, Dad." The son shook his head, obviously thinking along the same lines as Jackson. "She loves her career."

"She'll love her husband and children more."

George's adamancy seemed to be a long-standing argument.

An argument Jackson didn't want to be a part of. "What can I help you with?"

Besides making sure Emory stayed away from Ryder.

George put both of his palms flat on the desk. "Your mother is harassing me with phone calls and demands."

Jackson's eyebrows flew high. After her two surprise visits here and her insinuations, he'd done some research and scheduled a meeting with the woman. He had to find out what she was up to. "And?"

"I want to know what's going on with her, and if she has anything to do with your company. I like to know who I'm going to bed with."

The choice of words cold-cocked him. Fear and anger swelled in his midsection into a turmoil of fury. He'd done so many bad things to make this deal happen, including sleeping with Emory. He wouldn't let anything stop it now. "My mother has nothing to do with Croft Industries. I'm meeting with her early next week, and I'll get everything straightened out."

"Good, because between your brother and your mother, I'm not sure we can do business with you."

Jackson was tired of the threats, tired of the hoops he had to jump through, tired of the dirty deeds he'd done. He agreed with Chance. The deal shouldn't be contingent on a marriage. Jackson wasn't his brother's or his mother's keeper.

But he'd come too far. "I'll take care of everything." He always did.

"A man who can't handle his family, can't handle his business." George's warning rang in Jackson's ears.

Blaring an alarm of his faults and failures.

Announcing his scars and sins.

Trumpeting his derelictions and deficiencies.

Maybe it was time his family took care of themselves.

Chapter Fifteen

Emory sat back in the booth at The Heights restaurant in the Castle Ridge Lodge the following day. The meeting with Dani Marstrand and Luke Logan was going well. They only needed to discuss scheduling for the interior design at their new bed and breakfast. Emory was on her way to a good start for her interior design firm without any promotion. Two solid clients, with the bed and breakfast and Jackson's penthouse. When she finished the penthouse, she could work on her business plan and securing additional clients. Then, she could find a combined living and office space for herself. One step at a time.

Just how she planned to pursue things with Jackson.

Internally, she sighed. Yesterday and this morning had been divine. He'd worked on business while she worked on his home. A home she'd begun to think she'd be spending a lot of time in. Not saying they were ready to take any major steps, yet she could see they were headed in that direction. She could sense it. Excitement tingled along her skin. She wanted to take the next step, wanted to tell her mom and Ryder about their relationship, wanted to be together in the open.

"Will the timeline work for you?" Dani tapped a pencil on her paper calendar, bringing Emory back to the present conversation.

She wouldn't be starting on their bed and breakfast until late summer. The old farmhouse needed major renovations. Once those were complete, she'd step in to decorate the kitchen and bathrooms, and choose the internal furnishings of every room in the house.

"Yes."

Dani grabbed Luke's hand on the table. Her skin glowed with happiness. "Our goal is to be open by ski season."

A man swooped down and planted a friendly kiss on Dani's cheek. "Trying to take away business from me, Dani?"

The man's grin revealed he had no bad will. A tease. His three-piece designer suit reminded Emory of Jackson's normal attire. This morning, he'd been wearing a T-shirt and jeans. She sucked in a breath, remembering how he'd been out of place, and yet handsome and virile.

She noticed the woman standing slightly behind him. Shey Webber.

Swallowing uncomfortably, Emory lowered her gaze to take in the very expensive heels her one-time-imagined nemesis wore. To think she'd tried to date Ryder when the two of them had just broken up. Silly, really. Rebounds were never a good idea.

"Stop teasing, Parker. You know the more luxury accommodations available in Castle Ridge, the better it is for business." Dani slapped his arm playfully, understanding the tease.

Emory knew the man only by reputation. His family had owned the Castle Ridge Lodge for decades.

Pushing a stray lock of blond hair out of his face, Luke stood and held out his hand. "Plus, you always have overbookings. We're hoping you recommend us when you do."

The two men shook hands, seeming to be friends.

"Or us." Shey stuck her hand out to Luke and Dani. Shey's friendly, non-competitive smile caused uneasiness in Emory. "Hi. Shey Webber with Webber Resorts."

Emory kept her glance down, waiting for her introduction.

Dani shook the new woman's hand with a tight expression, not exhibiting the same friendliness to this announcement "Are you opening a Webber property in Castle Ridge?"

Emory knew the merger with Croft Industries would impact any new property development.

"Not at this time." A neutral answer. Shey was a business-savvy professional. "We are down the road, though, at Powder Mountain. Emory. How're you doing?" The conversation redirected toward her. "Where's Jackson?"

One person knew about their relationship.

Her cheeks heated, knowing exactly what the woman thought. And she'd be right. "He's working from home today, I believe."

"So you know Emory is the interior designer for Jackson Croft's penthouse in Denver. She showed me the designs. They're amazing." Dani's compliment had Emory's shoulders straightening, until Shey's brows arched, communicating she knew there was more than designing going on.

"You're a designer?" Her question added a layer of unease to the conversation.

Dani must be wondering if Shey didn't know Emory was a designer, then why had she asked her about Jackson Croft? How many designers went dancing with their clients?

Wanting to ward off any personal questions, Emory took out a business card and handed it to Shey. "I've just started my business. I'll be designing the interior for Dani and Luke's bed and breakfast."

"Ski Race Inn."

Parker choked out a laugh. "Ski Race Inn? You're playing off Luke's celebrity."

"Stop teasing." Dani put her hand on her husband's arm and squeezed with affection. "It's a great name."

The friendly argument continued around Emory. She loved seeing how close they were. Competitors and friends. Once her business became more established in Castle Ridge and her and Jackson's relationship was out in the open, they could hang out together. Go out to dinner. It would be great to have a girlfriend like Dani, and a possible sister-in-law like Shey, for Jackson to have friends his own age, and not the stuffy older businessmen he tended to hang out with at the country club.

"Emory, do you have a minute to talk?" Shey's request caught her off guard. "Are you done with your meeting?"

"Um, sure." Emory shifted in the booth. She didn't know what the woman wanted to say. Was she going to ask about her relationship with Jackson? Or Ryder?

"Parker and I finished our meeting, and I could use a coffee." Shey gave the lodge owner a glance of dismissal. "Do you mind telling the waiter?"

"Of course not." Parker said his goodbyes, and headed toward the kitchen.

Emory stood to shake hands with her new clients and arrange the next step in the process, and then Luke and Dani were off. She sat back down, and Shey took the seat Luke had vacated. The silence stretched, and Emory didn't know how to break it.

"I understand you live at the Croft mansion." Shey's tone was even, not giving anything away.

"With my mom. She's the housekeeper." Emory spoke confidently about her mom's position. She wasn't embarrassed by the fact any longer, even in front of a rich woman. And soon, she'd have her own place.

"Right." Shey took a sip of the coffee placed before her. She fidgeted with the white mug, running her finger around and around the edge of the cup. "My father said Ryder danced with you at Lexi's wedding reception."

Was this an interrogation? "I did."

Dancing wasn't a big deal.

"My father said he saw you kiss him."

Her stomach dropped. She had kissed Ryder, except so much had changed in the last week. At the time, she hadn't met Shey, and had only heard about the big break-up.

Emory wanted to explain, not wanting to cause either of them more agony. "Yes, I gave him a peck. I always had a huge crush on him."

"So did I." Shey's sarcasm held an edge of torment.

The woman's pain twisted inside Emory. She remembered the hurt of Alejandro's betrayal with other women. His hadn't been as innocent.

"How's Ryder feeling?"

"I haven't seen much of him lately." She emphasized this point. "His allergic reaction is getting better."

"Good." The woman didn't sound good. Grief flashed in her expression.

Hating to see the torture caused by a lover's rift, she leaned forward. "I'm not interested in Ryder."

"You're not?"

She shook her head. "Croft men have many layers and are hard to pin down." She thought about Jackson's secret painting, and smiled. "Go after what you want."

She'd been attracted to Ryder for her entire life, and yet, ended up with Jackson. Because she'd dug deeper and she couldn't be happier. Once they explained things to his brother, they could tell her mom, and the world.

"I can't believe you got us in to the back." Emory's happy-surprised voice rang through the cavernous room of the art museum's storage area early Monday morning. "No one ever gets to see this amazing stuff."

Calling in a favor had been the right thing to do.

Jackson's gaze wandered. This room wasn't the dreary storage room of most businesses. Lines of ceiling-high shelves were filled with furniture and accessories, protected with clear plastic wrap and tagged. This section was the decorative arts storage.

"When you're a large donor to a museum they tend to help out with special requests." He'd learned early how money could buy anything.

Anyone.

Except his family. And now Emory.

A surge of pride ran through him at the image of her turning down his initial offer in the garden. His life would've been easier if she'd taken the money, he'd have no guilt. His emotions wouldn't be stirred into a maelstrom. There'd be none of the soul searching he'd found himself doing at odd moments. And yet, he couldn't deny spending time with her had widened his perspectives.

"Oh my! This is a Gehry chair." She pointed to a chair with a wiggling structure beneath the seat.

Her fascination with art and design filled him with a sense of wonderment. The wonderment had sparked his own inspiration. He'd painted again because of her. She didn't realize the gift she'd given. Given him a small slice of what he used to see and feel.

And if he could give her this tiny thing, an experience she'd never have the chance at again, it might make up for the anguish he'd cause when he ended things. Because this weekend he'd understood she wouldn't have a fling without her heart being involved.

While he didn't have a heart.

The organ pounded, denying his internal claim.

Obviously, he had the organ. He needed one to live. But the emotional heart with honor, the one connected to his soul and spirit? That heart had died when he'd taken charge of the business, lost his ethics and his art.

He hoped giving her new experiences and using his penthouse in her design portfolio was a good enough consolation prize.

Maybe someday she'd forgive him.

Like gnats buzzing his brain, he understood her forgiveness mattered. Mattered more than most people's opinions. More than his billions sitting in the bank.

"Look at this." She trailed her delicate fingers over the plastic formed shape of a modern hanging lamp.

He imagined her trailing her fingers across his skin. His chest thunked, and he wanted to draw nearer. He was the one being wooed by her, not the opposite. He was falling under her spell. A hazy, dreamy sensation surrounded him when she was near. And when they parted, he'd become cold and hard again.

A chill raked across his skin. He'd lose the creativeness, too. He'd clean up the art studio at his penthouse and never paint again, because he didn't deserve to. He'd move to Denver to avoid the wrath of her mom. And to avoid Emory who planned to live in Castle Ridge.

Doubts chipped away at his spine, putting chinks in his plan. His tongue swirled in motion, wanting to tell her about the ploy. To let her know it was nothing personal. She'd gotten in the way of a merger, and he'd sent himself to deal with her.

Except it had become personal. Intimate.

Her smile appeared to be a permanent fixture this morning. She was happy. If he exposed his scheme, he'd ruin his plans for Ryder, and her mood. And the mood for later tonight.

Jackson wanted one more passionate night with her before he revealed his final vile act. One more night in her arms, savoring possibilities of things that would never come to fruition. One more night pretending she was the light in his life and would be there forever.

If that was terrible of him, so be it.

"I can't believe it!" She'd stopped in front of a crate left half open. Her expression of surprised-joy glowed on her skin. "It's an original Louis Comfort Tiffany lamp."

The lamp had more art than function. The brown base was sculpted into roots leading to a trunk. The shade resembled the overhang of a tree in varying shades of blue, green, purple, and golden-yellow blown glass.

Jackson's fingers itched. He wanted to capture the way the light from the bulb broke through the colors, spreading an effusion of peacefulness and serenity. "Special, I take it."

"Louis Tiffany was a master in decorative arts. His design skills, blending form with function, were renowned." Her enthusiasm struck a fanciful note in Jackson's mind. "I have a replica of this exact same lamp."

He appreciated the man's blending of colors. The way the free-flowing lines evoked nature. "Why do you like this lamp so much?"

"What it represents." She pointed to another example. "When Tiffany couldn't convince the finer manufacturers to leave the mineral impurities in the glass, he created his own glass company."

"Why would he want impurities in the glass?"

"Because the impurities gave the glass a uniqueness. Character."

Would she think Jackson's impurities gave him character? If he confessed everything he'd done up until this point, would she believe he still had honor?

He choked. No way. She'd be running in the other direction, because she was good and pure. She'd never accept his black soul.

"Tiffany created the copper foil technique for creating stained glass, which made possible the level of detail he was able to create. His work had emotional impact."

The explanation spoke to Jackson's own artistic endeavors. In the past, he'd used his paintings to communicate his emotions. He used to be able to see things in art, to be inspired by the shape of an item, the falling rain, and the formation of clouds. He'd lost the ability. Too busy concentrating on his spreadsheets and balance sheets and making money. Except the last few days his imagination had been sparked. His creativity recharged.

Had the last few days been an aberration? A whim? The urge to paint and express had poured out of him and onto the canvas. The exhilaration had brought him to a frenzy, with bold brushstrokes and tight focus. He struggled to breathe. His creativity returned because of Emory. What would happen when they were done?

"Mr. Croft. I hope you've gotten to see everything you wanted." The curator, who'd taken them into the backroom and given them privacy, returned to his side. "We're honored you've taken an interest in our decorative arts collection. Your very large donation will start us on our path to expand display space, and be able to showcase so much more of the collection."

"Thank you for letting us spend time here."

This man had had a price. "Is there something specific you're interested in?"

"Ask Miss Barrington." Because Jackson wanted to see her happy so he could remember these moments.

Emory waxed on about the lamp and various pieces the museum had from the artist. The curator pointed out a couple of additional pieces farther back.

Jackson glanced at his watch, wishing time could slow. Stop. "Sorry to break this up. I have a meeting I need to attend." His voice soured, because he really didn't want to go to his next meeting with Victoria Croft.

After dropping Emory off at the penthouse, he arrived at his office. His assistant bombarded him with a million messages, and paperwork, and things he needed to sign.

"Lastly, your mother is waiting for you in the conference room." Barbara sounded put out.

What had Victoria Croft said to his normally un-swayable assistant?

"Don't be so surprised." He remembered Webber's comment about him not having a mother.

"Nothing surprises me lately." Barbara's airiness wafted through Jackson.

"What's that supposed to mean?"

She pinched up her nose and narrowed her gaze. "Musical tickets and dinner reservations. Paint under your normally-clean nails. Early-morning trips to the museum."

Things had been different. He'd been different. Not his normal routine. He'd spent the weekend in Castle Ridge, not working the entire time. He'd spent time with his brother and Emory, although separately. She'd spent time with her mother and working on her website. She'd even met with clients on Friday. Out of respect for her mom, they hadn't slept together.

No one knew what they'd been doing in Denver, although Emory had pushed to share the news. He hadn't wanted to damage her reputation, so he'd insisted on secrecy. And instead of enduring the temptation of her being so close and yet untouchable, he'd headed down to Denver last night and painted. She'd drove from Castle Ridge this morning.

His assistant would be even more shocked at his next request. "I need you to get me two first-class tickets to Barcelona."

She didn't flinch. "For you?"

"For me and Emory Reese Barrington."

"Are you actually going on a vacation?" His assistant's tone went high, shock mixed with disapproval, as if she understood his sinister plan.

He flexed his fists. The trip was for work, for family. For the good of Croft Industries and his brother. "Of course not."

"How do you know the young lady will go with you?" Barbara's lips pinched.

"The same way I knew when to buy companies, when to sell, and when to break them apart." Weary resignation flowed through his veins. He'd used intuition to trick Emory into falling for him. He didn't know if she even realized his tactics. One more grand gesture, and she'd be putty in his hands. "I just know."

"When will you and Miss Barrington be leaving?" His assistant struggled to keep the curiosity from her voice. He could tell by the glint in her eyes, and the whiteness of her knuckles gripping a notepad.

He felt as if her knuckles gripped the center of his chest. Taking Emory on this trip was a huge step. A cruel stomp on her heart. She'd believe he wanted to experience life with her. That he was willing to walk away from Croft Industries. That she was saving him from himself.

Would he be able to take things this far and abandon her? To hurt her this much? To hurt himself?

Webber's threats banged in his head. The image of his team working hard on the merger flashed before him. The memory of his brother's smile the last time he'd been with Shey twisted inside. And the thought of his father's pride when the Croft-Webber merger went through filled his chest.

It had been a goal of his father's to purchase the land Webber Resorts now owned. Because of other questionable financial decisions, his father couldn't get the backing. George Webber had swooped in with better financing to secure the purchase. The man had developed the property into a resort, and now was wanting a partner. This deal would cement Jackson's father's dream.

Everything inside him hardened and solidified. He'd do what he had to do. "Two days."

Emory waited in the lobby of the nicest hotel in Denver. In her jeans and spring sweater, she felt out of place next to business executives, and smartly-dressed men and women. She was not out to impress.

The dark lobby had expensive reproductions of European furniture. Oriental rugs scattered across the floor. A large chandelier hung in the center near the elevator doors.

Her stomach churned with the thought of seeing Alejandro for the first time since their break up. Last night, he'd called the house phone in her mom's suite of rooms and she'd picked up. He'd traveled all this way, and he'd said it wasn't to talk about everything he'd done wrong in their relationship. He'd said he was sorry. She'd agreed to meet with him because she'd learned he could be persistent, and she didn't want him interfering with the new man in her life.

Knowing Jackson had an appointment, she'd arranged this meeting for the same time. She wasn't keeping her ex-boyfriend a secret, she just wanted to know what Alejandro wanted before telling Jackson.

The elevator dinged and the doors slid open, revealing Alejandro. Jet-black hair went past his shoulders. A full beard and mustache and dark sunglasses hid his face. He wore shiny leather shoes, and expensive mustard pants. His jacket was open, revealing a button-down shirt featuring a garish pattern.

Her pulse didn't race. Her heart didn't beat faster.

His haughty expression changed to welcoming when he spotted her. "Emory, my darling." He kissed her on both cheeks.

The contact of his lips on her skin, which used to send desire through her, did nothing. "Hi, Alejandro."

He grabbed her hands, pulled them together, and brought them to his lips. "So American you look now."

She no longer needed to compete with the stylish European women she'd worked with. Her business and her style were her own. "I've always been American."

"Your marvelous design ideas always made me forget." He spoke as if being American was a bad thing, and she had to wonder if he'd ever really knew her. "Let's get a drink."

"It's not even noon."

"Again, so American. In Barcelona, we enjoyed cocktails all the time." Tugging on her hand, he led her toward the bar off the lobby.

Maybe that's why she'd fallen for him. He'd seemed so exotic and sophisticated. It wasn't his wealth or even his title. It was his attitude. He loved life. He'd been fun and flirtatious and complimentary to her and her design skills.

The small bar was empty at this hour. Old-fashioned paintings of ships at sea hung on the walls. She slid onto a velvet-covered bench seat in a small booth with low light.

While he ordered a bottle of champagne, she checked her phone. No messages from Jackson. He'd said he had meetings the rest of the day, and wouldn't see her until around dinner. She was hoping to surprise him with a home-cooked meal.

"How have you been, my Emory?" Alejandro clinked his champagne flute to her glass of water. His long fingers sported several rings. His thin frame worked well with the designer fashions he preferred. He was attractive, suave, and she'd been blown away when he'd displayed interest in her.

She'd tried to retain his interest by dressing more European, drinking the drinks he enjoyed, and eating where he wanted, and by trying to fit in to his lifestyle. In a way, she'd become different from herself.

With Jackson, she'd also been blown away by his interest, yet she'd stayed true to herself, speaking her mind, and showing him things she enjoyed. She hadn't been intimidated by his power or wealth. They'd made a real connection because she hadn't pretended.

She couldn't stop her slight smile at the thought. "I'm good. How're you?"

Alejandro pursed his lips. "I've missed you. And I'm truly sorry for the distress I caused."

A chortle burst out, half pain and half funny. She would've loved to have heard those words right before she'd left Barcelona. Now, they meant nothing and were ludicrous in the current situation. "How can you miss one person from such a large harem?"

"Don't be mad." His pursed lips went from pouty

to annoyed. "How could I choose between you and Sofia and Luciana?"

If he was here to win her back, this wasn't the way to do it. Emory wanted to get to the point. She'd learned a few things from Jackson. "Why are you here, Alejandro?"

"Forceful and direct." Taking a sip of champagne, he shivered. "I like it."

Her head spun. So, if she would've been her true self and not tried to fit into his image of what a woman should be, he would've liked her better? She'd found her true self in Spain, and he'd headed her in the wrong direction. Through the hurt, she'd done a complete turnaround, rediscovering herself, and learning she'd never placate someone again. "What do you want?"

"I want you." He spoke causally.

"Excuse me?" The only explanation she could think of for him wanting to see her was to win her back. Yet even though he said he wanted her, he'd done or said nothing to try to impress her.

It didn't matter. She was making a new life for herself. Starting her own design firm and a new relationship with Jackson, a real relationship, one built on trust and mutual respect.

She'd never had that with Alejandro. Because she'd never been truly in love.

He leaned forward across the small bar table. "My *castillo* is a mess. Since you left, the design firm's ideas have fallen apart. The designs are no good. Nothing matches. The furniture being delivered to my home is late and sub-par."

Her gaze widened and she fell back in the cushy booth. "Are you asking me to come back to Barcelona and be your designer?"

"Of course." He swung his hand to emphasize his point. "I need you. Your designs, your organization, your attention to detail."

This time she laughed out loud. The offer lifted her spirits, yet she wasn't tempted. "Thanks, but—"

"Wait!" He held up his other hand in a stop motion, imitating a game show host or a cheesy salesman.

She waited to hear the words *and there's more.*

"You wouldn't need to work for Sofia or her firm. You'd work for me. I'll pay you an outrageous amount of money. You'd stay at the *castillo,* or my flat downtown, depending on where you need to be to supervise the work. I'll give you complete authority." He placed a flat palm on his chest. "With no interference from me. I won't even ask you out, unless you want me to."

The wink at the end had her laughing again. He'd always been fun and frivolous. The life of a party. That wasn't her life anymore.

Alejandro's home was a dream job. The original project through her design firm had come with too many strings. Now, the strings would be cut. She'd be free to do as she wanted. Pick the best color palettes and style. Her designs and her decisions.

Still, she had a dream project with the penthouse. A great start to her portfolio, and starting her own design firm in Colorado. And she had a dream of a future with Jackson.

"I appreciate the offer, but I'm happy here."

His brown gaze narrowed, and he studied her intensely, making her uncomfortable. "You're sleeping with someone."

The accurate accusation prodded too deeply. She crossed her arms. "That has nothing to do with it."

But it did.

"George Webber is not happy with your brother right now." Victoria Croft sat across the desk from Jackson.

He hadn't invited her to sit on the more comfortable couches. She was an adversary, and he wanted a clear separation between them. Her short dress revealed too much of her overly-tan legs, proving she'd spent too much time in a tanning salon. She had her blonde hair in the too-young ponytail again. The ponytail didn't hide the wrinkles around her eyes and lips.

The moment was surreal. The woman hadn't been in his life since he was fourteen, and now she wanted a say in running the business.

His business.

Resentment built inside him, brick by solid brick. Question by question. Why was she trying to get involved now? What was her motivation? Money? Control? Revenge? This meeting would put an end to his questions. He needed to know what she was up to.

"I didn't realize how much you cared about Ryder." Jackson poured sarcasm into his tone.

"I care about the deal you're making with Webber Resorts." His mother's cold voice matched her cold expression. "You're going to need me to make the deal happen."

What the hell was she talking about? He didn't need her. He never had.

Under the desk he clenched his hands together. "I understand you own Croft Industries stock that at one time was worthless."

"I bet on you, though. I bought more Croft stock when it was barely worth the paper it was printed on." Her thin red lips lifted in a smile resembling a snarl.

Not revenge against him, if she trusted his business instincts.

"How much do you have? Five? Ten percent?" He knew exactly how many voting shares she'd received in the divorce. He'd had his team researching individuals and corporations buying their stock recently, and hiding the real investor in dummy companies. That's how he'd make good on a threat such as hers. Hide the shares until it was profitable to reveal.

His team had uncovered clues, although not a definitive number.

"Thirty-nine percent."

His stomach dropped, and he felt as if he'd lost his balance. If her claim was true, she'd be able to wrangle a seat at the boardroom table. He followed who bought and sold Croft stock. He also knew the way to hide identities. He'd used the same tactic several times.

Gritting his teeth, he slowly sucked in air. "You never declared your intentions."

The thin, red lips smirked. "I did everything by your playbook. Shadow companies. Dummy corporations. Maybe not ethical, but legal."

His brain scrambled. He'd never written a playbook. He'd tried to keep his tactics secret.

"Very similar to some of the schemes you used when you first took charge of Croft Industries." His mother spoke resembling a master manipulator, when that was his job.

How did she know about his tactics?

Panic roiled inside him, sending his thoughts teetering one way and then the other. He didn't know what to expect from this woman who'd given birth to him. She was an enigma. She'd already provided evidence proving the terrible financial state of the company when he'd taken over. Her claim of him using risky and borderline-ethical schemes was true. And somehow, she'd learned from him?

Guess she hadn't been as distant as he'd believed.

His mother pointed a sharp nail across the desk. "Time to stop telling me to mind my own business. I have every right to know what's going on, and if you're not going to fill me in I can call an emergency board meeting and let the board and stockholders know I have clout."

His mind blew. He tried to line up the arguments and legalities. He tried to focus on appealing to her better nature. He rejected everything. Pulling himself together, he knew he couldn't show his enemy weakness. She'd outmaneuvered him. This time. He'd treat her like any other business opponent.

"What do you want, Mother?" He wanted to be clear what her plan was.

She beamed. A brilliant, toothy smile. "I want Croft Industries to be successful."

A load of crap. He needed to dig deeper into what she'd been up to these past several years. He needed to poke and prod.

"If you're so business savvy, how would you handle the Webber Resorts merger?" He'd throw the problem right back at her.

"I'd start by analyzing the holdings of each family member, and what their goals are in the merger." Sound advice, but not earth-shattering.

He'd done his due diligence on the Webbers. "Are you referring to the son, Chance?"

"I'm thinking Shey can handle any trouble Chance might cause."

Jackson had witnessed how she handled a couple of her father's larger bunglings. "Agreed."

Victoria's gaze narrowed, trying to catch him off guard. "What about Emory Barrington?"

His muscles tightened, even though he fought to keep his expression blank. Using no inflection, he asked, "What about Emory?"

His mother slid her handbag on her shoulder. "When I met with George Webber, he told me his suspicions about her and Ryder."

A jagged green flash sliced through Jackson's muscles. He wasn't jealous. He had Emory where he wanted. Her feelings for his brother had been crushed. "She's not an issue."

His mother's perfectly-plucked eyebrows rose.

"Why? George said he saw them together at the house last week. Maybe we should force her to move out. She's not a child needing to live with her mother."

"No." Jackson got to his unsteady feet. She certainly wasn't a child. "The Emory issue is under control."

"How? What's going on I need to know?" His tenacious mother wasn't about to give up.

"Nothing for you to be concerned about."

"If it concerns the company, it concerns me. I'm a major investor. Silent, *at the moment.*"

The threat hung in the air between them. If he didn't tell his mother his strategy, she'd make her ownership public. He didn't want to hurt Emory any more than he was going to. Telling more people about his plot would embarrass her. "I'm handling her."

"Sorry to interrupt, Jackson. I need return dates for the plane tickets for you and Emory Barrington." His assistant spoke on the intercom.

His body jerked and he glanced at Victoria. "Now?" He gritted his teeth.

"If you want to leave in two days."

Victoria cranked her head toward the intercom, listening intently. By her expression, she was putting together the pieces.

He needed to give the information, without her learning anything more. "Open-ended on the round-trip tickets. And, I'll need a separate return ticket in three days." Guilt tugged at his conscience, as he finalized the plans. He glared at his mother, daring her to comment. "Sorry for the interruption."

"You and Emory are going on vacation together?"

Victoria studied him with a spiteful gleam. "Upstairs-downstairs has become into something more."

His relationship was none of her business. "I'm dating her."

She pointed an accusing finger. "This is not the time to leave the country, when the merger is at risk."

"I'm taking Emory with me."

Victoria's cold gaze calculated. "You're only dating the girl to keep her away from your brother."

Cringing, he stared her down, refusing to answer. He hadn't planned to tell anyone about his nefarious plan. That way only he'd know the depths to which he'd sunk.

Her lips moved slowly up, in a sniveling-superior smile. "I'm proud of you."

His shoulders scrunched high on his neck, and a dirtiness clung to his skin. He didn't want this terrible woman proud of him. If she could see through his scheme, so could others. He'd always known what he was doing was wrong, but he'd believed his justifications.

Now, he didn't trust his own dirty tactics.

<h1 style="text-align:center">Chapter Sixteen</h1>

Humming, Emory unwrapped a couple of accessories that had been delivered to Jackson's penthouse. A woven umbrella stand, a Nambe silver bowl, a coffee table book featuring surrealist paintings. The last item she'd bought on a whim, thinking he'd be interested.

The crinkling of the paper added merriment to the proceedings. The smell of fresh latex paint permeated most of the penthouse. The new color had been painted over the weekend, and it brought harmony to the main rooms. She'd kept the wood floors throughout the open space, and the original kitchen cabinets and counters, because they added to the overall expression of Mid-Century Modern.

She personally loved how the old mixed with the new. Loved everything they'd picked out, and couldn't wait to see the furniture in its place.

Pasta sauce wafted from the kitchen. After meeting with Alejandro, she'd stopped at the grocery store and bought a salad and pre-made lasagna for dinner. Jackson had made plans to meet her here early this evening to go out for dinner. She didn't want to go out, she wanted to surprise him and stay home.

The emotionally-charged word stamped in her brain.

Home.

This wasn't her home, and yet, glancing around, she realized she loved everything about it. She'd never done that with a client before. The furniture and the colors and the accents were about the client's needs. Not the designer's.

Letting out a breath, she regarded the room. This felt like home. Jackson felt like home. Of course, she wasn't willing to confess yet.

She didn't think of the large Castle Ridge house as her home. She'd been gone too long, and her and her mother only shared a suite of rooms. She planned to rent an apartment in town, where she could combine her office and living space. At the moment, she was truly homeless.

Except, she didn't feel as if she wandered from place to place. Castle Ridge, and by extension, Denver, were her hometown. She needed to find the perfect place to live, spending part of her time here, and part in the mountain town. And hopefully, many nights in Jackson's penthouse. And his arms.

Her head drifted in the clouds, similar to the late-afternoon sun shining through the windows, casting a beam of light across the living room. A few of the lights were turning on in the other nearby highrises. A clear view of the snowcapped mountains centered through the floor-to-ceiling windows on two sides. The penthouse was a glass castle in the air.

She loved the combined living and dining space. Loved the modern kitchen with the clean lines. Loved how the elevator whisked you right up into the space. Loved the fact it had a study and three bedrooms.

Her survey stopped. Three bedrooms. She'd been in two of them. Her gaze strayed down the hall. She was alone, and a designer really needed to see the entire place. A rationalization. Even if she wasn't decorating the bedrooms, she wouldn't be doing her job, if she didn't make sure every room worked well together.

Her feet led her down the hallway, to the room with the locked door. The walls closed in on her. The staid artwork mocked, not at all like the paintings she'd found behind the couch on her first visit.

Reaching the door, she paused. Misgiving quivered through her body. He kept the door locked for a reason. But she had to know. Had to know what Jackson kept hidden from everyone. He'd asked her not to go in there on the day she measured, before they'd gotten to know each other, slept together, and started a relationship. Now that they were dating he wouldn't mind.

With shaking hands, she gripped the doorknob and turned.

Locked.

She should walk away and ask him tonight what was in the room. He'd always put her off in the past. If he had a big secret hidden, shouldn't she know? They were sleeping together and starting a relationship.

A small Chinese vase stood on the side table in the hall.

She picked up the vase and found nothing underneath. Flipping the vase upside down, she hoped a key fell out. It didn't. She looked around the hall searching for some other hiding place.

Her gaze went up, noting the door transom. Getting on her tiptoes, she stretched her arm toward the thin top ledge. She ran her fingers across the top.

A metal tinkling clinked. A small object hit the floor. A small key.

Breath whooshed out of her chest. She bent down and picked up the key, and contemplated it sitting in her palm. Her body swayed. Should she or shouldn't she? Before she could change her mind, she inserted the key in the lock and swung open the door.

The brightness hit her first. She blinked to adjust to the light. The same floor-to-ceiling windows combined with a roof of glass. More than a skylight, it was an opening to the sky.

The room had no furniture. Only easels and canvases facing the walls, and a drop cloth covering the floor. The easels held covered canvases, and next to them, a stool or two. Some of the stools were empty, and others held wooden boxes holding a multitude of paint containers. And palettes. Some on the stools or boxes, others on the floor.

Wonderment and shock and confusion charged through her body, giving her a shock. Who was the mysterious painter? It couldn't be Jackson. He was too straight and businesslike. And yet, she'd seen glimpses of light and color.

The light gleam in his eyes when he beheld her. The subtle colors hidden in his stoic personality.

Colors and interests he was beginning to show her.

She moved toward the stacked canvases leaning against the closest wall. Her stiff fingers sorted through the paintings. Landscapes and still-life and abstracts and photorealism. Different styles, as though the artist couldn't decide which style was preferred.

Her fingers fumbled when she recognized one of the paintings. The painting had been balanced on the sofa table behind the old couch her first time here. The artist had depicted the scenery outside the window with passion. She'd loved the colors and the depth of emotion, and had told Jackson she'd love to feature the work in the new interior design. He'd mumbled something about the painting being amateurish, and it had disappeared.

Disappeared into the artist's cavern.

She strolled farther into the room. Stopping at a covered canvas on an easel, she slid off the tarp. Vibrant purple screamed from the canvas. Rounded brushstrokes and black flecks. A deep, dark center with shadows of gray. She peered closer, trying to make out the image in the painted reflection. Gigantic violet eyes stared back.

Clutching her chest, she almost fainted. Her eyes. Those were her eyes reflected back at her. Eyes filled with desire and longing. Eyes painted with passion and talent. The piece confirmed what she knew in her heart.

Jackson was the painter.

Everything inside her vibrated, shaking up her preconceived notions. He'd presented himself one way his entire life. Recently, she'd seen deeper into his core, uncovered hints of another truth. The façade he presented to the world had cracked in front of her. And now, the pieces making up the man had settled into place.

Jackson was an artist. And he was good.

She studied the painting. He'd used a texturing technique to bring depth to the irises. A shiny, flat black ringed the pupils, before graduating into shades of gray. Even though the painting wasn't complete, she could tell it was of excellent quality. Could see the emotion reflected in the gaze.

Were her eyes really that expressive? Did Jackson see the longing and love for him? All the blood drained from her head and pooled in her heart, swelling to gigantic proportions. Her pulse beat loudly, booming in her chest.

She loved Jackson.

A real, grown-up type of love. Not the silly crush she'd had for his brother. Or the friendly-lust she'd held for Alejandro.

Real love.

The booming grew louder, echoing in her head. She slapped her palms to her cheeks, trying to shake herself out of the realization.

Had he seen the extent of her emotions? From this painting, apparently he did. Her entire body trembled. For her, things had progressed fast. She'd known she'd been falling for him since the incident with the dogs, because she'd learned he wasn't the man he pretended to be. He was special.

Picking up a paint brush, she studied the piece of art. The work revealed passion. Passion for the subject, her, or the painting itself?

"What the hell are you doing in here?" The deep, dark voice sliced through the atmosphere.

Jackson.

Her swollen heart dropped into her belly. Guilt churned, making her slightly ill. She clutched the paintbrush. Still dazed, she slowly turned toward the doorway.

His dark brows thundered over stormy gray eyes. His mouth pinched together, trying to hold in the anger. He didn't do a very good job. "I forbade you to come in this room."

"I'm not your servant." Her indignant response caused her dazedness to fade. The order hurt, because she believed they were beyond the client stage. It reminded her of how Alejandro treated *the help* at his *castillo*. He'd made her feel inferior, like she had in school as the housekeeper's daughter. She didn't feel inferior anymore, because Jackson had showed her she was her own person. "I'm sorry I came in, and yet I'm not."

He stomped forward and yanked the tarp, covering the painting she'd been studying.

"That's why you had a purple spot on you the other morning." She forced her trembling body to stand tough. He'd painted after they made love. "You're an artist."

Scowling, he glared. He snatched the brush out of her hands.

"A painter." She wanted him to know she knew, wondering why he'd felt the need to keep the secret. Especially from her.

"No." He firmed his lips and stood frozen. "I used to dabble."

She refused to let him dismiss his talent. "This isn't dabbling."

"It's an old hobby." He put his hand on her lower back and tried to usher her out of the room.

She spun out of his grip. "Old? You painted this the other night." Her hand waved at the canvas.

What did it mean when a man painted after making love? And why hadn't he shared? She thought she knew the real Jackson. Yet, she'd only touched the surface.

"For the first time in years." His low inflection had ragged edges of anger and shame, and possibly fear.

Fear of discovery?

How could they have a real, loving relationship if they didn't know everything about each other? Guilt butted up against justification, causing an emotional grinding. He should've told her he was an artist.

She removed the tarp from the canvas. "They're my eyes, aren't they?"

He grimaced with a half-smile. "Shows how good I am, if you can't immediately recognize your own eyes." The tease fell flat.

She grabbed both his shoulders, digging her fingers into him to get his attention "You're good. You're very good."

He moved out of her hold and stood by the open door, trying to escape. Trying to get her out of the room. His expression was a dark mask. "Your opinion."

Bravely, she stepped closer. Closer to the door and

closer to him. She refused to be intimidated by his anger. "My educated opinion."

"Biased opinion."

"Biased? How can you say that?" She thought about the paintings. "The paintings I found by the couch the first time I visited. Those were yours."

Nodding, he jerked his hand and pointed to the hallway, indicating she should step out of the room. She radiated with hurt. He wanted her out of his secrets.

"I told you those paintings were good. I didn't know they were yours. I didn't know you." Still didn't, if the work scattered around the room was anything to go by.

Her lungs pumped hard once, swirling the ache around. The discovery of his artistic sensibilities made her love him more. The sensitive man she'd come to know went even deeper. The man who appreciated her, appreciated art.

Her gaze linked with stormy gray orbs. She put her hands back on his upper arms trying to keep this connection. "You're really good."

The anger in his pupils swirled into a sexy smoldering. He glanced at her hands gripping his arms, and his gaze lifted to hers. His gray eyes lit with tiny flecks of black, hinting at sudden, smoldering desire. He wrapped his arms around her and shoved her body against his. His manhood rubbed against her, igniting her own desire.

"Show me how good." The suggestive voice had her insides flaming, but something in his tone sounded off.

He must be angry at her for breaking into his painting studio. And she understood why. What she didn't understand is why he didn't want to share this part of him. They were good together.

She ground against him, hinting how much she desired. Wanting to take him up on his suggestion. Wanting him. He'd painted her eyes with strong emotion. Surely, that meant he felt deeply for her? Certainty settled the doubts inside her. First, he painted her eyes, next her body. The paintings would prove what he felt about her, and she wanted to demonstrate how she felt about him.

Their first time together, she'd wanted to take control and he wouldn't let her. This time she refused to release the power. Her hands flew to his waistband, and she undid his belt and unsnapped his pants. Tugging down the pants and underwear, she lowered herself. She wanted to show him her passion. Her knees hit the splattered tarp protecting the floor. Her mouth positioned at cock level.

This specific part of his anatomy was beautiful. Long and smooth and large.

My, oh my. To please him and take control of his pleasure sent a shaft of heat through her body.

She wrapped her hands around his balls and stroked the hairy skin. Her hand massaged the area and went up to stroke his sleek cock. His body trembled beneath her hands. The display of this strong man weakening, had her own body reacting. Power and redemption surged through her veins. Liquid pooled at her core.

Licking her lips, she lowered her head. She wanted

him to be as turned on as her. She wanted him to want her the same way she wanted him. She wanted to indicate how much she cared without saying the words.

Kissing the tip of his penis, she ran her tongue along the top, tasting his rich taste. Her mouth widened and she went down. She sucked with her mouth. She laved with her tongue. She stroked with her hands.

"Emory." His hands dug into her short hair. His fingers massaged her scalp. Hard.

His cock grew.

She couldn't stop the smile curling on her lips, around *him*. He was under her domination. She might be the one on her knees, but she was bringing this man to his knees.

Sucking harder, she felt his body tense. He went up on his toes. His muscles strained.

"Emory." He sounded out of breath. He pulled on her hair trying to raise her head. Not a chance. "If you don't stop now, I won't be able to stop."

She didn't want him to stop. She wanted him to come. Wanted him to fly.

His muscles strained tighter. His hand gripped her hair harder. His fingers dug into her scalp. "Emory. Emory. Emory."

Each call of her name was a promising declaration. Satisfaction filled her spirit. The anger was gone, and they were going to be okay.

His body jerked and spasmed. "Emory!"

And he came.

Pulling her up into his arms, his head fell against

the top of hers. "Not fair. You didn't give me a chance."

"A chance at what," she purred.

"To please you." His lazy tone matched the lazy caress of his fingers on her bare arm.

She smirked. "You will." She wasn't done with him yet.

Together, they lay on the floor on the tarp covered with paint. His chest moved up and down in an even beat. Sweat shone on his face.

"Now." With a sudden urgency, he got to his knees. He quickly removed her jeans, panties, blouse, and bra.

The quick and masterful maneuver caused her pulse to quicken. She'd thought he'd been exhausted. She'd believed he'd need time to recover. Nope. He was fully erect.

He took both of her hands into his large one and held her arms above her head. "You're naked now. What should I do with you?"

His gaze blazed into her. The dominant expression had her lower lips throbbing. A simple look, and she was a goner. He made her feel beautiful and sexy and wanton.

And loved?

Her earlier thoughts about reading his emotions through his art returned. "Paint me. I want you to paint me naked."

Jackson's cock twitched, dangling close to Emory's body, knowing instinctually where it wanted to be. Which infuriated him. She'd broken into his private sanctum. She'd viewed his paintings. She'd broken his trust.

And then she'd gone down on him.

He tried to rebuild his anger, yet the only thing hard was his cock. Her actions had been conniving, like most people he associated with. He'd been fooled by her sweetness and light. By what he believed was her honesty. Why had he felt guilty about his plan to divert her from his brother?

Hell, he'd been thinking about confessing everything to her.

Why should he? If he couldn't trust her, why should he be honest with her? Why shouldn't he enjoy what she offered?

He had her hands pinned above her head. His naked body loomed over her naked body. "Paint you?"

"A portrait." Her body wiggled, bringing attention to her jiggling breasts. "A nude."

"That's not what you said." Time for payback.

Not the mean, scheming payback he employed in his business transactions. This was different. With Emory, everything was different.

He reached under the closest easel with his free hand, and grabbed a container of acrylic paint. She wanted to be painted, did she?

Her eyes widened and her expression grew wary. "What're you doing?"

"As requested, I'm going to paint you." He flipped open the paint cap and squeezed red onto her belly.

"Ah!" A slight scream combined with a giggle. Her legs came up trying to protect herself. "Is this safe?"

"It's acrylic paint. Completely safe."

Was he safe? Safe from her laughter and her love? Safe from a bleak future where she'd hate him? Probably not.

Not wanting to think about the future, he drizzled more paint on her stomach and her breasts. Those lovely, jiggling, distracting breasts. After setting down the paint, he used the flat of his palm to spread the red across her stomach. His hand massaged and stroked, contrasting the silkiness of her skin with the cool texture of the paint. The familiar scent intermingled with the smell of sex.

He used a finger to trace a heart on her skin.

Her snort interrupted. "That's your art? A five-year old can finger-paint."

He froze. She must be teasing and not talking about his real art. Right?

"Can a five-year-old do this?" He scooped his now-red hand around her breasts, and tweaked the tip.

She moaned and arched toward him. Lust combusted, setting off small blasts beneath his skin. He needed her.

His finger curved between her luscious mounds and went across her ribcage. Using a cross-hatching technique, he swished his fingers, imitating a brush erasing the heart, but not erasing the feelings in his own heart.

A warmth stole through him. Not the heat of lust. A warmth toward her, toward them. He wanted to please her, to make an impact. He wanted her to remember him and this moment.

His fingers brushed lower and she trembled. Palpitating each finger against her skin, he created a pattern of desire. She moaned and the moan hit his gut—a mating call only he could hear.

Swirling his fingers back up to her breasts, he didn't want to get paint in her most intimate of spots. That was for him and him alone. The possessiveness of the thought struck him and his fingers stalled. He didn't want anyone else touching her, being intimate with her.

"Jackson?" Her half question-half moan nearly caused him to collapse on top of her.

Not a bad idea.

Letting go of her trapped hands, he lowered himself on to her body. The paint oozed between them, creating a sensual experience. Relighting his fuse of lust, he moved his body up and down, creating tension. Stimulating, exciting tension.

His chest rubbed against her wet breasts. His midsection stroked against hers. His cock poked at her wet core. Sprinkles of anticipation shivered across his skin, building into frantic desire. He strained to stay in control, even after his earlier release he couldn't wait. He needed to be inside her.

He grabbed his pants and reached in his pocket for a condom. Being careful not to get paint on the latex, he rolled it on his penis. "Can I stroke inside you now?"

"Yes, yes, yes." The yearning in her voice took him closer to the edge.

Pausing at her entrance, he anticipated their coming together. Unable to wait, he sunk into her warmth and pumped, working toward their completeness. He wanted to please her and protect her and conquer her. He wanted to hold her and never let go.

But he knew that was impossible.

Chapter Seventeen

Emory melted when, after making love, Jackson picked her up off the floor and carried her to the shower. A shower she'd thought about being naked in with him. Another fantasy come true. He set her on the built-in bench as if she was a precious package, and gently used a wash cloth to wipe away the paint from her body. Deliciously spent from their lovemaking, she sagged against the marble wall and enjoyed each touch and caress.

Once she was clean and smelling of his crisp soap, he quickly rinsed himself off before getting to his knees. With the rain shower trickling down, he suckled at her feet, swirled his tongue around her ankles, and trailed kisses up her calf to her inner thigh. He was trying to please her.

Again.

Or make up for something. Or make her go crazy. Indelibly etching himself into her psyche. Her mind dazed, her thoughts wandered down a path of bliss. Together, with Jackson.

When his tongue flicked out and stroked her nub, her entire body went taut. Tingles shot from her core up her spine and alerted her brain.

"What're you doing?" Her mind hadn't wrapped around the idea their lovemaking wasn't complete, because they'd both come to a satisfied conclusion.

"I want you to orgasm. For me." His words steamed through her wet skin like the hot air in the bathroom surrounding them. "Would you enjoy that?" His tongue flicked out again.

She arched toward him, showing him how much she wanted. Her legs spread open. "Yessss."

His mouth settled on her lower lips, and pleasure flashed through her. His tongue circled and stroked and sucked, causing wave upon wave of sensation.

"Ahhh!" Every inch of her skin sparked and prickled and flamed. She was probably spouting steam. Her body was a mass of sexual nerves with the water coming down, and him *going down.*

One of his hands cupped her breast. "You taste so good."

Her stomach clenched. Pleasure exploded inside her, resembling her own internal fireworks. She felt so good. So ready. She wanted him to come with her. "I want you."

"This is for you." His lips moved against her clitoris as he spoke, triggering another onslaught of quivering.

She moaned, unable to control anything. Not her words or her body. Not her emotions. "Jackson, I—"

"That's the way, Emory." The way he said her name propelled tremors to form an earthquake.

A full-on seismic event.

Her entire body shook and rocked. Tremors undulated from her core, and she burst into a million pieces. A million pieces held together by his love.

Moonlight glinted off the glass skylights, casting light across the room. The light hit the wet canvas and traveled through the paint and reflected back to Jackson. The barely off-white color glowed.

Glowed like Emory's skin after making love.

On this very floor, with the paint squishing between their skin while they'd had sex. The canvas they laid on had the outline of their bodies connecting on canvas. Another piece of his art no one would ever see. The tarp painting would become his greatest unknown masterpiece.

While showering, he'd pleased her to make up for the way he'd been thinking. Her betrayal of breaking into his studio was nothing compared to the betrayal he had planned. After showering, he'd made love to her again, with desperation burning inside him. A desperation he understood because that would be the last time. He might have no honor and a black soul, still, he couldn't take advantage of the gift of her body again. They'd travel soon to Barcelona, and he'd only stay with her three days. Then, he'd leave her forever.

Sadness flowed in his bloodstream and changed into a river crashing over rapids of his own making. He had to be hard similar to a roaring river. He had to be resolute.

If she returned to Castle Ridge before the merger, and before Ryder and Shey were engaged, Jackson would force Emory out of the house. No way would his brother be interested in her once he knew the scope of their relationship.

His hand slipped on the canvas, and the skin-colored mixture of paint went outside the line.

He'd crossed the line. Several, actually.

His guilt wouldn't allow him to sleep. Dreams of what could be taunted. If he really was this person who wanted to see more of life, if he was willing to abandon the Webber deal, if he pursued Emory for real and not for business, could this dream become reality?

The wood brush handle snapped between his fingers. He wasn't that man. Not the man she believed in. He had obligations to the business and his family. He needed to make this deal, and when Emory discovered the truth, she'd hate him.

He wanted her, but he couldn't keep her. There'd be no future for them.

Tossing the broken brush to the floor, he studied the new painting he'd started. The nude exposed the backside of a petite woman whose head was turned to appear like a seductive whisper. Short, muscular legs that had gripped him around the waist. A luscious ass where he'd used a glazing technique to intensify the shadows and modulate the color. Slim waist leading to soft shoulders. Short, springy hair framing an angelic face. Vibrant, violet eyes swirling with desire.

Emory.

She'd requested the nude in a tease. The compulsion to paint it for her, and for his own pleasure, had driven him out of their warm bed. Something he'd pull out in the dark days he knew would come when he stomped on her heart.

The stage was set for the final act.

Jackson had cleared his calendar for a few days, and two first class tickets to Barcelona sat on his desk. Those tickets had no return date to prove the truth of the lie. A third ticket was in his desk drawer.

He'd left Emory sleeping this morning, after their long and amazing night together. She would be meeting him for lunch at his office any minute. He'd thought of more romantic places for his proposal, and had rejected them because this was a business deal.

Nothing more.

A ragged breath escaped from his lungs, and his chest pounded at a rapid pace. Only because he was sealing the best fake-deal ever. The deal for her heart, and it had to go off without a hitch. She had to believe the proposal was real. Had to believe him.

The sad part was, he believed him, too. Which was bad.

This was just business, he kept telling himself.

She believed she loved him, she'd go away with him. What was love, anyway?

The rapid beating of the heart when that special someone was near? The way the soul lit up in the lover's presence. The way making love was sweeter.

He broke out in a cold sweat. His body slumped,

leaning against the edge of his desk. The skyline of Denver was sharp lines and angles. So different from what they'd see in Barcelona.

"Is there anything else you need me to take care of, before you leave on your trip?" Barbara's disapproval rang in her voice.

Ignoring her tone, he thought about the actual question. He wanted Emory to be comfortable when he abandoned her. "You leased the furnished apartment?"

"Yes."

"What about setting up the grocery delivery service for three months?" He didn't want her starving as well as sad.

"You'll only be in Barcelona a few days." His assistant knew about the separate return ticket he'd purchased.

"Emory will be there for at least three months." Possibly longer.

When he broke things off with her, he planned to tell her it was best if she didn't return to Castle Ridge for a few months, that she couldn't live in his house. As a parting gift, he'd pay for an apartment in Barcelona, and whatever else she needed. It was the least he could do.

She could come back in the fall and work on Dani and Luke's bed and breakfast, restart her business, and be with her mom. Jackson would only delay her plans by a few months. Maybe he'd be ready to face her by then, too.

His assistant tapped on the tablet. "I'll change the grocery service."

"And what about the bank transfer?" His stomach roiled. He'd offered her money once before, and she'd rejected it. Except he didn't want her to be destitute, and the money would come with the condition she stay in Spain.

"Done." His assistant's disapproval rang higher. Her protruding, pinched mouth showed she was gathering courage to speak her mind. "Is this really necessary?"

He knew his assistant well. His mind tossed in a frenzy, and his entire midsection churned. His emotions changed with every second the moment drew closer. Ripping off his tie, he wasn't sure what was necessary any longer. He wanted, needed, Emory to be happy. To survive the deep cut he'd make with his fake romantic pursuit.

The urge to throw the last part of his scheme in the trash pulsed in his fingers and swelled in his chest. He'd promised to take care of the Emory issue. Except, could he take care of the issue by keeping her close by his side? Why did he have to send her away and break her heart?

Because if he didn't break her heart in Barcelona, he'd do it eventually. He wasn't the man she thought he was. He didn't plan to take vacations and see the world. Going back to school with his experience and at his age would be ridiculous. Since finishing the nude painting of Emory, he knew he would never paint again.

Because while painting, he'd realized he was falling under her spell. If he kept her by his side and continued this charade, it wouldn't be a charade any longer. And she'd find out the truth about him. That he couldn't live up to her expectations.

His life was his business, and taking care of Ryder and Lexi. And now Emory. Jackson would take care of her from a distance. If she was nearby, he'd only be distracted.

He'd make sure she was able to move on with her life, move on to other men, and possibly find a husband. His heart cracked, and he was physically ill. His blood changed to an envious green, and the urge to halt the next step in his ploy slammed into him.

No. He needed to end this charade sooner rather than later. "Of course, it is necessary."

"It seems…" His assistant tapped her finger against the tablet. "…sick, even for your standards."

Everything inside hardened. "It's business."

"They didn't teach you this in business school."

The joke was on his assistant, because he'd never graduated from business school.

"Hello, Jackson. Barbara." Emory knocked on the open office door and stepped inside, wearing a bright, beautiful, blazing smile, which caused desire to leap inside him.

Dread knocked the desire down.

Staring, he wanted to remember the smile. Her violet eyes lightened to lavender when they connected with his. Her cheeks had a warm glow about them, a glow displaying her love.

For him.

A lump lodged in his throat. He'd tricked her into loving him.

"Hello, Emory." His tight-lipped assistant reeled and headed toward the door. "I'll take care of those final details for you."

His assistant's disapproval settled in his bones. Another blow to bear for the sake of Croft Industries.

"Everything all right?" Emory slid her arms around his neck and kissed him on the mouth. She wore a soft sweater he wanted to continue to caress. And then remove to caress her skin, instead.

Her lips stayed smiling while she kissed. The scorch from her mouth and her emotions sent a heat wave through his body. Of lust and shame. He clung to her mouth, wanting the kiss to go on forever, so he didn't need to pull the last trick out of his nasty bag of deception.

She leaned away and quirked her head. "Everything okay?"

"Fine. Everything's fine." Plastering a smile on his face, he knew he needed to get this over with, or his mask would slip. He stepped back, letting his arms fall. "Honestly, I've got a surprise for you."

The word surprise knifed through him, as if this was a happy surprise, and not a Trojan horse. How would he be able to keep up the pretense for the few days he'd be in Barcelona, without telling her the ugly truth?

"A surprise? How wonderful." The questioning expression was gone, replaced by a grin. She kissed him again.

"We talked about going on a trip." That was truth. If he kept this short, maybe he wouldn't lie too frequently.

Except being with her was a lie. He was a lie.

"A vacation? You're really going?" Her disbelief was palpable.

Maybe she knew him better than he thought. Maybe she'd already seen through his lies.

"Say you'll come with me." He gripped her upper arms and focused, willing her to do what he commanded. "Say yes."

"When?"

"Tomorrow." He had to get her out of the way now. Before Ryder was one hundred percent better and figured everything out. Before Jackson lost his own mind and heart in the deal. "Say you'll go. Say you'll fly with me."

Standing on her tiptoes, she wrapped her arms around his neck. She whispered in his ear. "Where? Where are we going to fly?"

The tickle of her breath and the longing in her voice reminded him of when they'd discussed flying before. The first time they'd made sweet love. His blood ignited, rushing to his cock. He wanted her. Wanted her now. But, he'd already decided they wouldn't make love again. Not now. Not in Spain.

"To Barcelona."

"I love Barcelona." Her joy was a song. Her gaze lit up, and she beamed. "I can show you the things we talked about. You're going to love the city."

Like he loved her.

His body numbed. He stopped breathing. His brain wouldn't function because his heart had taken control. Squeezing his eyelids tight, he fought the realization. Love? His head spun, and his chest overflowed with emotions. While he'd been tricking her into falling for him, he'd fallen for her. He was in love with Emory.

It wasn't lust and desire. It wasn't loneliness. It was love.

Real love. First love. Forever love.

Stumbling away from her, he opened his eyes.

She stood before him. Her image glimmered in the fluorescent office lighting. Her chin tilted in that endearing way. Her orbs glowed with a knowing, as if she'd realized all along what a fool he was. Her dark hair highlighted her face like a halo. Similar to how he'd painted her.

"I never really thought you'd take a vacation. And with me." Dancing to the desk, she picked up her plane ticket. "You've made me deliriously happy."

Her happiness shot holes through his soul. He'd made her happy in this moment, knowing he'd break her heart later. He was a terrible person. His evilness was blatant, laid out before him in a sinister plan. The reason why she'd never really love him. The real him. The monster behind the mask.

Cracks formed in the mask. The old Jackson leaked through. Not enough to be worthy of her, but enough to stop the madness.

"No!" He grabbed her shoulders and shook her. The cracks in his monster mask widened and baked with the painful realization. The cold monster was melting. She'd done this to him. Made him see more than the world around them. She'd made him see how true happiness looked.

"Yes, you have." Happy tears streamed, apparently from some sort of epiphany. A misconstrued epiphany. "I can't believe this is happening. I mean, I thought I loved Ryder, but I didn't. It had only been a silly crush. And then you hired me, and showed me your world, and your paintings, and I fell in love. Fell in love with you."

Her confession of love sent a shard of torture through his body. He trembled, and the heart he'd never believed he had shattered. He couldn't do this to her. She didn't love him because she didn't know the real him. He couldn't lead her on any longer.

"No. You don't love me." His voice sounded ragged and raw, resembling how he felt on the inside. He yanked his hands off her shoulders, not wanting to touch something so precious.

She quirked her head again. The tears dried. "Jackson?"

"I can't do this." Tears burned in his own eyes. The agony of what he planned to admit ripped his soul. He couldn't go through with it. He needed to break her heart now. "It was a trick. A lie. A billionaire's ploy to get you away from Ryder."

Chapter Eighteen

Emory heard Jackson.

She heard him. She didn't believe him. He loved her. She could see it in his eyes, sense it in his touch, feel it when they made love.

Desperation and confusion clawed at her lungs, each emotion fighting for a breath. "Jackson. I don't understand."

His gray gaze morphed to cold slate, chilling her skin. His mouth pinched into an ugly, flat line. His brows arched in a menacing shape. He held his body in a stiff pose, not wanting to get near. So different from only seconds ago.

"You got in the way of the merger with Webber Resorts." His hard, matter-of-fact tone knocked into her. "I sent myself to deal with you."

The confusion smashed to dust, leaving her throat dry. The desperation scratched and flared, causing every muscle and tendon to ache. Her chest shredded, and she wanted to collapse to the ground. Instead, she straightened and took stock of him.

"What about Barcelona? You were going to go to Barcelona with me." The desperation traveled to her voice. She recognized the edge, almost shifting into hysteria. Trying to control her deteriorating emotions, she couldn't believe this was happening. He loved her. She knew it to the depths of her being.

"For a few days. To get you out of the way."

She backed away from his statement. Maybe if she ignored him, ignored the cold glint in his gaze, he'd reveal the truth. She'd seen the plane tickets. One in her name and one in his. "The plane tickets have no return date."

Because he wanted to be on a trip with her for a long time.

The coldness expressed in his hard chin and hard lips. Lips she'd kissed and worshipped. "I've got another ticket. A return ticket. In three days."

Three days?

He yanked another airline ticket out of his desk, displaying the hard evidence. Proof he spoke truth. Even so, did he sense the same truth?

She blinked away the sudden tears. How could the man she loved treat her this way? She'd dreamed of a future. Now, her thoughts ran as fast as her pulse. Confused, wild, simmering with anger. How could he be false to her?

"So everything between us was a lie?" She needed him to state the bald facts. "The trip. The dating? The making love?" The simmering started to boil, agitating with her anger and her fury and her hurt and her pain. She'd been a fool. Believed his lies from his lips and his caresses. "The interior decorating?"

"Not the interior decorating."

"Ha." She pointed a finger, wishing she could stab him. "You didn't need your penthouse decorated, you were trying to get me out of the house in Castle Ridge. *Away* from Ryder."

And she'd fallen for it. Fallen for him. Or the him she believed him to be. Where was the artist? The lost soul? The man she saw underneath the façade?

His gaze flickered, and she knew she'd hit on the truth. "It was only business."

"You blame everything on business. Sometimes, you have to take responsibility for yourself and your actions." Hysteria whipped around in her head and her chest and her gut. He couldn't place the blame on his stupid company, and she was tired of hearing the same excuse. "So you didn't get your college degree. Do it now. So you didn't have a choice for your career. Make a choice now. So you don't have time to see the world and take a vacation." She struggled to take a breath. "Do it now."

The fury boiled over and out with her words, leaving her depleted and lost. He was the guy she'd come to know, she was sure of it. But he wasn't sure. He didn't recognize himself.

"You could still come to Barcelona with me." She'd help him find his true self.

She knew he loved her, even if they had many things to figure out. They'd make it work. This might've begun as a business tactic. It didn't have to end that way. In the process of his detestable actions, they'd found each other.

Except not if he couldn't recognize himself. Understand who he was beneath the mean business persona. Know his own soul.

His head moved back and forth in a slow shake. He wouldn't even look at her. He was building a wall between them. She could feel the hardness form in the air as if steel surrounded him and his heart. "Impossible. I have a company to run and a merger to manage."

And that's when she knew she'd lost him.

Lost him to this fake Jackson. Or maybe he'd played the role for so long, he'd truly become the ruthless businessman. Which was too bad, because who she believed was the real Jackson was worth fighting for. This shell of a man was not.

Her shoulders slumped, and her energy slowed. The anger faded, to be replaced with sorrow. Sorrow for him. Firming her spine, she refused to show this shell of a man weakness. She would maintain her dignity. "What other things was your assistant going to take care of?"

Redness stole up his cheeks. "An apartment, groceries, money transfer."

"I don't need anything from you." *Except you.*

Betrayal stabbed in a physical wound. Betrayal of her, and also of his true self. Betrayal of what they could've had together, if only he could search deep into his soul.

Wheeling away from him, she picked up the ticket with her name on it. She clenched the thin paper between her fingers, knowing her nerves were just as thin. Blowing out puffs of air, she needed to stay calm.

His hands raised and dropped in a helpless gesture. "I want to take care of you."

Her laugh sounded brittle, breakable, snappable by a thin thread. The lie he spoke was a joke. He'd never wanted to take care of her. It had always been about what was best for the business. Not her. And not him either.

His loss.

"And I wanted to take care of you. The real you." Her voice cracked. "You would've been happy in Barcelona on vacation. And, with me forever."

"You're back." Ryder leaned against the kitchen counter, reading a financial newspaper. The recycling bin sat on top of the counter, with other business papers and magazines.

Emory sniffled and tried to hide the redness of her cheeks. After making a couple of logistical calls, she'd cried on the long drive to Castle Ridge. She'd had to pull over several times, thought about finding a hotel room so she could hide in an anonymous bed and cry herself to sleep, but she had to pack. She'd stopped at a rest stop to wash her face and reapply her make-up, not wanting her mom to see her upset.

Ryder set down the newspaper and studied her.

Bittersweetness swept through her. Her crush on him had been so innocent and simple. Nothing like the roiling stew of emotions churning and slashing inside her now. "Home only for the night."

Except this wasn't home, and never would be again.

"Where are you going?" He slid off the counter slowly, sensing her upset.

She forced a grin, even while tears pooled in her eyes. "Barcelona. I have a plane ticket."

He nodded. "Is Jackson going with you?"

The name, *his name*, assaulted her calm exterior, and she almost gave in to the tears. She sucked in a long, slow breath trying to control her emotions. "No. He has a previous engagement."

Ryder blanched and took a step back. "Engagement."

A hysterical giggle escaped. He must be allergic to the word. Even if her life was a disaster, maybe she could help him. "I ran into Shey on Friday."

His gray gaze flickered with interest.

"I told her the same thing I'm going to tell you." With her current situation, giving love advice was stupid. And yet, she believed she understood what both Ryder and Shey were going through. "Go after what you want. Don't let expectations or outside pressure get in your way."

Even though Jackson had caved to the pressure, didn't mean Ryder should.

Stepping up to him, Emory bussed him on the cheek before heading out of the kitchen, toward her mother's suite of rooms. The house was dark and quiet. She preferred it that way. It matched the dark and empty thoughts in her head. Opening the door to the suite, she stopped when she saw the small light.

Her mom sat in the corner, reading a romance novel.

Another hysterical-ironic giggle escaped.

"What's wrong?" Her mother slapped the book down and stood.

She'd never told her mother about her relationship with Jackson, even so the woman's intuition was accurate. Mom knew something was going on.

"Alejandro offered me a job and I'm going to take it." Emory controlled her quivering lips. One of the people she'd called before leaving Denver, to ask if his offer was still available.

"In Barcelona?" The surprised tone said her mother knew something was wrong.

"Yes." The change would be good. Nothing to remind her of Jackson or their love. She'd be in control of the entire design aspect of his *castillo*. She'd be in charge. Because clearly, she wasn't in charge of her life.

"What about Jackson's penthouse interior decorating?" Her mother's examination made her fidget.

She couldn't talk about her love life with her mother. What a fool she'd been. How she'd believed Jackson loved her, and wanted to grow and change. "Everything is picked out and ordered for the penthouse project. I can oversee everything else from Spain."

And she'd use photos of his penthouse in her portfolio, because it would help her business. And be a constant reminder of his betrayal. Her skin went cold and clammy. Business was more important than her emotions. Her heart pinched, denying the claim. Now, she sounded like Jackson.

"What about Dani and Luke's bed and breakfast?" The intent expression on her mother's face told Emory she wasn't going to let her flounce out of the room, or out of the country, without an explanation. "Your meeting went well."

"Yes, it did." She quickly calculated excuses. "They don't need me to start until late summer. I'll be back."

She'd come back to Castle Ridge and start her business as planned, only a few months delayed. With Alejandro's project, she'd have a bigger budget, she'd have the penthouse project complete, and she'd have one current project. Better than starting from scratch.

And living and working in Barcelona would give her time to heal her wounds.

Her mother's brows furrowed. "I thought you didn't want anything to do with Alejandro?"

"That was before…" Shuddering, she reminded herself of her plans. "Before Alejandro gave me full authority for his entire *castillo*."

"What about your relationship with him?

"Alejandro doesn't want to date me."

Nobody did.

Jackson spent the night in his office. Not his penthouse. Too many memories. His fingers had itched to put his emotions on canvas, except he didn't deserve even that relief. He'd been an ass to Emory.

And not only last night.

He never should've started this evil game.

Barbara strolled into the office. "Good morning, Jackson. Shouldn't you be packing?"

"Plans changed. I need you to get in contact with Victoria Croft." Jackson grabbed the remaining tickets. He didn't want to think of what those changing plans did to his to-do list. The egos he'd have to soothe, another person he'd have to hurt. "And take this first-class ticket and change it to my brother's name."

His heart, a heart he realized he actually possessed when he set Emory free, seized up and throttled, ricocheting torment around his chest.

Knowing it was a long shot, he had to convince Ryder to go to Barcelona. Even if only to keep Emory company. Jackson didn't want her traveling alone when she was upset. And then, he'd have to break the news to Shey.

"Jackson." His brother stomped into the room wearing business-casual clothes. He didn't even know his brother owned business casual, and must not enjoy wearing them, by the furious expression. "What the hell did you do?"

Picturing Ryder and Emory together seeing the sights of Spain made the pressure around Jackson's heart tighter like a python squeezing its prey.

"I'll let you two...talk." His assistant fled from the room and slammed the door.

He clapped his hands together. "Ryder. Great news." For him.

"How could you do this to Emory? You hurt her, and you kicked her out of the house." The glare shooting from Ryder's gaze proved he wasn't a little kid anymore. He was an adult. The hard expression resembled Jackson's, and threw him off-kilter.

Maybe he didn't need to protect his little brother anymore.

For one last time, he was going to make everything right. He'd get his brother to Spain to be with Emory, and he'd deal with the fallout with Webber Resorts. And Shey. "It was a business tactic that got out of hand."

"Business." His brother spat the word, making Jackson feel like slime.

"I'm going to fix this." It's what he did. "You need to go to Barcelona this afternoon with Emory. I'm changing the airline ticket. You can meet her at the airport."

"Emory doesn't want me. She wants you." The disgust on Ryder's face revealed he'd figured out everything. "God help her."

The python in Jackson's chest wrapped around his ribcage, making his bones crush. After everything he did, she couldn't want him. He wasn't worthy. She'd fallen for the sensitive artist, not him. She deserved more than Jackson or his brother. Ryder would make her happy for now, and heal her sorrow. Ryder would make her fall in love with him.

And if he didn't, he could keep her happy for a week or two in Spain. Keep her mind off what Jackson had done.

Claws raked his lungs. He needed to convince his brother to go to Barcelona. "My relationship with Emory was a ploy. I used my money and my charm to trick her. She's loved you since she was a kid. She's always loved you."

"You told me yourself that I love Shey." Ryder's intensity grew. He lurched forward resembling a warrior. "You said Shey was the best thing that ever happened to me."

"I was wrong." Jackson had been wrong about many things.

About his brother.

About Emory.

About himself.

"You're admitting you're wrong?" Ryder's incredulous expression changed to sly. His gaze narrowed, and a mischievous smirk appeared. "I think Emory's gotten into your head."

Jackson ignored the taunt. "You were attracted to Emory, and I ruined it. Go with her to Barcelona, and I guarantee you'll fall in love with her."

Like Jackson had.

His spirits plummeted down a cliff. He'd lost her. He'd lost himself. He'd lost.

"Why would she change her mind and be interested in the lowly Croft brother?" The evident hurt in his brother's tone demonstrated how his brother really felt.

Had he been the cause for making his brother feel inferior? When they'd been kids Ryder used to emulate him. He'd follow Jackson around the house, always wanting to know what he was doing. His little brother would study his textbooks, and always got great grades. The divorce had created a rift, each one hiding from their pain.

"You're not lowly. Just uncommitted."

Ryder's eyes gleamed in a *got you* stare. "I committed to Shey. You helped me pick out the ring."

"And you returned it."

"Because she broke up with me." He ran a hand through his long hair, clearly upset. "I wasn't going to propose to a woman who broke up with me."

"Maybe it was for the best." Jackson needed to convince his brother to go and win the woman *he* loved.

"How can you say that?" His brother strode toward the window and surveyed the Denver skyline.

"You have to understand." Hurrying to his brother's side, he grabbed Ryder's arm, forcing him to turn around. "I manipulated her. I confused her. You're what she wants. What she's always wanted."

The crack in Jackson's heart grew into a fissure the size of the Grand Canyon. Not that he'd ever seen the Grand Canyon. He pushed the thought aside. He wasn't a poor little rich kid, as a lot of people thought. He was his own man, and took responsibilities for his actions.

Look at how he'd driven a stake through Emory's love for him. Plus, it probably wasn't real love, because he'd manipulated her feelings, pretended to be someone he wasn't, told her the things she wanted to hear.

His brother's doubting face swam before him. He loved his brother and wanted him to be happy, too.

"She'll make you happy. I want you to make her happy." The plea sounded raw. He couldn't let Emory fly to Barcelona, upset and alone. She needed a friend, if nothing else.

The yearning to see her one more time tugged at him. He had to stand strong. He was doing what was best for her.

"What about Shey and the merger?" Ryder examined Jackson, as if he was an insect on a rug.

Watching, analyzing, assessing. Like he was the latest stock acquisition, and his brother could see deep inside him, as Emory did. The fissure fractured further, causing ravines of emptiness. He already missed her smile and her warmth. "I'll deal with the outcome."

"You'd blow a million dollars for this?" His brother's assessment continued.

Jackson had never noticed how shrewd Ryder had become. Adept at interpretation. Smart. His gaze narrowed and dissected.

The inspection sliced Jackson on the inside, a burning agony. His body slumped in dejection. He was going to lose the deal of a lifetime, and yet, it didn't matter. He'd already lost the love of his life.

"I see."

The meaning Ryder put into two words, stretching the vowels and consonants, had Jackson's insides straining and tensing. He felt exposed and vulnerable, as if his plans, his new plans, were about to fail.

"I had an emergency board teleconference this morning." His brother's matter-of-fact statement kicked him in the gut.

"You can't just call a board meeting." He didn't realize his brother even knew how to coordinate a board meeting.

"I own half of our family's stock. I have a seat on the board."

"You never sit on it."

"Because I never saw a need. You always took care

of everything." Ryder's eyebrows gathered in a fierce line. "Not anymore."

Good news. Ryder would take on some of the responsibility of running the company. Jackson could take things a bit easier. Maybe he'd find a little time to paint.

No. Painting would remind him of Emory.

His brother clasped his hand around his shoulder. "Jackson, I'm sorry. I'm taking the chair position on the board."

He wanted to stumble, yet he held his body completely still. Frozen in shock. Helping was one thing. Taking over the board something completely different. And wrong. He was the chairman of the board. He made the final decisions. "You can't do that."

"Article seven, paragraph five. I've discussed the issue with the other board members, and we've decided you're overworked and making bad judgement calls."

Each word punched him, and vibrated to his brain. He couldn't wrap his head around the meaning. "Bad judgement?"

"Look what you did to Emory."

He winced. A low blow.

Ryder dropped his hand. His mouth softened, and his gray eyes rounded with concern. "The board is willing to give you a leave of absence."

A leave of absence? The words tangled around Jackson's tongue. He'd been outmaneuvered and outplayed. "Where did you learn how to do this?"

"From you." His brother sounded proud to be

related to him, and he couldn't comprehend why. "And from my master's degree in business. As well as reading every financial report you've copied me on for the last several years."

He was proud of his brother, and maybe always trying to help him and cushioning his blows had held him back. "I didn't know."

"Of course you didn't." Ryder's smug smile said he wasn't offended. At least, not anymore. "You barely registered my existence."

"Not true." The sentiment rubbed Jackson's nerves. "I wanted to protect you from what I'd endured over the years."

"And now you'll have time to do what you want." His brother took a set of rolled-up papers out of his back pocket. "After you sign the legal documents giving me authority and a raise."

The crinkling legal documents crackled in his lungs. He struggled to breathe, watching his brother wave the roll of papers back and forth. He became dizzy. Freedom or exile? His sight glazed, and his thoughts ran in panicked circles. If he refused to sign the papers, his brother would believe he didn't trust him. Ryder would hate him and continue with his frivolous life. Jackson's life would be chained to his desk and the business.

"It's really your choice." Ryder held the documents out. "I won't force you. I'm only presenting another option. You need to do what's best for you."

Jackson took another shallow breath, continuing to contemplate the paperwork. His stomach coiled into a tight knot. Tension tugged every muscle in a different direction. This was his choice. His brother wouldn't railroad him out of a job. If he signed the papers, he could do whatever he wanted. Travel wherever in the world.

Barcelona.

The thought pounded.

Emory.

He snatched the papers and flattened them on his desk. A tiny light of hope flared. He'd been given a second chance at life. "I can't believe I'm doing this."

"Good decision." Ryder shoved a pen at him, wielding it like a sword. "And if you hate your time off, you can come back."

Jackson seized the pen. His brother wasn't completely uncaring. Neither was he. "What about the Webber deal?"

"I've already scheduled a meeting with George and Shey." Ryder was already a step ahead.

Jackson signed the documents with a flourish. An artistic flourish. His body was lighter. He could breathe easier. Easier than he had in a long time. "You need to know what our mother has been up to."

Another complication his brother would need to deal with. Not him.

"Nothing good, I'm sure." Ryder hadn't been taken in by Victoria Croft's sudden appearance. He winked at Jackson. "You can send me an email filling me in from the plane."

His shoulders dropped and any hope he'd had snuffed out. "I missed the plane." And the boat with Emory. "She'll never forgive me."

He felt as if his heart had been fed through a paper shredder. He'd driven a wedge so deep between them, he didn't know if the rift could ever be healed.

"Look at what you did to me." Ryder swung an arm around his shoulders. "Stole a girl I thought I wanted, and exposed me to shellfish."

A stunned shock went through Jackson, electrifying each and every nerve. "You knew?"

His brother twisted his lips in a sardonic grin. "Between the timing of the allergic reaction, the over-prescribing of medication, and something Shey said, I concluded it hadn't been an accident."

His brother had been talking to Shey more than he realized. "You must hate me."

"No. I forgive you." Ryder's familiar-relaxed expression returned. "That's what family does."

Their gazes connected. So alike, yet so different. Brotherly love swelled in Jackson's chest. He loved his brother, and knew Ryder would do a great job. Jackson wrapped both his arms around his brother's shoulders and brought him in for a hug. A deep, meaningful hug.

Pulling apart, his eyes burned. "Thanks."

"You're welcome." Ryder must think he was crazy, running after a woman in Europe.

Emory wasn't any woman, though. She was his woman. They were meant for each other. When he was with her he became a better person. He wanted to become that good man permanently.

"Sometimes you have to go for it." Ryder's smile said more than words, obviously keeping a secret.

Jackson glanced around his office one last time. He'd spent hours and hours working and plotting and making deals. Unhappy hours.

He wasn't going to miss it. "I should be on my way."

He knew he headed in the right direction. Emory's direction. He only hoped she'd take him back.

Chapter Nineteen

"Who was at the door?" Emory lifted her head from the sketchbook, the bright sun causing a glare on the paper. Sitting in Alejandro's garden was worth the eye strain. The Spanish heat helped warm her cold heart.

Colorful blooms from exotic flowers soothed. Butterflies flew past, and bees buzzed from flower to flower. The Olympic-length swimming pool stretched out before her in a cool invitation.

Alejandro handed her a glass of iced lemonade, and flopped on the lounge chair beside her. His long, slim frame was covered by a tiny swimsuit. "Salesman."

His gaze darted away, reminding her of when she'd caught him lying about his other women. It didn't matter. She wasn't dating Alejandro, she was working for him. What did she care who was knocking at his door?

She hadn't cared about a lot of things since returning to Barcelona a week ago. The sharp, ragged pain of hurt and betrayal had dulled into a numbing chill. She'd barely left his grand mansion, preferring to sit in the garden or the solarium and concentrate on her designs.

"What was he selling?"

"Nothing special." Alejandro relaxed in the chair in a languid pose. So different from…other men. More intense men, who had a million things to accomplish, who had to conquer, who had to trick a woman into falling in love. Who, beneath the tough exterior, were soft and soulful.

He watched her nervously. "You've been here for eight days. You're already working on my designs." He tapped the sketchbook, ruining her concentration. "Isn't it time you signed the contract?"

There was a part of her that had hoped Jackson would come to his senses and follow her to Spain. He'd hurt her, yet she believed he had loved her. If only he'd realize it himself. He'd tricked her into falling for him, yet she'd discovered new things about herself. He'd made her dig deeper into her goals for her business and her life.

Her eyes prickled, and sadness whispered inside. Or maybe he hadn't learned and grown. Maybe he loved Croft Industries more than her. Or maybe she was wrong, and the only thing Jackson loved was himself.

She peered at the contract laying on the small table between the chairs. "I can't commit to being an exclusive designer to you, Alejandro."

He chuckled. "You, saying that to me, is ironic."

She smirked realizing the truth of his observation. "I'm working on the Croft penthouse." Her heart stirred, mentioning the name. "And a bed and breakfast."

"Pfft. Small jobs."

"I plan to return to Castle Ridge to start my interior design business." After she healed.

She might run away to heal her wounds, but she wouldn't stay hidden. She wanted to live and work in Castle Ridge. After her internship, she'd researched the market, and knew she could be successful and expand into the Denver area.

"Why? When you can stay here." He waved at the colorful gardens. "Once you finish my *castillo*, you'll get multiple projects from my friends."

She wanted to design for more than large mansions. She enjoyed the variety between the bed and breakfast and penthouse. She wanted to plant roots and make real friends. She missed the scent of evergreens and the view of the snowcapped mountains. She missed the crisp, cold mornings. She missed her mother.

"I've committed, and I keep my commitments." She was firm. "I'm here. I'm working on your house." She held up the sketchbook. "And I will finish the Croft penthouse and start the bed and breakfast in the States."

No matter how much it hurt.

Standing, she flung the sketchbook back on the chair and straightened her skirt. "I'm going to walk in the garden for inspiration."

Orange trees surrounded her, wafting their fruitful scent into the air. She inhaled deeply, finding the fragrance relaxing and healing. Roses grew in abundance, and several statues were placed in spots along the path. She strolled here several times a day, trying to soothe her spirit.

A crunching caught her attention. The birds tweeting covered the sharp noise.

Moving closer toward the back of the garden, she watched a big bee land on a purple flower. The continuity of nature amazed. No matter what happened, the cycle of life continued.

"Emory." Her name drifted on a slight breeze. The deep voice reminded her of Jackson.

Maybe she'd had too much sun today. She put her hand to her forehead, and went to turn back toward the house. Surely, she was daydreaming.

"Emory!" Louder and more insistent. Just as deep.

She stopped and pivoted toward the wall growing with vines.

A man's leg was thrown across the top. The vines shook with the weight of a body.

Alarm bells rang in her head. She needed to call Alejandro's security. Someone was breaking into the walled garden. Before she had a chance to run, a man pulled his body onto the top of the wall. His gray gaze connected with hers.

Jackson.

Her lungs constricted painfully tight, causing her entire body to shiver. What was he doing here? And why was he climbing the back wall? Hope hovered, calming the shaking. How could she have hope when he'd rejected her, betrayed her?

"Emory." He straddled the wall, imitating a conqueror from ancient times. His gaze shot Cupid's arrows straight at her heart.

Dizziness overtook her, and she swayed. She grabbed the top of a wrought-iron bench. "Jackson."

His body started to teeter. Bending into a crouch, he jumped to the ground. Landing, his ankle gave, and he tilted into a bush. His pants were torn, and his shirt untucked. Sweat dripped from his forehead, mingling with the dirt.

"Jackson!" She rushed forward. "What're you doing...?" She perused the height of the twelve-foot wall. "Are you all right?"

"I thought I could fly." His sensuous tone belied his precarious position.

Remembering their teases while making love, she forced down the immediate lust throbbing in her body. "You could've been injured."

"I've had more serious wounds. Like my heart." The sweet words were a balm. He continued to stare.

Her spirits swooshed, sending hope fluttering. Similar to the flowers nearby, she bloomed inside with love and joy, but...she loved Jackson. *The real Jackson.* Not the façade he put on for the world. And the day she'd departed, he'd had the ruthless Jackson fully in place.

What mask did he wear today?

She firmed her back and didn't help him to his feet. "What're are you doing here? Why did you climb the wall?"

He struggled to stand, and brushed a few loose leaves from his clothes. A thin cut on his cheek bled. His appearance was a drastic change from the fully-put-together man she'd known. "I've been searching for you."

"Why didn't you ring the doorbell?"

He took a step closer. "I did."

The salesman Alejandro hadn't wanted to discuss. She'd need to have a talk with him. She didn't need a man protecting her. She could take care of herself.

"I've called your cell phone." Jackson's voice rang higher.

"I don't have international calling." She'd been using the house phone to talk to her mom.

"I've stalked Vizconde Alejandro's office." Jackson took another step toward her, leaving only a foot between them.

Heat emanated off his body. Familiar and potent warmth flashed through her. She wasn't nervous or intimidated. She and Jackson had been much closer before. Intimate. She stood her ground. "I work here at the *castillo*."

He leaned closer. "Are you a prisoner?"

The seriousness of the question and his concerned expression put a chink in her defenses and she laughed. "Don't be ridiculous."

She hadn't gone out much. Alejandro had invited her to parties and polo meets and other social gatherings. She hadn't wanted to join the festivities.

"The Vizconde said you weren't here. He lied." Jackson had lied plenty of times. Their entire relationship had been a lie.

"Alejandro is protecting me."

"From me." Jackson's eyebrows flattened in understanding.

"Yes." Her eyes burned, and she tried to control the tears. She hadn't fully recovered, which was evidenced by her fluctuating emotions. The ups and downs, and highs and lows. He couldn't come here and turn her life upside down again.

What did him coming here really mean? She'd let go of the dream of them being together to face reality of the past week alone. The hope of her romantic fantasy she'd tried to squash attempted to take flight again, because it lived and breathed in her psyche. Except this dream featured the Jackson she'd fallen in love with. Was this that man standing before her?

Words weren't good enough. He had to prove he'd changed and grown. Become a man with a heart, not a business automaton. A man who was interested in people and things.

She took a step back. "Why are you here?"

His slate gaze deepened, and his brows flattened into a serious line. His mouth opened slightly, except he didn't speak. His hand reached into his pants pocket and pulled out a small blue box.

An expensive ring box.

She sucked in a shaky breath.

He flipped open the lid to reveal a perfect ring, with a center diamond in a frame of intertwining strands of silver and sapphires. "For you."

Jackson's hand started steady, but began trembling as he waited. And waited. He hated the show of weakness. Surely, Emory would say yes.

He'd flown to Barcelona the day after her, and moved into the apartment he'd rented. He had no idea where she was staying. He'd spent the week searching for her, even hiring a private detective. The detective had found Vizconde Alejandro, and Jackson had to believe the man had helped her hide.

Mrs. Barrington had assured him Emory was okay and told him to leave her alone.

He couldn't leave her alone. He loved her. He'd left Croft Industries to be with her, proof he was willing to change. With her help. He needed her help. He needed her.

His lungs screamed for air. Even oxygen wouldn't help if she said no.

Between searching for her, he'd spent his days wandering the streets, seeing the sights she'd mentioned, and painting. He'd thought about their future together.

And it all came down to Emory's response.

His pulse pounded, crashing against his skin. He hadn't actually asked her anything yet. She'd understand by the ring.

Her skin was paler and the glow he remembered was missing. The violet of her eyes wasn't as sharp. And her ever-present smile hadn't made an appearance. Her furrowed brow alluded to her racing mind.

His stomach churned. Dropping the ring box back into his pocket, he grabbed her hands and stood. "I'm sorry for what I did to you. The ploy was wrong, and the entire scheme exploded in my face."

It had. He'd fallen for her, and quite possibly, she'd fallen out of love with him. His ribcage tightened, poking his internal organs with sharp jabs of knowing he'd done wrong. He had to continue explaining.

"That day in my office, I knew I couldn't go through with it because..." He squeezed her hands tighter, and willed her gaze to connect with his. No matter the outcome he needed to tell her. "Because I love you."

Her eyes shimmered. "You lied to me from the beginning."

"No. I lied to myself." The bald truth sliced through him. When he'd laughed with her or kissed her or made love to her, he'd pretended it was part of the ploy.

"Our entire relationship was based on a falsehood." She slipped her hands from his, and tucked them beneath her arms in a cross-armed position. A defensive position.

"Without it we never would've gotten together." He had to convince her to give him a chance to prove himself worthy.

"We're not together. Never truly were." Her tortured cry mauled his hope.

Was he too late? Had he caused too much damage?

"We were together. I might've been lying to myself, but my heart knew how I felt. I loved you. Still love you." He had to make her understand. This was the most important negotiation in his life, and it had nothing to do with business. "I loved you so much I tried to send Ryder to be with you. So he could take care of you. Make you happy because I knew I never could."

"Ryder could never make me happy." Her angst ripped at Jackson.

"I know that now. Then, I wasn't thinking straight. I knew the anguish I was going through and figured you'd be feeling the same. Worse because I betrayed you." His heart squeezed in a painful fist. He laid himself and his emotions out there, exposing himself to her. For her.

"You hurt me."

"I know, and I'm sorry."

"You can't come here and say you're sorry and expect me to fall at your feet." She whirled and paced a few paces away. "Sorry isn't good enough."

Shock reverberated through his body. He went hot and then cold and then frozen. A numbness traveled from his head to his toes as he took in what she said. He'd lost her.

He didn't know what to say to make it up to her. He'd never been in this position with someone who was the other half of his soul. He had no plan of action, and nothing left to bargain.

Grabbing her shoulder, he faced her toward him. "I know you have feelings for me. What can I do to win your love?"

Emory's heart wept.

She did have feelings for Jackson. She loved him. Did he love and believe in his true self, or was this another trick to get her to believe him?

Doubts and hopes crashed like waves on a shore, undulating inside her and making her sick. She wanted a future with him, except what if the cutthroat Jackson returned? She balanced on a thin line. She loved him but did she trust him? Trust this man who so easily fooled her into seeing what she wanted to see?

"Which man is asking?" Her throat scraped raw from holding in the tears. "The man who played me for a fool, or the man who paints in the night, who expresses his emotions, who is willing to step out of his business suit and appreciate life?"

"The man I am when I'm with you." There was no hesitation or doubt. Honest gray eyes held her gaze steady. "A better man."

Hope fought doubt, creating an internal war. She wanted to believe him. "How do I know you really are that man?"

"I can prove it." His expression animated, with a spark in his pupils and a determined angle to his chin. "I left Croft Industries in Ryder's hands the day I flew to Spain."

She arched one eyebrow. "You haven't checked in?"

His head dipped. "Ryder has had a few questions, though mostly he's running the company on his own."

She believed him. There was something in his voice and his expression. Hope escalated winning the battle. "What have you been doing for the last week?"

"Looking for you, wandering around the streets of Barcelona." His lips lifted in the soft, persuasive smile she loved. "I went to the *Parc Guell* you talked about so much."

Her breath caught in her throat. He had listened to her, not pretended to hear.

"I climbed the steps of *La Sagrada Familia*. I ate tapas and took siestas." He waved his hand in a brushstroke gesture. "I painted." Bewilderment and satisfaction mixed through the tone of his speech.

He'd been discovering himself, discovering life. She was happy for him.

He took hold of her hand again, holding it gently. "I soul-searched. A lot."

Hope didn't escalate and build, it sprung like a fountain. "What did you find?"

"Me." Again, the certainty in his tone and expression. His gaze held no tricks. His smile was true. "I found I love seeing new places and experiencing new things. I love painting and never want to stop, even if it's a hobby. I want to go back to school and finish my degree."

The fountain overflowed. She'd wanted him to find himself, and going back to get his degree was part of the process. "That's what I want for you. I want you to do what you love, and enjoy life."

He gripped her hand tighter and his lips firmed with intensity. "I can't enjoy life without you."

His intensity struck in her chest. The weeping changed to rejoicing. The fountain turned warm and colorful and filled with light. She leaned toward him, needing his lips on hers. Everything wasn't settled. They had so much to discuss. But they loved each other, and she believed they had a future.

The touch of his lips launched celebratory fireworks inside her body. Her mouth melted against his, and he wrapped his arms around her in slow motion, as if afraid of being rejected. She tilted into his body, loving the familiar heat. She wanted the kiss, this kiss, to never end, because she knew there was more needing to be repaired.

"I love you, Emory." His normally-hard voice went

quiet. His slate eyes softened. He took the ring box out of his pocket, and flipped open the lid. "I want to spend the rest of my life with you."

This was the moment she'd dreamed about. She was ready to commit to forever. Doubt skirmished with her joy, because something held her back. "I love you, Jackson. Love you with all my heart...but—"

"There's that but again." His humorous response tinged with worry.

She needed to be sure.

"I've lived life. Finished college, lived in Spain to do my internship." She'd committed to finishing the *castillo*. "I know what I want. To start my business, to live in Castle Ridge, to be with you."

"Good to hear." His lips quivered.

"You've accomplished so much in the business world, yet you haven't experienced much of anything else. I want you to be sure about what you want to do with your life. About us. About everything." She couldn't stop herself from running a hand down his cheek. "You need to do those things."

"I want to do those things with you." The finality didn't put her off. Neither did the shininess of his gaze, or the way his words stumbled.

A new kind of torment walloped in her chest. Sadness. Wistfulness. She would love to be with him while he found himself, except this was something he needed to do alone. "I've committed to finishing Alejandro's home."

Jackson's nose scrunched in distaste. "That man who tried to keep you away from me."

"And you need to spend time on your own." A

purple butterfly flew past them in the garden, and she remembered the saying about setting a butterfly free. "Go back to the States, get your degree, truly find yourself."

His body tensed. "What about us?"

"When you finish finding yourself, you'll find us."

Chapter Twenty

"Awarded a Bachelor of Science in Business Administration, and a Bachelor of Arts in Fine Arts, Jackson Croft."

The applause thundered in Jackson's ears, and boosted his pride. He'd done it. He'd attended the local university, and between the old credits that transferred and the full credit load he took during summer and fall, he'd graduated in six months. Six long months.

Between missing Emory, helping his brother learn the ropes managing Croft Industries without getting too involved, his mother's continuing interference in the merger with Webber Resorts, and Ryder's evolving relationship with Shey, it was a wonder how Jackson graduated at all. But that was another story.

He walked across the stage, shook the dean's hand, and gripped the two gold diplomas. The diplomas were worth as much as gold. They were proof he'd found himself.

He scanned the audience at the ceremony, spotting

Ryder, Lexi, Dax, and Mrs. Barrington. His scanning stopped at a woman with short, dark curls. Emory, his magical fairy. His accomplishments slid into place beside the space he held for her in his heart. He'd barely seen her in six months. They'd talked and video chatted, and now she'd finished decorating the *castillo* and had flown in this morning for good.

She seemed to clap the loudest. His personal cheering section, always boosting him higher, pushing him farther, making him better. She sat straight and her gaze followed him. He couldn't wait to hold her in his arms.

Their long-distance relationship had been tough. She'd worked long hours to get the *castillo* done. He'd been studying and painting. The time difference had interfered with communication. In spite of the difficulties, they'd both grown stronger, and their love had cemented into the foreverness people deeply in love understood.

The rest of the ceremony passed in a haze. The double major had started as an art minor to fulfill the business requirements, and had become a passion. He'd actually sold a few of his paintings with the help of a local agent. And he planned to get involved in the local art scene. Finance a gallery, or maybe open one of his own. He'd continue his position on the board at Croft Industries, but Ryder was doing a great job, and it was his turn to man the helm. Jackson only had one destination in mind: Emory's arms.

At the end of the ceremony, he jumped off the stage and into her embrace. The sensation of her arms centered him. Her body against his felt right. When their lips met everything around faded and it was perfect. Magical. He'd found himself and his home.

Because of Emory.

"Congratulations, Jackson!" Another quick kiss and tight hug, and he knew he'd never get enough of her. "You did it!"

"We did it!" He glowed from the inside. She'd made this possible. He wouldn't have been brave enough to leave his position at Croft Industries, to go back to college, to paint. She'd given that gift to him. The gift of himself. "I couldn't have done any of this without knowing you were there waiting for me."

Her eyes gleamed with lavender luster. Her cheeks shone with the light of happiness. And her radiant smile blazed with joy. He wanted to paint her looking like this.

"I love you, Emory. My life has revolved full circle, and I've realized what's important. And the most important thing is you." He reached beneath the graduation gown and pulled out the same ring box he'd held in trembling hands in Barcelona. This time his hands were sure.

"I love you, Jackson." Her smile bloomed expressing her happiness. "The real you. The you that combines business with art. That works hard, and also stops to appreciate life. The you that's proved who you are, and who you want to become."

He dropped to his knee and held the ring box up high. "Will you make me even more complete by marrying me?"

She paused for a beat, but he saw the twinkle of a tease in her gaze. "Yes!"

Jumping to his feet, he slipped the ring on her finger, and sealed the deal with a kiss. The best deal he'd made in his entire life.

*Read on for excerpts from other books
in the Castle Ridge series.*

Dear Reader,

Thanks so much for reading *The Billionaire's Ploy*! If you enjoyed the book, please consider leaving a review at your place of purchase. Word of mouth is crucial for any author to succeed so she can continue bringing you more stories you love.

And don't forget to join my newsletter for a free book, the latest news, and contests! You can join at www.allieburton.com.

Allie

The Heartbreak Contract
A Castle Ridge Small Town Romance, Book 6

by ALLIE BURTON

Love on the dotted line.

Self-made sports and entertainment agent Vivienne Tucker knows no one in the frozen town of Castle Ridge is going to melt her heart. No one can. She's been on her own for too long and while her skin might appear soft, she's as tough as nails.

Paul Bradford is a devoted family man to his younger siblings, whose heart and life belong to the town he grew up in. He's not used to taking time for himself or relationships, but after an anonymous one-night stand, he can't forget the ice queen who heated at his touch and ignited a passion he thought he'd lost. Until the next day when he spies her kissing someone else.

Vivienne never expected to see Paul again until she discovers he's the older brother of her newest client. An older brother who doesn't approve of her client's career choice. An older brother who stirs up desire she's tried so hard to forget.

When her client is involved in a possibly career-ending accident, Vivienne and Paul must put aside their differences and work together. But what if working together makes them both re-think the heartbreak contract they'd agreed upon?

COMING SOON IN THE CASTLE RIDGE SERIES!
The Marriage Merger
The Runaway Royal

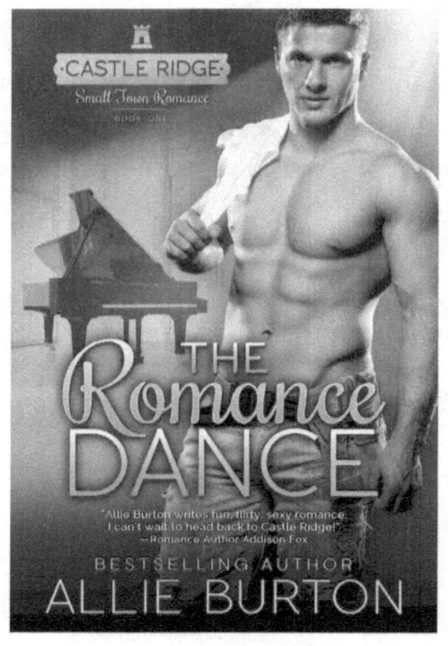

A slow sashay to desire.

After being abandoned by his fiancée and his fans because of a disfiguring accident, former classical pianist Reed O'Donnell returns home to hide. He's pieced his life back together becoming a landlord and remodel construction specialist, but shies away from a social life.

Ex-ballerina Quinn Petrov moved to Castle Ridge and invested her money to start a dance studio with plans to put down roots. She wants to get involved in the community to promote her business and make real friends, not the acquaintances she'd made in New York. When she meets her secretive and sexy landlord, she's intrigued but he always seems to be hiding behind a mask.

Reed can't stop the attraction he feels toward his new tenant, but she's beautiful and outgoing, while he is not. When his younger brother begs him to help impress Quinn, Reed can't say no. Using the musical language of love, he woos Quinn for his brother, but when his own mask slips will he reveal his secrets?

In this modern take of Cyrano de Bergerac meets Beauty and the Beast, Quinn and Reed dance their way into each other's hearts.

EXCERPT:

Quinn lay on her back and scooted farther under the sink. The warmth from her body slid along his skin, sending tingles of attraction to his loins. Her long leg lay next to his damaged one. Perfection next to destruction. Reed was a grotesque monster next to her doll-like body.

"What do you need me to do?" The soft lilt at the end of her question sent a shiver up his spine.

"Point the light at this joint." He handed her the flashlight and the beam swung around. He'd have to show her the joint. Reluctantly, he took her hand and guided it into position. Locked together, her delicate hand hid the scars on his. He didn't appear so hideous.

"Is this good?" Again, the sexy lilt playing to his lust.

"That's what she said." His brother Dax chimed in, and pounded on the top of the sink. "Ba-dum-bum."

Fever flushed through Reed at his brother's lame joke. He hadn't heard his brother come in. He dropped the wrench again.

The tool fell and smacked Quinn on the forehead.

"Ouch." She held her other hand at the spot.

"Oh, shit. I'm sorry. Are you okay?" He stroked her forehead where the angry bruise formed. "Dax! What're you doing messing around? I wanted your help, not a comedian."

"I'm fine." Lifting her arm, she rubbed her forehead. Her upper arm smashed against her breasts, making them jiggle and pushing them up higher in the low-cut camisole.

His cock noticed, hardening into a bigger shaft. He tightened his muscles, trying to control the anger surging inside him. As well as other things. He didn't want this attraction, and he certainly didn't deserve a woman so beautiful. And he'd hurt her. "I'm sorry. My idiot brother surprised me."

"You asked me to come. What's going on down there?" His brother peered under the sink. "Is this a new, kinky way to—"

"Dax, dammit." Reed shoved himself out from underneath the sink. Reaching back around, he held his hands out for Quinn. She placed her slim hands in his. Like a monster, his ugly, scarred hand swallowed her tiny one. The earlier image of her hand making his look better slipped away. He had too much ugliness to cover up.

He helped Quinn out. "Thanks."

"You called me." Dax took her elbows and helped her to her feet. A knight helping an injured princess being held captive by a monster. His sexy smirk enhanced his handsome face. "Who is this beautiful—" His gaze traveled the length of her body. "—and wet woman?"

Reed stiffened and clenched his hands into fists. His little brother shouldn't be ogling her. Not with her perky breasts sticking out of the soft silk material, not with the way the wet cloth clung to her slight curves and hugged her hips. He grabbed Quinn's wet robe and held it in front, covering most of her. "Here."

Her relaxed, answering grin showed she wasn't concerned with how much of her body was displayed. As a dancer, she was probably used to people staring at her. "I'm Quinn Petrov."

His brother's charm was already working. Annoyance pulsed at Reed's temples.

Besides their green eyes, it was hard to tell Dax was his brother. Dax had longer, blond hair while Reed's was dark and curly. Dax's lanky and able body was the opposite of Reed's thick trunk exterior and his limp. Dax's fun attitude toward life contrasted with Reed's darker views.

"Bro, why didn't you tell me about your new woman?" His brother gave an exaggerated wink, trying to embarrass Reed.

If Dax stayed in town longer than his ski patrol shift, he'd know who Quinn was. "She's not my woman." He sounded grouchy and short, and he hated himself for it. This woman didn't matter to him. Not what skimpy clothes she wore, or who she dated. "She's my tenant."

"Interesting." His brother's eyebrows rose and lowered in a more-than-interested action.

"I should get changed." Quinn's soft smile had his insides twisting. "Nice meeting you, Dax."

"I'll be seeing you around." The suggestiveness said more than his words.

The twisting inside Reed's gut pulled tighter, watching Quinn's wet backside sway out of the bathroom. He couldn't pull his gaze away from the mesmerizing move.

"Getting out of bed was worth it for the view." His brother's face took on a wolfish expression. "I want to be a landlord, if I can have hot tenants like her."

"Stick to blowing avalanches up." He wanted to blow up. At his brother, at Quinn, at the situation. He never should've called Dax. "Help me finish fixing the leak."

Dax crouched down by the sink and picked up the flashlight. "So what's going on between you two?"

"Nothing." Reed climbed back under the sink, with a caulk gun in hand.

Why would his brother think he'd have anything going on with a woman as beautiful as Quinn? He hadn't dated anyone since his fiancée. He only socialized with his family, rarely talked to anyone else except his construction clients.

"It's the middle of the night." Using a suggestive tone, his brother pointed the light at the pipe connection. "You're dressed in only shorts. She's in a sexy nightie."

He strangled the caulk gun like he wanted to strangle his brother. "Shut up, Dax. Nothing is going on between Quinn and I."

Dax wiggled his eyebrows. "Then, you won't mind if I ask her out."

The season for second chances.

After heartache at a young age, single mother Danielle Marstrand has finally found her place in her hometown. A good job, a good home, a great daughter—nothing can sway her from her course until Luke Logan returns to their small Colorado mountain ski town.

Champion skier Luke Logan is ready to return home to Castle Ridge, even if he's not quite sure the town's ready to welcome him. Especially his high school sweetheart Danielle. Nursing an injury that nearly ended his career, Luke's struggling to get back more than his range of motion...he's hoping returning to where his career began might help reignite the passion he's lost. But instead of discovering his passion for skiing he discovered the daughter he never knew he had.

Hurt that Danielle never told him about Brianna, Luke is determined to know his child. Danielle's reluctant to allow Luke in, fearing he'll just leave again, but she's willing to compromise when Luke suggests fake dating with Brianna tagging along. Why then, does a kiss for show feel oh so real?

In this classic reunion story, love finds a second chance.

EXCERPT:

"You're single. I'm single. You've changed. I've changed. You asked to meet *me*." His voice rose in accusation. "Nothing smarmy about that."

Her eyebrows rose. "Every time a woman asks you to meet does it mean having sex?"

"Pretty much." His cockiness caused the wine to burn in her chest.

Disgust made it travel the wrong direction. "Not with me."

His eyes blinked. For a second she thought she'd seen hurt on his expression, but then the suave-macho guy she'd seen in interviews on TV made his reappearance. "Then what do I owe this... pleasure?"

His hesitation told her he meant the opposite of pleasure, but again the imagined images of the two of them together burned. Her entire body felt as if she sat in the fire, not next to the fireplace. She blew out a breath and focused on what she came to do.

Tell Luke. Tell Luke. Tell Luke.

The room seemed to close in on them. The few people in the dining area were normal people having normal conversations. They weren't about to change someone's life. They weren't about to alter their own reality. And their daughter's.

The fire roared louder. The flames spurted higher, taunting. Other people's laughter spiked through her head. The clanging dishes echoed and burst in her brain.

She blew out a slow breath, knowing she just needed to spit it out. "I need to tell you something and I want a promise you won't yell or make a scene."

"I promise." His snippiness set the wrong tone.

Nerves scraped in her stomach making the wine go sour. Nausea rumbled and burned up her chest. She felt as if she was going to heave on the table. She pinched her lips together and then forced her mouth to open. To speak.

Nothing came out.

"I haven't seen you in thirteen years. There's nothing you could say that would make me angry." He grabbed his mug and took a long pull.

She froze at his statement and his casual action. *He didn't believe anything she said mattered?* Her iced body cracked and heated. Fissures formed with her fury. *He didn't think she mattered?* Her brain popped and her veins burst in a torrent. *He probably wouldn't think their daughter mattered either.* Her hands curled into cold claws. She wanted to scrape the annoying expression off his handsome face.

Instead, she scooped up her coat and lunged out of the booth. "Oh!"

To hell with him.

"Well?" His impatient tone yanked her to a stop, goaded her.

Her heart thumped once. Deviousness had her swirling back around. So, he didn't think anything she said would affect him, did he? She was going to give him the shock of his life.

She took a step forward, leaned toward him, and whispered, "Brianna is your daughter."

Excerpt from

The Flirtation Game
A Castle Ridge Small Town Romance, Book 3

by ALLIE BURTON

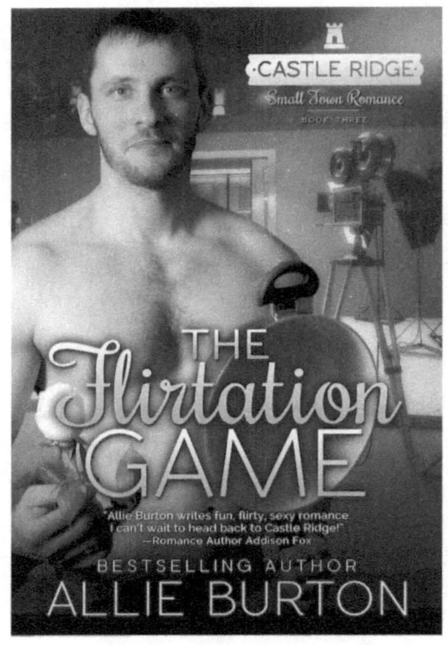

Love isn't all that's cooking.

After a scandal in Hollywood, celebrity chef Michael Marstrand accepts a position to be head chef at Castle Ridge Lodge and star in a television program about re-opening a five-star restaurant. He believes returning to his hometown to help the struggling restaurant will earn him public relations points and help an old friend. What he doesn't know is the sous chef expected to be named head chef and the television series is a reality show called *Kitchen Catastrophe*.

Sous Chef Isabel O'Donnell returned from vacation to discover the restaurant kitchen remodeled and a new head chef. With contracts already signed, she has no choice but to work for Chef Michael, a man she'd had a crush on since middle school. A man who'd stolen her job.

With the hidden cameras rolling, Michael tries to make the day-to-day routine boring so *Kitchen Catastrophe* will never be shown, but an interfering producer introduces a bridezilla and an employee who causes trouble. Add the simmering attraction between Michael and Isabel and the reality show has everything: drama, fights, and sex.

In this best friend's brother conflict, will a fake flirtation produce the perfect recipe or enflame desire?

EXCERPT:

Michael stepped away from Isabel and straightened his shirt. A shirt she hadn't even realized she'd messed.

She ran her fingers through her hair, trying to pull herself together. She was going to be head chef; she couldn't be caught making out in the kitchen. Not only was it unsanitary, it was unprofessional.

Parker, the lodge owner, observed the two of them, a glint of confusion on his face. His perfectly-coiffed hair appeared tame compared to the man she just kissed.

"What do you need?" Michael's voice sounded normal. He obviously had more control over his libido.

Her skin cooled. Maybe he wasn't as attracted to her.

"Good. You two are getting reacquainted." Parker wrung his hands together. He seemed more together than on New Year's Eve, but still jumpy.

Why would he be nervous of either one of them? In high school, Michael and Parker had been best friends. Now, they acted like strangers.

Michael's face was a complete mask. What was he hiding?

"I'm glad you're going to be okay with this decision, Isabel." Parker's shoulders relaxed.

She tilted her head, trying to figure his puzzling words out. "What decision?"

"Now that Chef Françoise has retired, I'll be announcing the new head chef."

Her chest pounded. She stood straighter, and pulled back her shoulders. This was it. Parker was going to tell her the head chef position belonged to her.

He waved his hand in a vague fashion. "The press release with head shots will go out today."

Air caught in her lungs. "I didn't take new photos."

Michael jerked beside her. He gaped at her with raised eyebrows and tightened facial muscles. "What?"

"No need for the sous chef to take head shots." Parker avoided her gaze like a guilty man.

"But...but." The catch in her chest morphed into a

fissure, a fissure cracking and widening with each of her panicked thoughts. "I'm the new head chef."

Michael's shoulders hunched, and he took a step back, as if he'd taken a punch to his midsection. Except she was the one who'd taken the punch, because something was wrong. Parker acted nervous. Michael shocked.

She sucked in a sharp, jagged breath, ignoring the pain. "Chef Françoise promised me the position."

Michael's skin had gone white as a chef's coat. His round eyes had dimmed of color. "What?"

Parker's expression softened, except for his pinched mouth. "I'm sorry, Isabel. I thought Michael told you. I thought that's why you two were talking in the kitchen together."

Her breath spasmed, sending alarms throughout her body. Her gaze switched back and forth, between Michael and Parker. "Told me? Told me what?"

Parker touched her arm. "The new head chef at the Castle Ridge Lodge is celebrity chef Michael Marstrand."

Excerpt from

The Playboy Switch
A Castle Ridge Small Town Romance, Book 4

by ALLIE BURTON

Instructed in fun. Schooled in love.

After almost dying in an avalanche, Dax O'Donnell makes a promise to himself: get serious about life and his career. His playboy ways might be fun, but he needs to plan for his future. Applying to paramedic school has always been a dream, but is he smart enough to succeed?

Lexi Henderson has loved Dax since joining the ski patrol team at Castle Ridge Resort. Knowing he's a playboy, she's kept her distance, but when he's rescued from an avalanche she kisses him and sparks both of their desires. But he thinks she has a boyfriend—another playboy, and she keeps a major secret. Or two.

Dax suggests *fun lessons* to turn Lexi's quiet and rigid attitude around. But when fun turns to passion, he must ask, is she willing to make the playboy switch?

In this secret identity tale, love overcomes secrets and lies.

EXCERPT:

"That guy will break your heart." Dax eased up next to her with a drink, but no woman in hand. His carefree expression was gone and the light had dimmed from his green gaze.

"Will he?" She was curious to see where this was going. He must not realize Ryder was her brother and would never hurt her. Not like others in her past.

"Ryder Croft is a playboy with no serious career or goals."

She glared. Her brother loved coaching the kids on his ski team. Sure, he was a little lost when it came to a career. Dax had no right to judge. "Really?"

"Croft is a gazillionaire." Dax sounded as if his beer went sour. "If I had as much money, I'd quit my job and ski around the world."

"Sounds as if you want to be just like him." His sour tone filled her mouth with a bitterness that burned down her throat. He was jealous of Ryder's wealth, not because he'd been dancing with her. Dax reminded her of her ex-fiancé Andrew who had only been interested in her money and her family's connections. Pursing her lips, she tried to control her annoyance. "You don't care about your job?"

She had a passion for saving people which is why she'd joined the ski patrol and become a paramedic. She didn't want anyone else to unnecessarily lose their life on the mountain. The invention she'd been working on and trying to get developed would help her mission.

"I care about my job. I don't want to see you get hurt." He took her hand and patted it like she was a cowering puppy. "Croft's a playboy."

"And you can say this because you have the greatest dating record?" Overplaying her sarcasm, she let her pessimism come out in her voice. She'd always been attracted to Dax, yet kept her distance knowing his true personality. "You're a playboy."

His eyes morphed into chipped emeralds. He gripped her hand tighter and pulled her against him. "Then go out with me instead."

The whispered words sent a tingle down her spine.

She'd longed to hear a declaration from Dax. A sexual tease or an invitation. Except this was a declaration of competition because he was jealous of her brother. The moment he learned about her background, she wouldn't know if he liked her or her money. Plus, what exactly was he asking for? A date or a night in bed?

Stopping the tingles before they reached her heart, she forced a sappily sweet smirk. "So I should dump Ryder and start dating you, doing a playboy switch?"

About

Atlantis Riptide
Lost Daughters of Atlantis, Book 1

by ALLIE BURTON

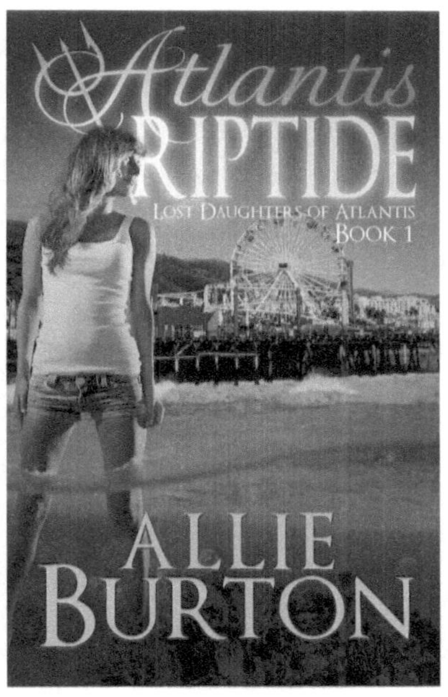

When a girl runs away from the circus…

For all her sixteen years, Pearl Poseidon has been a fish out of water. A freak on display for her adoptive parents' profit. Running away from her horrible life, she craves one thing—anonymity. But when she saves a small boy from drowning she exposes herself and her mutant abilities to Chase, a budding investigative reporter.

Now, he has questions. And so do the police.

Once Pearl discovers her secret identity, she learns she's part of a larger war between battling Atlanteans. A battle that will decide who rules the oceans. A battle raging between evil and her true family. Will she find a way to use her powers in time to save a kingdom she never knew existed?

This is the start of a young adult fantasy action adventure novel series. "Free sweet summer young adult paranormal with death-defying underwater rescues."

– Reviewer

his place to inherit King Tut's soul and justly rule. He knows nothing about the society's evil plan to control the world or the curse. Now, he must deal with the female thief who stole the amulet.

When the two teens find themselves up against the secret society, they reluctantly join forces and must figure out how to end the curse before it turns deadly. On the run and unable to touch because of the curse, Olivia and Xander develop a connection during their quest.

As the mystery surrounding the amulet unfolds, Olivia and Xander fall for each other. But is love enough to save them and the world from destruction?

"If you are a fan of Rick Riordan books about a quest with love and history thrown in…this is for you!"
– Hooked In A Book Review

Other Books by Allie Burton

CASTLE RIDGE SMALL TOWN ROMANCE SERIES
The Romance Dance
The Christmas Match
The Flirtation Game
The Playboy Switch
The Billionaire's Ploy
The Heartbreak Contract
The Marriage Merger (*coming soon*)
The Runaway Royal (*coming soon*)

LOST DAUGHTERS OF ATLANTIS SERIES
Atlantis Riptide
Atlantis Red Tide
Atlantis Rising Tide
Atlantis Tide Breaker
Atlantis Dark Tides
Atlantis Twisting Tides
Atlantis Glacial Tides

SOUL WARRIORS SERIES
Soul Slam
Tut's Trumpet
Peace Piper
Cleo's Curse

Find all of Allie's books on her website.
http://www.allieburton.com/books.html

Allie Burton has always been a reader and writer. She wrote her first novel at the age of twelve when she was stranded at a hospital by a snowstorm. Receiving her first romance from her grandmother, she fell in love with the genre. As an adult, she read young adult books with her own teens and was excited to find something fresh and new. Now, she writes both.

Having so many jobs as a teen and adult became great research material for the stories she writes. She has been everything from a bike police officer to a professional mascot escort to an advertising executive. She has lived on three continents and in four states and has studied art, fashion design, and marine biology.

Allie is a member of the Society of Children's Book Writers & Illustrators and Romance Writers of America. She loves to ski, golf, and run. Currently, she lives in Colorado with her husband and two children.